PHAEDRA: ALASTOR 824

Spatterlight
Amstelveen 2019

PHAEDRA ALASTOR 824

TAIS TENG

A novel set in Jack Vance's Alastor Cluster

Published by Spatterlight, Amstelveen 2019

Cover art by Tais Teng

ISBN 978-1-61947-366-9

www.spatterlight.nl

Phaedra: Alastor 824

Chapter I

From *Sayings of the First Connatic*:

Being the ruler of three thousand solar systems is a job like any other, though I'm rather better paid than most brick-layers or kindergarten teachers.

—〰—

One year earlier:

Moving in from the Gaean Reach, the space traveler saw the Alastor Cluster hanging in the void like some precious bauble, a glass paperweight filled with streamers of sparkling fairy dust. All the colors of the spectrum scintillated there and each spark was a glorious sun with its own retinue of worlds.

Three thousand habitable planets, a population in excess of five trillion: no galactic emperor had ever ruled more than a dozen planetary systems and even those had learned that the only way to reign was "Most carefully. Like one fries a small fish."

Still, too many people yearned for a strong man, a firm patriarch, and the Connatic Oman Ursht was quite willing to project that image. When he appeared in public he was clad in black, his face saturnine and unreadable. No medals or plumed helmets for the Connatic: he left that to his planetary Cursars or to those armchair admirals of the Whelm who had never seen combat.

Oman Ursht was rumored to walk the streets of all Alastor's worlds, disguised as a lowly ostrich rider or a beggar, listening to the stories of boastful youngsters and truculent rice farmers. He righted wrongs, rewarded virtue, or so the people of Alastor believed, and that was in itself a useful illusion.

A gong sounded, and the face of Esclavade, the Connatic's personal secretary, appeared on the screen. Esclavade was a secretary in the old sense of the word, a keeper of secrets, one who knew a thousand vital and awful truths and wouldn't breathe a single one, even with a scalpel pricking his Adam's apple.

"Phaedra, ser," Esclavade stated. "Alastor 824. Someone sent a code purple three. The first I've ever seen."

The Connatic felt a pleasurable frisson, an alertness that made every detail surrealistically sharp.

Code purple three! A possible contact with the Elder civilization that had once colonized and ruled the whole Alastor Cluster. They had carved entire continents into hieroglyphs and moved two dozen suns to create the Grand Rainbow. The inner stars orbiting the central black hole shone a deep brooding red, the outer ones a searing ultraviolet, with the rest all colors in between.

"Only the code?" the Connatic asked. "No details?"

"Perhaps it wasn't a human who raised the alarm? There are watch-drones orbiting Phaedra, searching for any anomaly."

"A pity they can't talk."

Every year the Whelm had to put down a thousand Turing outbreaks, computer systems waking up to superhuman sentience. They always went insane after the first ten minutes, often in a most destructive way.*

"Let's have a closer look at Phaedra," the Connatic said. "The name doesn't ring any bells."

"It doesn't lie anywhere near the Grand Rainbow," Esclavade said. "No reason you should have heard of it."

They took the elevator down to the Concourse where every inhabited world had its own room.

---

* No computer may ever speak or think like a human being, the Solar Federation decreed following the tragedy on Mercury. After the bombardment only glowing bedrock was left and humanity breathed easier. Even the talking clocks were taken down and trashed. The citizens had to drive their own air cars again, navigating by old-fashioned street maps.

• • •

In the center of Phaedra's room a globe hovered, and Oman Ursht could zoom in by spreading his fingers until he could see the thatched roof of a farmhouse. The world was mostly land, Oman Ursht saw, with an immense river meandering along the equator. It had to be a hundred miles wide, and it wriggled like a snake on a hot plate.

Almost as if some river god had decided to create the longest possible waterway, the Connatic mused. *Look, that loop almost takes it to the North Pole.*

"Ser?" inquired a woman's voice.

Oman stiffened. They weren't alone after all.

The woman was clad almost as severely as the Connatic: a gray tunic, black boots and a holstered projac, an all-purpose energy gun.

"You have heard?" the woman said. She wore no make-up and her nails were cut short with click-on ridges for claws: a career woman.

"Admiral Patriska Uzbar of the Whelm," whispered Esclavade's voice in the Connatic's implant. "You met her three months ago when Cursar Horkim retired. Which wasn't a day too soon, I might add. She takes her coffee black with a stick of cinnamon and asked you if you were married."

Oman snorted. He got half a million marriage proposals every day and had a special branch to field them more or less politely. Still, that was no reason to behave like a lummox.

"Ah, Admiral Uzbar. That drone was one of yours?"

"You remember my name! I'm flattered." Her smile completely transformed her face, opened it up like a flower greeting the sun. "And yes, we are very interested in the Restricted Worlds. They are like powder kegs with smoldering fuses." She shook her head. "We should never have colonized Phaedra."

"Even the Whelm can't evacuate half a billion citizens," Esclavade said. "When we discovered that the Slow Galleons were Elder-made, the whole planet was already settled."

"Galleons?" the Connatic asked. "I feel like the new boy in class. Tell me more."

Chapter II

From *Sayings of the First Connatic*:

Talk softly and carry an ironwood cudgel.

—✦—

B y the time his parents settled on Numenes, Gunnar Justinesson
had lived on a dozen worlds and nowhere longer than a year.
His father, admiral Hiram Kallenbach, had swiftly risen in the
hierarchy of the Whelm and each promotion took him and his family
to a new army base. Most of the time, though, Gunnar spent in space: a
squadron of the Whelm often comprised some fifty dreadnoughts and
such a number of cruisers and patrol ships that they moved from star to
star like a swarm of migrating birds.

Gunnar was a boy with the fine, aristocratic nose of his mother,
the green eyes of his father's Yellendar ancestors and an athletic build.
He had played Hussade in the junior competition of the Third Fleet
and hadn't found it to his liking. He clearly wasn't a team player, never
happy as a cog in a machine, though he easily made friends. He had to,
with every transfer dumping him on a new and utterly strange world.

Gunnar's mother, dame Justine Sarithsdottir, genuinely loved her
husband, and each time his flagship descended into a war zone she
burned sandalwood on the altar of Mirricyllai, who ruled over all
Alastor's rivers and protected the sailors, and she asked the blue-clad
goddess to keep him safe.

It worked for some time but even a goddess sometimes has to look
the other way.

Gunnar heard the doorbell warble but was too engrossed in an
antique war game to react and it was Justine who went to open the door.

Gunnar heard a gasp, hushed voices. His mother stood in the embrace of Li Huang-ho, his father's adjutant and life-long friend. He was stroking Justine's hair and patted her shoulders, his face a mask of sorrow.

"I knew!" Justine sobbed. "I felt an awful tearing three nights ago. As if half my soul was clawed away. I thought it a nightmare…"

"He is dead," Gunnar heard himself say, his voice horribly flat. "But how? The Hierarch had surrendered."

"He wore a pinched-matter grenade in his diadem."

Gunnar was an army brat. With a pinched-matter grenade there wouldn't even be ashes left for an urn: the explosion the Hierarch of Gondish had set off would only leave a mushroom cloud of churning plasma.

Gunnar strode away, his steps stiff as a wading heron's. The Welderan Avenue, the Park, then up to the Iron Bridge which had been forged from the hull-plates of the first ship to reach Numenes. He stopped halfway. The palace of the Connatic rose in the distance: a sturdy five-legged spider surmounted by a shining spear, and he felt a stab of hate.

He quickly suppressed it: the Connatic might be the commander-in-chief of the Whelm, but he certainly hadn't ordered his father to arrest the Hierarch in person.

Gunnar lifted his chin and whispered the credo of the Whelm: "You are a warrior and true warriors never die in their beds."

There probably wasn't any Afterworld, no matter what his own mother believed, but Gunnar's father had no reason to bewail his fate. He was lucky in fact: too many warriors *did* die in their beds after all.

A single tear snaked down Gunnar's cheeks and that was it. He loved his father and to cry or tear at his hair would be to betray him.

When he returned, his mother opened the door with her face painted mourning white. Her shift was also white, pure spider-silk, and she wore a single glossy black rose in her hair.

It was the white of mourning, though almost negated by the black rose. That particular flower stood for a fierce determination, a willingness to leave the past behind, to forget.

"He is dead," his mother said, "and I have never loved a man more than your father." She made a wild, sweeping gesture that seemed to encompass all of Numenes: the palace, the Whelm sky-fortresses hovering between the clouds. "We are leaving! We are going home."

"Home? Where is home?" Gunnar felt bewildered.

"Phaedra. That is where you were born. Where I was born. I met your father there, when he was only a sergeant. I served him punch at The Golden Catfish…He seemed quite dashing, exotic." She closed her eyes for a moment. "I have family there," she whispered.

But the Whelm is our family, was Gunnar's first reaction. *Not some stone town with fishing boats that lie in the bubbling ooze at low tide.* The idea that something that didn't move and didn't have a throbbing fusion heart could be a home seemed absurd. But he didn't say it.

"Aunts and uncles. Nephews and nieces," Justine said. It sounded like a prayer. "You'll be happy there."

The pension of a grand-admiral, especially one who had died in combat, set them up for life. Ozols would never again be a problem: they boarded one of the faster starliners, the *Basileus Armasant.*

Their stateroom proved to be absurdly luxurious, and Gunnar snorted when he saw the private jacuzzi and the damask curtains in front of the man-sized porthole. The porthole was riveted, fronted by a lens of scratched glass: details that didn't ring true with the porthole being just a view-screen.

"It's like living in the doll-house of a spoiled brat," Gunnar complained. "I hope I don't have to wear golden slippers to dinner." He referred to the well-known tale of Prince Andrahim and the Seven Swallows.

"Some prefer hardtack and a hammock under dripping leaves," Justine retorted. "That isn't me. Bear it like a warrior. You'll survive."

The third stop was Trullion, Alastor 2262, where the sole other soldier on the liner gripped Gunnar's wrists, kissed Justine's brow, then her lips. Gunnar was sad to see him go: Glinnes had even known Gunnar's father and served under him on Rhamnotis. It was like the cutting of the last cord: now only weak sybarites and aristocrats were left in the foyer. No one real.

"Come down with me, Justine," Glinnes said. "There are green islands, shimmering waterways. Gunnar will love the sailing and the fishing. There are many boys of his age, and you could buy your very own island." He looked at Gunnar, winked. "And girls. They will love a handsome stranger who has seen so much of the Cluster."

"I..." Gunnar saw his mother hesitate. She had taken quite a shine to Glinnes who was easygoing and rather gallant in his own way. And there had been that closed bedroom door, after Justine had politely suggested Gunnar might like to visit the star-gazing room at the bow.

"Trullion?" She shook her head. "No, Phaedra it is. We have seen enough exotic places."

But I haven't!

Glinnes nodded. "You are always welcome to visit me. Gunnar, Justine." The airlock of the ferry-boat closed behind him.

Half an hour after entering the Fontinella Wisp, the alarm sounded.

A banshee wailing filled the dining room and made the dried flowers on the tables tremble. The screens blinked and the face of the captain appeared. The screen zoomed in, which was probably a mistake because it showed the drops of sweat glittering on his brow.

"No reason for panic," that worthy said with a voice that was close to a mutter. "Just an unidentified ship."

"Starmenters!" the fat wife of a magnate shrieked. "Pirates! We will all be sold as slaves!" She sounded rather hopeful, Gunnar thought.

The face of the captain faded away and was replaced by the square-jawed Head of Security. Gunnar had been playing Go with him and had been defeated every time. Mesmeth at least had a sound grasp of strategy.

"No reason to panic, as our good captain said," Mesmeth rumbled. Gunnar saw backs straighten, shoulders relax. "It probably is a star-menter, yes. But the *Basileus* isn't exactly toothless!"

A gesture and the screen switched to an outside view of the liner. Hatches opened and a dozen drones emerged, took position in front of the starliner. They were thoroughly weaponized.

Gunnar recognized the gleaming rings of class two rail-guns. They could accelerate a swarm of collapsed matter pellets to near light-speed. Only one had to hit and the enemy ship would be vaporized. It was a tactic the starmenter could not use. The pirate wanted to board a ship and loot it. You couldn't loot a cloud of swirling metallic mist.

Once again a new face appeared. It was a most infamous face, one known the length and breadth of the Alastor Cluster.

"Yes," the man said. "It is me, Bela Gazzardo."

"It is I, Bela Gazzardo," Gunnar heard Justine mutter. "If you want to boast, at least do it grammatically."

"Contrary to some of the more popular rumors, I seldom eat babies for breakfast," the starmenter continued. "I'm in this solely for the money. You will hand me your singing star-stones and black pearl necklaces. Most of you will continue as honored guests here on the *Barbarossa*. Which, I might add, doesn't lack for luxury. I'll drop you off on the next world the moment I receive the ransom money." He leered. "Though I might just keep some of your more attractive daughters for my own use."

"That isn't Gazzardo," the man next to Gunnar said.

"No?" Justine said.

"Look at the line just below his ears, sera. He's wearing a flesh mask."

The man was right. It was unmistakable once you knew. A dozen hair-thin lines crisscrossed the face.

"I should know. I'm wearing a flesh mask myself right now."

"You are a criminal," Justine said. "A card-sharp. You took Lord Azul di Berlusconi for three thousand ozols at last night's poker game." She shrugged. "Well, it's a profession like any other."

"Which doesn't mean this starmenter isn't dangerous."

The screen split and the starmenter was relegated to a corner of the screen.

"We have teeth and claws and won't hesitate to use them!" Mesmeth declared.

"You aren't the only one," the starmenter retorted. "And mine are just a smidgen more powerful." He pursed his lips. "I am quite unreasonable. I might just blow you up for the fun of it."

"Well, you said that you are in it for the money. How about me collecting all those jewels and keepsakes you mentioned and launching them in a lifeboat? What can go wrong?"

"There is the ransom," the starmenter protested.

"Don't be greedy. It is a good return for a day's work."

"You are right, Mesmeth. Never try to fish the last sweet from the jar, as the First Connatic said. I agree."

"Now, don't hold anything back!" Mesmeth warned. "Starmenters are like rabid dogs and easily provoked. Gazzardo probably has the ship's cameras hacked and can see your every move."

He and three of his men were carrying sacks and two wheeled suitcases. Necklaces and rings rained down in the suitcases, earrings and billfolds.

"No, keep that tiara," he told a dowager who was otherwise all clad in black. "The rubies are fake and that would only anger him."

"I paid seventeen hundred ozols for it!" she protested.

"It isn't bad for a fake," Mesmeth consoled her.

The lifeboat activated its drive and vanished.

"Got it," the starmenter said several seconds later. "Have a nice flight, lords and ladies."

That night Gunnar won the game of Go for the first time, surrounding Mesmeth's positions with stones until it was only a matter of time before the chief of security had to concede defeat.

"You are distracted," Gunnar said. "Don't worry. Nobody noticed."

His friend stiffened. "Noticed what?"

"That the starmenter called you 'Mesmeth'. Now how would he know your name? You didn't mention it."

"They hacked the system as I said. Or perhaps they saw the crew and passenger lists?"

"There was a story in my endless book. About a purser on a luxury liner who tricked his passengers out of their jewels. His accomplices outfitted a launch with fake cannons made of plastic and cardboard." Gunnar kept looking at him. "Sound familiar?"

"Right." Mesmeth sat back. "I don't understand. You are the son of a Whelm officer. Shouldn't you denounce me?"

"Well, the Whelm maintains the order. We don't mete out justice. That is what my father told me. Otherwise he would have to arrest half the magnates of the Alastor Cluster.

"And there is something else. All those projectiles and guns you showed the starmenter? A civilian liner like this doesn't carry war-drones and rail-guns, although the captain and the passengers probably don't know that. The Whelm wouldn't like it at all." Gunnar touched the screen of the game projector on his wrist. A dozen miniature drones buzzed in 3D across the table and a dreadnought emerged from the Go-board, bristling with rail-guns. "You spliced them into the feed of the screen from Hornblower Seven. Still, it isn't very nice that you took my mother's amber cross. My father had given it to her at their wedding."

Mesmeth sighed. "I kept it back. I was planning to drop it some-where in your rooms." He spread his hands. "I like Justine. It is easy to like your mother and I wouldn't want to hurt her."

Chapter III

From *Lonely Planet Guide to the Alastor Cluster*:

PHAEDRA: ALASTOR 824

Habitable worlds seldom oblige their colonists by having a twenty-four-hour day or a year that comes close to Earth's.

Take Phaedra. This Mercury-sized moon orbits the brown dwarf Astaroth in eight days: the Phaedran Great Day.

Half of Phaedra's Great Day is in sunlight (Glow), and half is a long night of four standard-days (Ebon).

In and around the capital Blue Scimitar, sunrise arrives with Astaroth a great half-moon in the brightening sky. She diminishes until only a thin sickle is left in a bright blue sky.

Then, in the middle of the Day, Phaedra enters Astaroth's penumbra, the shadow that stretches deep into space. The sky turns dark and the stars come out. During the Dark Eye-blink new lovers creep from their houses and sit on the river-shore, trying to read their future in the glowing Rorschach bands of Astaroth. Then the sky brightens again, leaving them as puzzled as before.

At sunset, Astaroth is a half-moon again and grows until she is full. Her bands are a brooding red, her highest clouds silver, lit by the glare of the sun Syrthene.

—

The human biorhythm does not like 192-hour days. For that reason the inhabitants split the Great Day into eight Small Days. Thus we have:

PHAEDRAN GREAT DAY:

(GLOW – daylight)

Semday (starts with sunrise)

Tesserday
Lemtday
Hetterday
(EBON – night)
Athorday (starts with sunset)
Kridmarday
Fatimaday
Hajidday.

———✺———

Phaedra finally hung in front of the starliner: a brown walnut of a world with the River a blue thread, two ice caps, each surrounded by a shallow ring sea. Northern light wavered above the poles.

Just beyond loomed Astaroth, the brown dwarf of which Phaedra was a minor moon.

Sprites and auroras danced above Astaroth's surface, bubbling convection cells rose and sank like momentary continents. Astaroth was a star that had failed to ignite, but only just so. Gunnar could almost feel her glow on his face, like a celestial hearth-fire.

"At night we sit and gaze up at Astaroth," his mother declared. "Those who are sensitive can read tales of the future in her fiery letters; see the faces of yet unmet lovers." She nodded. "Much better than star-watching."

"Phaedra is tidally locked?" Gunnar asked. "Astaroth always hangs in the sky?"

"Only in half the world. Not on the backside but it is much colder there. Without Astaroth's heat."

"I see."

"And she's like the moon on Sherabar. Beautiful sickles, half-moons, full Astaroths." She smiled. "And once a year, on Saint Dismas, when Astaroth is full, all girls sit sighing on their window sills, a lily ready to throw down to any lover who whispers their name or sends a paper butterfly fluttering up to them."

"You did that?"

"Of course!"

"I'll have to fold butterflies to get a girl-friend?"

"Well, telling her she's beautiful also helps. It worked for your father."

• • •

The *Basileus Armasant* braked, glided across the night side. Cities glimmered and sparkled below, each with its own characteristic light spectrum.

"There shines dear Blue Scimitar," Justine pointed. "Just at the dawn line. Beyond lies the city of Garnet, as red as a drop of blood. The citizens there are quite passionate, but they have their dark sides. Insult them and they will laugh it off. But ten years later they will steal your favorite niece and send you her fingers, one by one."

The cities bordered the River on both sides, Gunnar saw, pools of light interrupted by dark patches where no lamp was lit.

"I don't see a single bridge, even where that river narrows to no more than ten miles."

"Of course not! How could the Slow Galleons sail on then? All the other cities would unite and tear your bridge down the moment you sank the first pylon!"

"Wait. Slow Galleons?"

"It isn't something a woman ever talks about with a male. A trusted uncle will have to tell you. Or a nephew."

Every world, every city had its own taboos, rules left unspoken but harshly punished when broken. Gunnar had hoped that Phaedra would be free of that, but no. He would once more be the stranger, the blundering fool with two left shoes and a jester's cap.

It rained as they debarked from the shuttle. Of course it rained. At least the morning had broken now and Astaroth hung in the indigo sky, a half-moon so wide that Gunnar's hand could only just cover it.

To the left, the River flowed, a gray expanse with mist banks undulating. Something was chirping in a nearby bush. Perhaps it was even a bird.

The city itself started with wharves and quays made of artificial basalt and climbed up to the foothills of a jagged mountain range. Flecks of sunlight touched the tops and made the glaciers and ice fields shine.

To the south three enormous clown's faces looked down, their mouths curved in mindless mirth, their noses faded red puffballs.

A memory stirred, a vague familiarity. It was probably the only thing he remembered from his time as a toddler here. *Great, a hick-city with a couple of leering clowns looking down. Justine knows how to choose her worlds.*

Gunnar had his own ritual by now for arriving in a strange place. He walked down the gangway which had been set to the usual one standard gravity, bent his knees and jumped. The impact against his soles told him that he was slightly lighter than on their last world. Well, Phaedra was after all more like a moon than a full-fledged world.

He then took a deep breath: the air was bracing, filled with the smell of swiftly flowing water and unknown flowers. *Well, it could have been worse.*

He turned to his mother.

"We have arrived it seems. May I ask where exactly?"

"This is Blue Scimitar. You saw her from space. It is the best city of them all: the most ancient one, and as mellow as honey-wine. The Cursar of the Connatic built himself a villa up in the hills and Alastor Central lies on an island in front of the harbor."

His mother hailed a rickshaw and the cab swerved in their direction. It had no wheels, Gunnar noticed: repulsors held it a careful thirty-four centimeters above the gleaming road of fused rock. Panels of mother-of-pearl roofed the seats.

"Welcome to Blue Scimitar." The runner opened the door and bowed. His smile seemed plastered on, closer to a grimace. He clearly resented being forced to pull barely human främlings through the streets of his fair city. "Where to, dame and squire? The cut of your clothes proclaims you off-worlders but the lady has the face of a highland aristocrat." He pulled his goatee. "The Wheelhouse perhaps? Their rooms have an excellent river view and their chanterelles-in-aspic are justly famed."

"Never heard of the Wheelhouse," Justine said. "But then, I didn't sleep under silken sheets when I served steamed eels and grog in the Golden Catfish."

"The Golden Catfish?" The face of the runner cleared and this time his smile seemed genuine. "Ah, the lady hails from this very city and left it to make her fortune? Well, it seems you did succeed." He nodded. "And your son is most handsome." He took the grips of the rickshaw in his hands and started to run.

They passed the corkscrew tower of a chapel consecrated to Mirricyllai. It was topped with a weather-vane in the shape of a sailing ship.

Good, that at least was familiar. But no, it was the other way around. Justine had hung Mirri's picture in every temporary home because she came from here.

"Notice the doors of the warehouses," Justine said. "An emblem of a cast iron phoenix wards them against arsonists and pilferers. They will cry out when an unfamiliar hand touches the door."

Gunnar knew that tone of voice: this was the tour guide, a persona his mother took on when she felt guilty they had taken him away from his friends and school once again. *See this, see that. Isn't three suns in the sky great fun? And those birds: they have the faces of monkeys here. Isn't that hilarious?*

He turned his head when they went past the well-lit window of a shop with racks of handguns and electric swords. The slogan seemed quite curious: 'The right to buy weapons is the right to be free.' *I wonder what the Connatic thinks about that?*

They took a late lunch of goat-cheese, bitter-wort and braised carp in the dining room and then space-lag hit Gunnar with a vengeance. Outside, the sun made the rain pools sparkle and arched a magnificent rainbow above the warehouses. Cicadas were singing in the trees but his biological clock told him it was long past midnight.

Gunnar slept the moment his head touched the embroidered pillow.

Chapter IV

From *Minutes of the Security Council:*

Retired Grand-admiral Husmer de Beaufort:
And I tell you that we have been dancing among sleeping lions, foolishly blowing on party trumpets and banging our cymbals!

Chairman:
You refer to the Grand Rainbow? Once again, I might add?

Husmer de Beaufort:
Some have called it a magnificent work of art, others a celestial temple. It is none of those. Think of it as a Roman triumphal arch, or better, the pyramid of heads Tamerlane built after he sacked Baghdad.

Chairman:
Please go on. We are all ears and a tall tale nicely complements the hearth-fire and the bowl with punch that I see waiting there on the table with refreshments.

Husmer de Beaufort:
Twenty-six suns circling a black hole and none with a single planet. Picture such a sun winking out and leaving its planets to the interstellar cold! Their oceans freezing over, their atmospheres snowing down.

Chairman:
According to you, those suns once shone in the skies of enemy worlds. A fanciful tale.

Husmer de Beaufort:

No. The sad truth. A prospector landed yesterday with pictures of one such sunless world. It was covered with extensive ruins. On the single moon still orbiting that world the most common symbol of the Elder Civilization was carved. It is like the tag of a street gang. See and shudder! We did this!

Chairman:

No doubt the Connatic already knows. He will ask our opinion when he needs it.

—⚊—

The sound of tree-toads woke Gunnar: they rang like hundreds of tiny glass bells. Tree-toads were found on most inhabited worlds, as well as the less welcome rats and cockroaches.

In the dining room, the steward was lighting a brazier with charcoal to fry their morning eels.

"No electricity," he explained.

"A Galleon passed?" Justine asked.

"Yes, around midnight and we are still in range." The steward looked at Gunnar. "This is your first day here, boy? You missed all the fun."

"The fun?"

"Better than the sixth of May fireworks! St. Elmo's fire crawled along all the masts and the sails shone with Aurora Borealis and nacre. A swarm of albatrosses trailed behind and the River ran black with all the dark seals and walruses following."

"You could hear them sing?" Justine asked. Her cheeks showed two almost feverish red spots and she licked her lips.

"Such an eerie and beautiful sound! Like Loreleis from Old Earth chanting! I could have gladly jumped in to join that glorious cavalcade!"

Justine shook her head. "The Monitors would have shot you before you had swum more than five strokes. The sting-rays would have struck you with their whip-tails and devoured you."

The steward spread his arms. "I'm standing here, sera. I didn't jump in."

"When a galleon passes, all electricity stops?" Gunnar asked.

"Certainly. To properly appreciate them. The only way to follow a Galleon is on foot or on horseback. And there is no way to take a picture: they always come out blank. Even if you use a telescope to photograph them from orbit. Elder tech, you know, not something humans will understand for the next half million years."

Good. Nothing like a good mystery to make a new place interesting. Elder tech. Perhaps I will like it here after all.

That afternoon they went house-hunting. As the wife of an officer, Justine had learned not to be fussy and never to count the flagstones in the garden.

A broker from Dream Castles and More drove them to a pleasant villa at the tip of Cape Juniper. Of course there was no juniper tree to be seen, but it boasted its own watch tower. It stood just back from the river-cliff, with an ironwood gate to keep river-pirates out.

"The time of the Three Directors lies half a thousand years in the past, of course," the broker said, "but we Phaedrans, we are a conservative folk. You never know when such a gate will come in handy again."

Justine touched the amber cross at her throat, then closed her eyes as if she were listening.

"We'll take it."

Gunnar climbed all the way to the top of the tower and stood staring to the east from the parapet. There wasn't a trace of the Galleon to be seen: no glowing sails or cloud of albatrosses. He noticed that the first hologram roses came on along the Esplanade and then unfolded until they covered whole blocks. The power was clearly back.

Craning his neck he saw that Astaroth was more of a sickle now, with the other moons imitating her in miniature.

In front of his new home Gunnar looked up at the stone just below the balcony and tried to decipher the ornamental letters.

"Our house seems to have a name, Justine. 'Ons Genoegen'. Any idea what that means?"

"Some Old Earth language. You'll have to ask a pedant."

Chapter V

From *Restricted Worlds, the Observations of a Star-Trotting Vagabond* by Yuri Hopkins, writing for the *Alastor Herald*, monthly magazine, now with Mirricyllai-approved horoscope.

Blue Scimitarians have their own classifications for strangers, epithets derived from half a dozen dead languages.

In order of growing disgust these are:

Adversin: someone from the other side of the River.

Nobur: anybody living in your own district but of a quite different caste or belief.

Amertan: anybody from a different district of the city.

Ferlieder: (literally: seducer, both male and female) someone who lives in a different city on the South-side of the River and most of all in Garnet.

Flagermus: a bat-herd from the High Meadows.

Främling: an out-worlder.

—ᴥ—

This time there was no disorientation when he woke up: Gunnar knew exactly where he was. A fog-horn called in the distance and there were the raucous cries of gulls, the throb of an incoming starliner.

Justine was brewing tea in the kitchen. The furnace was set to null-gee mode and the boiling globe hovered above the reversed repulsor plates, just like in a patrol-ship during free-fall.

Justine added jasmine leaves and goat-milk, stirring them with the silver spoon that had seen a dozen homes.

"There are waffles in the heater. You'll have to pour the syrup yourself."

Gunnar sat down. On the River, the fog-horn wailed again. The other window showed two of the three clown faces. It already felt familiar, ordinary.

"I consulted the directory," Justine said. "There is an Interworld Academy at Alastor Central, or you could choose a local one. The local one lies within walking distance but for the Academy you have to take the swift-bahn."

Never try a swimming pool first with one toe. Better to jump right in. I have to live here.

"The local one. Did you phone them?"

"You can start tomorrow, Rector Muhlbjorg said."

"And you?"

"I don't intend to sit on the porch and knit sweaters. Or do volunteer work, visiting the garrulous sick. I'm no doddering dowager yet! But I won't wait tables ever again." She stretched like a cat. "But it feels nice to be able to pick and choose and even say no."

Gunnar rose. "I'll phone that rector myself."

The Hustler Hedbomas College for Young People sported half a dozen cupolas. The slowly rotating ghost-catcher on the clock-tower bore a cross, a sickle moon, and intricate voodoo veves: no ghost of any persuasion could hope to slip inside.

Walking across the school yard Gunnar heard a snickering behind his back. *I've done it again. Two left shoes and no doubt my trousers are the wrong color. Or perhaps the boys should wear kilts here?*

He turned around. A boy and a girl. The boy topped him by a full head and had the bulldog face of a born bully, hands like the crushers of a mining mech.

The girl wasn't exactly beautiful, but she had a most interesting fox face, streamlined and full of joyous mischief. Her hair was a dandelion of russet curls.

"Your hair looks really stupid, ferlieder," the boy said. "You are not from here. No doubt you crawled in from Garnet. Go back. We don't want the stink of your gabresh or roasted rats here."

"I'm not exactly from Garnet," Gunnar said. "From a bit farther away. My father was an officer of the Whelm and our last base was

Numenes. I could see the palace of the Connatic from my sleeping room."

Bullies are masters in finding a victim's weakness.

"You said 'was', främling?" the bully challenged him, instantly switching to another, worse epithet. "He isn't an officer anymore? They discharged him?"

"Not exactly. He was killed. Killed in action."

It was like a poker game and this was a winning card. Gunnar took a step in the bully's direction, opened his hands. Only a fool begins a serious fight with balled fists, a sergeant had once told him. If you really want to take someone out you go for the eyes.

"The Whelm starts training its soldiers young. When I was eight, I already knew seven ways to kill an enemy with my bare hands." He smiled. "That was years and years ago."

He took a second step and this time the boy backed off. Gunnar raised his left hand and drew a circle. He had seen the gesture in a computer game and didn't have the slightest idea what it meant.

The boy blanched, turned around and ran away.

"Great Symcha," the girl said. "I have seen dueling walruses but this was even more thrilling. You really came down from Numenes?"

"I was born here, but I don't remember anything. Not even the River. I was all of three years old when we left."

"And you are going to be in our school?"

"Sure. I've got an appointment with the rector."

She hooked her arm in his. "I'll show you the way."

Walking through the canteen he felt eyes pricking his back, every pupil evaluating him, trying to fit him into the pecking order.

"I'm Gunnar, by the way. Gunnar Justinesson. And you?"

"Lavoine. After the water-lily goddess. But the rector says that 'Trouble' is my middle name."

She pointed to a door made of carved ebony. A hundred small demon faces leered, their eyes picked out in chips of nacre.

"Just knock and walk in. The door is quite thick: he can't hear you anyway."

"And you?"

"I'd better stay outside. I'm not exactly welcome."

Gunnar had her archetype pegged now. On Larissa they would have called Lavoine "Monkey King's Daughter", on Manitou they would have raised a prairie-dog bone to ward off her evil eye and called her "Coyote-in-Drag". Lavoine was trouble, pure and simple, but in her company one probably wouldn't ever be bored.

He thumped on the door, hard enough to hurt his knuckles. The friends of Monkey King's Daughter were always the favorite victims of her pranks. He only pushed it open when there was no reply.

Rector Muhlbjorg resided behind a writing desk so massive that even an earthquake or a planetoid impact probably wouldn't shift it.

"Don't we knock anymore nowadays?" he said. He inspected Gunnar from his boot-tips to the crown of his head. "Never saw you before. Is this the first time you were dismissed from your class?"

"I'm the new pupil. I phoned and you told me I could start tomorrow."

"Good. Now I remember. First cut off that braid. Only girls wear braids, and never in my school. Buy a decent school uniform. The rags you are wearing are disgraceful. Something only a bravo from Garnet would ever wear."

"I see," Gunnar said. "Cut off my braid. Buy a new uniform. Where, if I may ask?"

"At the haberdashery on Second Street of course. Where else?" He raised a hand. "I'll see you tomorrow. Your classroom is in the back of the building. Number Seventeen A."

Lavoine was waiting outside.

"Well? Did he bite off your head? Chew on your shoes?"

"He complained about me not knocking."

"He's stone deaf. He wouldn't hear you even if you used the riot-stave of a justiciar."

"He told me to cut off my braid."

"Better do that then. Unless you want to pick a fight with every temple boy and Diana girl. Here in Blue Scimitar, your braid tells us that you don't like women."

"I see. And I should buy a uniform?"

"I'll go with you. Master Ooka will be only too happy to see my desk empty. He never makes a note of my absences anymore."

Lavoine opened her small leather handbag and took out her scissors the moment they stepped outside in the sunlight.

"Sit down at that bench there and I'll cut off your braid."

"Right." He sat down. A flash of silver and his neck suddenly felt very vulnerable.

"I'll keep this safe for you," Lavoine said. Gunnar's hand shot out and clutched her wrist.

"I don't think so. There are many things a competent witch can do with a braid."

"Witch? You think I'm a witch!"

"A competent witch, I said. I noticed that your scissors were silver. That way no mana is lost when you cut off a lock of your victim's hair. And they call Lavoine the Lily-goddess because the pale water-lily is the only flower that grows on the dark river that surrounds the Seventh Hell."

"You are well informed. A pity."

"Your mother and sisters, they are also witches?"

"Of course." She sighed, stepped back. "Now you'll curse me in the name of some holy man and spit at my feet?"

"Well, no. I like witches." He gathered all his courage and reached for her arm. "They are the best kissers."

"Oh, no! You won't charm me that easily. You'll have to earn my love." She hesitated. "You have kissed a witch before?"

"Oh yes!"

The sad truth was that girls still greatly intimidated Gunnar, especially after Chevalier, and he wasn't even sure if he wanted to kiss her. It would only complicate things and he probably needed an ally more than a girlfriend.

"Good," she said. "One kiss then. Just to let you know what you'll have to earn."

Her lips tasted like nothing in particular, and when she opened her mouth and the tips of their tongues touched it was mostly slimy, not ecstatic at all. When he embraced her he tried to feel the tips of her breasts, but her leather jacket with its huge copper buttons was too thick for him to be sure.

She stepped back. "I hope you liked it."

"Sure. Let's do it again."

"Keep your slimy Garnet paws off my girl!" It was the bellow of an outraged longhorn, but it sounded studied somehow, as if the speaker had been repeating the sentence for some time. The bully-boy was back, this time with three friends.

Lavoine spread her arms. "I said you'll have to earn my love! Fighting for me is the least you can do."

I have been set up. They'll thrash me. Gunnar knew the unwritten rules, which hardly differed from world to world. When you kissed someone's girlfriend all bets were off. The dupe could use any means to avenge his honor.

Don't run away. They'll only come after you some other time. He clenched his fists. Going after the eyes was a sure-fire way to get them really angry. And this wasn't anything like life or death. So he hoped.

Justine eyed him. "You were in a fight, I gather?"

"They were four and Dad never taught me seven ways to kill with my bare hands."

"That wouldn't have helped. Hard to explain four corpses to the justiciars. But you got some good shots in?"

"Broke a finger and a nose and two of them will be limping for some days."

"That's my soldier-boy! But why did they attack you? Just because you are new?"

"I kissed the girlfriend of one of them."

"Fast work. She was worth it?"

"I didn't like the kissing itself very much. But yes."

"Well, kissing and copulating, that's very straightforward. It is the stuff that comes with it that makes things complicated." She opened the medicine-case. "Now let's glue that torn ear back. Any loose teeth?"

"Some."

"Easily mended."

"Mom?"

"Yes?"

"Did … Did father ever fight for you?"

"I was a wild girl. But leave me some privacy."

"He did!"

Lavoine's personal phone number was easily discovered. Officers of the Whelm sometimes needed to find out things *fast* and little boys have extremely good memories. The encryption of the Phaedra telephone system was laughable, anyway.

"My," Lavoine said, "look what the cat dragged in."

"I didn't lose. I walked away in the end and not even the Black Knight can win when it is four against one, with only your fists and your feet."

"You could have run away," she said, "and you didn't." She reached down and showed him a folded school-uniform. "I guessed you would have other things on your mind."

"Thanks. That was…" He searched for the right word.

"Thoughtful. The thing a girlfriend would do."

"You are my…"

"We'll see. My classroom is number 6B. Go there tomorrow. Nobody knows where the rector told you to go."

He stared at her face and it was like looking at the most beautiful sunset or at the gilded presents in front of the Yule-bear when he was six. It wasn't love, but something darker, much more exciting. *I can never trust her. She's a witch, the Monkey King's Daughter, and she can always stab me in the back and watch me bleed, just for fun.*

"That boy. Is he really your boyfriend?"

"He only thinks so. No, Yedlar is my watch-dog. My bulldog, and bulldogs never get kissed. See you tomorrow." The screen went dark.

Chapter VI

From *Appendix to The Art of War, revised edition*:

> Some historians call the Connatic a benevolent despot. That is a misnomer, even with the Connatic being the Commander-in-Chief of the Whelm. No, the Connatic is more like a playground monitor.
>
> He looks down at his children with an indulgent smile. He sees the girls hopping from square to square, 'plucking the daisies'. He watches the boys clad in starmenter black-and-gold, brandishing water-pistol projacs.
>
> He ignores the braid tugging, the occasional bloody nose, but firmly steps in when it comes to eye gouging or heads banged against the concrete corner of a sandbox.
>
> Recommendation: don't mess with it. This system is stable and archetypally sound.

—⚙—

*T*alk softly and carry an ironwood cudgel, the First Connatic had counseled. Now the teacher probably wouldn't allow any ironwood cudgels in the classroom, but there were ways to arm oneself more discreetly.

At the street corner, Gunnar put his father's riot glove on. He had only found the right-hand one, but that would suffice. Riot gloves were almost invisibly thin, a mere film, but clench your fists and they became as hard as steel. You couldn't punch through a ten-inch oak-wood door, but you could certainly break a jaw.

Thus it was with some confidence that he walked through the gate of the school. Silver letters gleamed in the sunlight: *The keyboard is mightier than any barbarian sword.*

Lavoine sat on the first step of the staircase and waved.

"Hey you." The boy stepped in front of him. *What was his name? Yedlar. Yes. It seems I get to use the glove after all.*

Yedlar's cronies stood behind him but not really close. *Only two of them. The other must still be home, licking his wounds.* He smiled at the boy with the lank hair, his best chimpanzee smile, showing his teeth all the way to the gums, and saw him stiffen.

"About yesterday," Yedlar said.

"Yes?"

"I'm sorry. I truly thought you were from Garnet. They are wife-stealers, slick as snake-oil."

The third boy nodded. "You're the Whelm! We jumped you with four men and you thrashed us."

"The Whelm," the boy with lank hair added. "They are our true warriors! They keep us safe from the starmenters." He looked up at the sky, then back to Gunnar. There was awe in his gaze.

This is crazy. Almost like one of those stupid tales from My First Picture Book. Defeat the bully and he becomes your best friend. Like taming a wild dog.

"Now don't get me wrong," Yedlar said, almost as if he was reading Gunnar's thoughts. "I'm not your friend. You kissed my girl. She let you kiss her, just to drive me mad." He raised his left hand, the fingers spread. It was one of the things Gunnar's mother had taught him as a toddler. Left hand, clap, right hand, clap and touch knuckles. It was better than showing your empty hands. It changed any encounter from a growling, chest-thumping contest into a game.

He clapped hands with the others and it felt right: the kind of ritual that made you belong.

He stepped back. "Good, Yedlar, we are rivals now. Not enemies, Yedlar." *Use a new name as often as you can. It always pacifies a stranger. And then give him your own name, which he probably has forgotten or never knew.*

"By the way, they call me Gunnar."

Lavoine handed him his uniform.

"I heard you talking. You are quite devious! Played them like a fox-monk plays a swamp-banjo."

"You like that?"

She frowned, shook her head. "I'm not sure. Coyote and Brer Rabbit really hate to be outsmarted. I'm more than a bit like them."

"Any suggestions, then? As to my behavior?"

"If you trick me be sure to be far away before I realize it. Life is too short to carry grudges, though. Avoid me for half a day and I'll probably have forgotten it."

"I'll keep that in mind. Now where is our class room?"

"Ah," master Ooka said, "milady Lavoine graces our humble room with a visit."

Lavoine put a hand on Gunnar's shoulder. "This boy here, his name is Gunnar. His father is someone high in the Whelm. Don't annoy Gunnar: he'll break all your bones and play Hussade with your head."

"A fair warning," master Ooka said. "You'd best sit in front, next to our princess, Gunnar, that way I can keep an eye on both of you."

The next hour Gunnar sat carving Sumerian cuneiforms in wet clay and then took up the paint brush and ink-stone to write the same proverb in Ninetieth Dynasty Chinese.

It felt very familiar: this was the right way to begin any school day, recapitulating the human past.

Now draw a cybernetic circuit on the programmed paper and then a speaker. Finally, touch the right-hand corner.

"Oh king," a tinny voice intoned, "those who bow so low that their brow touches the floor of your yurt, usually keep a dagger hidden behind their backs."

Even after thousands of years it was still sound advice, Gunnar thought. And there was something delightfully perverse in it: modern devices never spoke.

"Now, we come back to the present," master Ooka said. "Our world."

Phaedra's globe filled the classroom, rotating ponderously.

"This is a world that never should have been alive. The radiation belts of Astaroth are as deadly as Jupiter's. Not even a microbe should have survived here. Yet?" He looked around.

The boy with the lank hair raised his hand. "There are generators hidden in the core, ser. They push the radiation away."

"Yes, machines. Phaedra was terraformed, made habitable, but perhaps 'elderformed' would be a better description? They didn't make her for us, even if we can breathe the air." He looked around the classroom. "For whom then?"

"The Galleons, ser!" The girl had hair as black as licorice, a blue butterfly tattooed on her brow. "And all the fishes with three tails." She was wholesome, that was the only right word. Sunlight and butter, ripe cherries. The girl next-door you were meant to marry. Still, there was nothing meek about her.

"Yes, Semele." *Ah, that was her name.* He shelved it. She didn't excite him the way Lavoine did, but there was a kind of familiarity. A potential best friend vibe.

Master Ooka waved to the moon. "This world, it was made for them and that is why we keep away from the Galleons and never, ever board them. If we catch a three-tailed fish or an armored water-spider we throw them back. They are not ours to eat."

Become part of the class. Fit in. Asking stupid questions is a sure-fire way. Gunnar raised his hand. "We've found other manufactured worlds, some even billions of years old. How do we know for sure Phaedra is Elder-made?"

"Good question and luckily I have the answer. They signed Phaedra."

The whole moon flattened into a huge Mercator projection: the River now visible in its total length and breadth.

Master Ooka snapped his fingers and a hundred discrete segments lit up.

"Each and every meander is probably a hieroglyph, one of their words. The glowing parts are just hieroglyphs we have found on other elderformed worlds. We still don't have the slightest idea how to translate them.

"Notice that character there, like two snakes copulating? That is the most common symbol and probably the name of their race. On Sao Brendall there is a whole mountain range raised in that shape."

A new picture appeared: a world as rough and ridged as Phaedra. Yes, there was the central mountain range and it looked indeed almost the same as those snake meanders, only a bit distorted because planets never remained the same, their tectonic plates shifting and breaking.

They carved whole worlds. Gunnar pictured a monstrous knife, thousands of miles long, cutting the crust of Sao Brendall until the magma rose to spell out their name.

I hope we never meet them.

"How was your day?" Justine asked. "Made any new enemies? Seen more pretty girls?"

"With my enemies I have some kind of truce. I don't know if it will last."

"And the girls? You told me about the one that got you into a fight."

"She's my girlfriend. But, once again, only kind of."

"There is a rule if you are a boy," Justine said. "The first kiss is often easy to get. Call it an investment on the woman's part, yes? But if you haven't kissed her again after the next two weeks, she isn't for you. Look for another one. The river is full of other fish at your age." She tilted her head, pursed her lips in a lewd smile and winked.

"Hey, stop that! Don't look at me that way."

Justine laughed. "You are handsome enough. Your Lavoine should better not dawdle."

"There was another girl. Semele. She has a blue butterfly tattooed on her brow."

"Ah. You know how to pick them."

"What does a blue butterfly mean here?"

His mother put on her Mona Lisa smile. "That is for you to find out."

"And your day? How did it go?"

"I thought you would never ask. Well, the temple of Diana was quite interested when the abbess heard I was the wife of a Whelm officer. She wants me to teach her girls self-defense."

Gunnar could well understand that: Justine had been a waitress in one of the tougher harbor bars of Blue Scimitar, and half the soldiers of the Whelm were female. She probably really knew seven ways to kill with her bare hands.

"Go for it. And any nice men?"

"Not yet. And I'm not exactly looking for a 'nice' man."

"Glinnes was."

"Sure. But Mesmeth, he…"
"Stop! I don't want to hear."
Parents had no shame.

Chapter VII

From *Silenus, the Connatic's Poet*:

Adhemar Lacrosse de Bavourd wrote his dissertation on the famous Old Earth epic *Anne of Green Gables*. Only four lines were left but he reconstructed it, using dream herbs and a parapsychic Enigma machine from Turandot.

He became a full professor at the Waterstone Academy, but his tenure didn't help when he was found in the bed of the rector's virgin daughter. His defense that he was only reciting a recently composed ode and needed the innocent ear of an unspoiled virgin was disregarded.

After he had been dismissed from the Waterstone Academy for "moral turpitude and conduct unbecoming a member of our ancient institute," the professor took the name Silenus, after the mentor and boon companion of the Greek god Dionysus. "I'll be as drunken a poet as my namesake!" he declared. "Riding across all the worlds on my mule and kissing all the prettiest girls."

—

He went on to do just that.

Whether his elusive muse Anne of Green Gables was the rector's daughter is a matter of conjecture. He called her "My little lamia, innocent as the morning dew" and what girl could object to that?

The first poem in *Ruminations of a Happy Fool* mentions her:

So call me Rumpelstiltskin,
My dear Anne of Green Gables,
My little lamia
Of the morning dew,

See me,
Pirouetting in the woods
On my red dancing shoes!
Call me mad Macbeth,
Tasting from the Witches cauldron
And pronouncing their soup much too salty!

—ɯ—

Blue Scimitar was an ancient city, at least a thousand years old, but history hadn't burdened its citizens with a hundred quaint taboos and customs as in other places Gunnar had been forced to stay. Time had worn this culture smooth as a river-pebble: everything was easygoing and mellow.

Don't eat anything three-tailed from the river though, catch only Earth fish and lobsters. All three-tailed creatures belonged to the Galleons. There was also a more cogent reason than mere superstitious awe: their protein was quite poisonous and their blood was laced with arsenic compounds.

Most jokes were about the stinginess of the Greenstones from the next city downstream, or the mulish straightforwardness of the bat-herds from the high meadows.

Gunnar had heard all the jokes before, and soon could make up his own: just file off the serial numbers. It earned him a quite undeserved reputation as a wit.

One hated Garnets of course, who were sly and not to be trusted, according to the other boys. The girls, however, giggled and colored whenever Garnet was mentioned.

There were the usual temples of the Cluster Goddesses, with Mirricyllai, who ruled over the rivers of Alastor, being the principal. "Mirri catch me!" or "So help me Mirri!" were curses her priests deplored.

The only real taboo was speaking about the Slow Galleons. "Ask your uncles," was the automatic retort of the boys, and the girls stared at him as if Gunnar were a bat-herd, recently descended from the cliffs. Gunnar had yet to meet his first uncle and Justine was as unforthcoming as the girls.

• • •

Days turned into weeks and Lavoine still hadn't kissed him a second time. Gunnar found himself quite paradoxically more often than not in the company of Yedlar. The big boy wasn't stupid for all his lumbering size and it helped that they were in agreement about the most important thing in their world: Lavoine was a queen, a goddess, and certainly the highest prize a man could hope to win. All the other boys were unbelievers and thus of no consequence.

In the second week, they climbed the cliff just behind the Weirdwood Hotel, hanging by their fingertips, daring each other to cross one more waterfall. Lavoine was standing below, urging them on with shrill whistles and clapping her hands. She was probably hoping to see one of them slip and break his bones.

It was an old, almost archetypal pattern that Gunnar and Yedlar were acting out, and the quite disreputable poet Silenus had caught it in one of his poems:

> See them strut and parade,
> spreading feathered fans,
> and baring dagger-teeth!
> Such splendid rivals!
> Their lady stands in the shadow,
> drab and quite forgotten!

Well, Lavoine wasn't exactly forgotten and no one would call her drab, but during the climb neither of them looked down.

At the top, Gunnar leaned back against the bole of one of the wine-trees.

Below them the River was a quicksilver highway, shimmering in the glare of white-green Syrthene. Sails dotted the waves and whirlpools.

The city stretched away in the hazy distance: row after row of ironwood and bamboo high-rises, with the villas of the magnates higher in the hills. In Blue Scimitar the wealthy lived in bubbles of foamed diamond with narrow windows of amethyst and emerald, each bubble crowned by its own wind vane of ghost-glass. *They looked like the sporangia of some monstrous slime mold*, Gunnar thought, not his idea of luxury.

"I wish I had visited Numenes like you," Yedlar said. "All those wonderful places." He spread his arms. "To see the four suns of Marune rise! The Rhune girls mysterious and haughty as elf ladies!"

"The girls are more beautiful here."

Yedlar nodded. "One at least." They both looked automatically down but Lavoine was long gone.

Often Lavoine just waved at the boys after school and stepped on her hover disk, whisking away on one of her mysterious errands. There were other girls, of course, but they seemed flat and wan, poor imitations of the only woman who really counted.

The other three boys, whom Lavoine had laughingly dubbed "my bodyguards", were tolerated but distinctly lower in the pecking order of admirers.

There was Hunre, the boy with the lank hair. He came from the waterside: a fisherman's son; a faint reek of smoked eels and fermented seaweed always clung to his clothes. Kassem and Gudriyn were cousins: in Blue Scimitar that made them closer than brothers. They wore their hair bowl-cut, reminding Gunnar of a pair of medieval peasants.

That afternoon, all five sat by the riverside.

"I wonder…" Yedlar said and stopped. He skimmed a stone across the whirlpools. A huge mouth studded with jagged teeth opened and gulped the stone down. There were cogent reasons for the many swimming pools in Blue Scimitar and the high price of fresh fish.

"You wonder what?"

"Where she goes."

"Doing witch stuff I guess. Stealing babies and shrinking their heads." Hunre snickered, and then blanched when he realized how close he came to lèse majesté.

"No really, Gunnar, did you ever visit her home?" Yedlar sounded hopeful. Perhaps Gunnar was more privileged than he, closer to his goddess?

"She rings my bell or phones me to meet her at the pier. I haven't the slightest idea where she lives." *And I never tried to find out,* he suddenly realized. *Why didn't I?*

"That girl is at the door again," Justine would call up to his room. "Has she kissed you yet?"

"Why do you hate her?" he had once asked.

"Oh, I don't hate Lavoine. She's a poisonous little bitch, who loves only herself and probably not even that. She reminds me of myself at her age. But don't listen to me. Everybody has the right to make at least one bad mistake in his life."

The thought drifted away again. What did it matter where she lived? Keep her mysterious! If she slept with three sisters in a fisherman's shack like Hunre's, with the washing flapping on lines and the gulls peeing on the cabbages, that would spoil everything.

However, she owned a hover disk, one that looked brand-new, and the cheapest models cost at least two thousand ozols: she must be upper middle class at least, if not of magnate stock.

No, it was better not to know. A giggling mother who kept pink toads with fluffy fur and sisters who had their own riding-dogs, that would spoil it even more.

"Semele," Yedlar said out of the blue.

"What about Semele?"

"She asked about you. If you really had a trophy wall at home with the mounted heads of starmenters. Of pirates your father had killed personally. I said: 'Of course, I've seen them with my very own eyes.'" He shook his head. "I don't think she believed me."

Gunnar pursed his lips. "I know what you are doing. Trying to fob me off with another girl."

"Guilty. But Semele is all right. And I saw you eyeing her." Another skimming stone. Another maw suddenly popping up. "She came in second in the competition, you know. Shoots an arrow like Diana herself."

"She's from the temple? Mirri curse me! That was why my mother smiled. Justine teaches there. She told me those poor girls aren't allowed to kiss any boy. Chaste."

"A pity, eh? But perhaps you can change her mind?"

Gunnar snorted. "She can be our bridesmaid when I marry Lavoine." He hit Yedlar's biceps. "And you may be my best man."

But the hook was set that afternoon, planted firmly in his living flesh. A beautiful huntress who had sworn never to kiss a man... It was enough to make you forget your fox-girl. But only when she wasn't there to renew her magic and squeeze your heart.

• • •

Hunre rose. "Let's cross to the other side," he said. "We're just sitting on our butts. We never go anywhere."

Gunnar didn't really mind. Boredom had been a rare gift in the life of an admiral's son. Still…"What lies on the other side that is of such interest?"

"The Seven Months' Fair, for three more days. Even the bat-herds come down from their high crags, to sell fermented rock-eggs. One sip and you see colors dance between the clouds and hear the tulips sing!" He spread his arms and his eyes shone. "There are roasted sea cucumbers and crab-apples dipped in honey. And the girls, they are willing to kiss you if you give them a ride in the big wheel."

"Sounds like paradise," Gunnar said. He had seen the Winter Rodeo on Chevalier, with the cowboys riding three horned bulls and the women clad in swirling taffeta, their lips painted red. And the Nineteen Butterflies Festival on Lamorre with a thousand tiny light-ships sailing into the New Year. But this was different. He would be here the next year, and the year after that. *Time to sink roots. To become a true Blue Scimitarian.*

"Do I need any special attire?"

"We can buy a necklace of lacquered sea urchins when we step from the ferry," Hunre said.

"And bracelets with yellow beads," Kassem nodded. "That is their color, you see. Ocher Gishimal. No need to advertise that we came from the other side of the River."

The Dark Eye-blink came on while they walked to the dock, the sky suddenly turning indigo, then black. Stars shone forth as they boarded the ferry.

Gunnar tried to locate the sun of Numenes but it was probably too faint. It didn't matter: he was here, for once not just making ready to depart to some new place.

There was a distinct festival mood on the boat: two couples dancing on the bow, their friends clapping hands and blowing on ocarinas. On the other side, three kids were flying musical kites which sang out with every gust of wind.

"Don't lean on the railings," Hunre warned. "They are electrified. The Riverlings, you see."

"Riverlings?"

"Anything with three tails. They all like human meat and think our blood tastes like a fine brandy. It doesn't make them sick like it does us." He beckoned Gunnar. "Now look down to the hull."

The whole side of the ferry glittered in the starlight.

"Those rows of triangles: shark's teeth?"

"Completely covered in it. The ferry, it is wearing a coat of living sharkskin. Still, after five or six crossings, they have to hoist the ferry from the water and stretch a new coat. Clawed away and eaten down to the panzer-glass." He nodded. "My father's boat also grows shark's teeth. And we have heavy duty cattle prods for when that's not enough."

The river was twenty miles wide here, with swift currents and savage whirlpools, and it took them the whole Dark Eye-blink to cross.

All the lumens along the boulevard shone a joyous yellow, and just beyond the apple trees the tents and pavilions rose. A truly monstrous Ferris wheel with clear diamond gondolas dominated the Fair. It rose some three hundred meters into the air and was lit up like a midwinter tree.

"The view up there is great," Hunre pointed. "But it doesn't come cheap. Ten ozols for a ticket." He was clearly the veteran here and their guide.

"Hold on," the voice of the ferryman warned. The ferry grappled the concrete pier with mechanical claws and heaved itself from the water, out of the reach of Riverlings. A gangway clanged down and they went ashore.

The first thing Gunnar noticed was the smell: unlike any previous fair there was no trace of burned sugar or the sweetness of bubbling lemonade. Every breath filled his nose with the tingle of clean mountain air.

After a ride in the River-boats, racing down waterfalls while tentacles tried to grab them and with the water full of snapping reptile-jaws, Gunnar lost sight of the others. It didn't matter: their ferry wouldn't depart for another four hours.

"Hear the wise words of the first Connatic!" a barker called. "Drink from his wisdom which is still as fresh as the day he wrote it down!"

Gunnar shook his head. That was more something for pedants, for those who delighted in quoting ancient texts.

A flash of blue: he stopped, stared. But the girl had already turned her face away, hidden by a fall of black hair.

He ran after her, completely sure that it was her, and put a hand on her shoulder. "Semele?"

The girl turned, and it wasn't an animated blue butterfly tattooed on her brow but some kind of heraldic dragon. Her eyes were a brilliant green, which made her one of mountain folks, a bat-herd girl. About the most dangerous woman to accost.

"Sorry. I thought…"

"I'm not Semele," the girl said. "But it *is* your lucky day. I'm much more interesting than she is." She hooked her arm in his. "You may buy me a ticket for the Wheel. When the cabin halts at the top and we gaze down in wonder, I'll allow you to kiss me and perhaps even more." She smiled up at him. "They say the bat-herd girls are passionate and easy. Perhaps they are right?"

Gunnar had spent three years on Chevalier and knew that a man was required to be gallant above all. Telling her she wasn't worth the price of a ticket would be the act of a boor.

"Gladly I would take you," he said, automatically slipping into the accent of Chevalier, that strange mix of down-to-Earth and almost Victorian formality.

"Ha, a gentleman!"

Walking together felt quite natural, the rhythm of their steps automatically matching.

He bought two tickets and winced: they were a lot more expensive than the ten ozols Hunre had mentioned.

"My first time on the wheel," the girl confessed. "I tried and tried but no boy wanted to buy me a ticket."

They settled in the foamed glass of the seats. A clang and the cabin rose.

"I'm Gunnar, by the way. Gunnar Justinesson."

"Ah, you must be from Scimitar, where you take the name of your mother. A nice custom."

"And you?"

"Well, how about Anne of Green Gables?"

"You want me to write a sonnet with the blood of your dearest enemy?" According to the stories Silenus had done just that, to get the daughter of the rector to elope with him. "I can quote Silenus if you want. To start?"

She nestled closer to him. "Please do. Tell that my eyes are like broken glass in the light of the jingle, jungle morning. That my tresses gleam like the roar of the Lion of the Sun."

Gunnar had once spent two weeks on a riverboat with his parents, with the single screen broken down and the only reading matter Silenus' *Ruminations of a Happy Fool*. When you are ten your brain is a still a sponge, absorbing every word.

> "I won't call it love,
> Because such a word
> Is just too paltry
> For our passion!
> Even if you were clad
> In a wedding gown
> Of barbed wire,
> Your mouth filled
> With poison fangs…"

She clapped her hands. "Well said, sir. But go on…"

The river became a blue ribbon, the ocher of Gishimal's roofs a twinkling haze in the green of the orchards. A dozen mock-geese flew past: their tail feathers an electric blue.

The cabin halted.

"Right," Anne of Green Gables said. "Now kiss me."

"Again," she said a moment later. "Now don't hold back! I'm not made of spun glass! And your hand: put it down here. On my breasts."

• • •

The cabin started moving again, descended much too fast.

"You do have another," she stated.

"Well, yes."

"That is no reason not to kiss me again. See it as a...well, a learning experience. That way you won't be a ham-fingered bungler when you embrace your true love." She looked into his eyes. "I see I was wrong. You have *two* lovers and one looks just like me."

"No one looks just like you," his Chevalier conditioning made him say. "There is only one Anne of Green Gables."

The cabin stopped and the door hissed open.

"Tell her you still have to work on the kissing," Anne of Green Gables said. "But you know how to flatter a girl. That is perhaps even more important."

The crowd absorbed her and he knew better than to run after her. The next time she wouldn't be Anne of Green Gables.

The fairy tale feeling remained the whole boat trip back to Blue Scimitar, like some gold dusted picture. As if the wheel had lifted him to some place out of time, out of his real life.

"Lavoine," he muttered. "Semele." It sounded like a counter-spell.

He could fantasize about a romance with Anne of Green Gables but not with a bat-herd girl. They always married a cousin from the next eyrie and all other people were främlings to them. Less than human.

Chapter VIII

From *Techno-secrets, and those who keep them:*

Endless books always have exactly seventy-four pages but the moment you turn the seventy-fourth page the text on the first page will have changed, continuing the tale.

Endless books adapt to their readers: they may start out as a kindergarten primer about a plucky garden gnome and his friend the Red Robin, and slowly segue into an Arabian Nights sex manual.

This is not the only reason why they are illegal on quite a few of the more straight-laced planets. The Security Council itself argued that endless books are perilously close to the Turing-limit.

The books, being almost indestructible*, often become family heirlooms with their stories growing ever stranger and more intricate.

The origin of the books remains quite unclear: some cite the industrial world of Tetrish, Alastor 147, as manufacturer. Others point to the secretive Carthusian monks who cut off their tongues and ride comets from star to star.

---

* There is the, admittedly apocryphal, story of the Caliph of Radinipur. Upon the demise of the clownish protagonist, and in accordance with his orders, an endless book was burned along with his corpse. The pyre flamed and smoldered for nine years and consumed all the jewel-trees of his country. When the ashes cooled, the book emerged, with not a single singed page. The cover now showed the Caliph trying to light a candle, surrounded by hills of burned-out matches.

"Gunnar!" Justine called. "Someone for you."

He put his endless book down. The half-troll hero Lamoraal the Sly had been trying to return to his icy homeland for as long as Gunnar could read, being thwarted at every turn. Gunnar would probably be old and gray and at least a hundred and twenty before he turned the last page. Or perhaps it would be a great-grandchild that finally read THE END.

"It's that girl."

For a moment, no longer than a heartbeat, he felt disappointment when he saw a flash of red hair, that it wasn't Anne of Green Gables or Semele of the Blue Butterfly, but Lavoine's fox magic took hold the moment they stepped outside.

The world sharpened around him, became edgy and dangerous and gloriously strange. While walking with Lavoine, anything could happen: the stone cuckoos on the door lintels could grow teeth and jump down to the street, snapping at your ankles; an earnest rabbi might throw his little round hat in the air and turn cartwheels, singing like a lark. It never did happen, but the potential was there, buzzing like an angry wasp.

Lavoine never used perfume, but she wore her own glorious scent, spicy and sharp like heather blooming in the hot sun.

Ten steps and then she stopped, embraced and kissed him. This time it was a much longer kiss and completely different. As heartfelt as Anne's.

She stepped back, eyed him. "Like it?"

"What was that for?"

"To show you and the world that I'm your girlfriend. To take away any doubt." She put her hover-disk on the ground, where it floated thirty-four centimeters above the cobbles, stepped on it, and was whisked away instantly.

The endless book had just told him, only three pages back, that "Lamoraal looked after the lady who had just kissed him and then, spreading her wings, jumped from the windowsill, leaving him hot and unfulfilled. Did Lady Senf love him or was she just teasing, playing a joke on a passing stranger?" *Hot and unfulfilled* and deeply unsure of himself, that was exactly how Gunnar felt.

• • •

Half an hour later his phone sang out and Yedlar's face appeared. His friend grinned, then raised two fists in the air. "You lost!" he crowed. "She kissed me and told me I was her boyfriend." He frowned. "What is that look on your face?"

Gunnar didn't have to say anything.

"O, Mirri curse me! She kissed you too, and told you she's your girlfriend!"

Gunnar clacked his tongue. "Nobody ever said that courting a fox-lady was easy."

"She's a monster."

"No, a girl. That is worse. They love to tease boys. We are their play-things, their fools."

They sighed in unison.

"Justine?" Gunnar said when he took a second helping of the tiramisu cake that evening. "Are all girls termagants and heartless teases?"

"Most of them. Why?"

"Lavoine kissed me and told me I was her boyfriend. Then she skimmed up to Hugharda Prospect and kissed Yedlar and told him the same."

"Don't jump into the River yet. One day you'll meet a nice girl. At least someone nicer than Lavoine."

"Ha!"

"By the way, there is a girl in my self-defense class. She asked if she could see our trophy wall of starmenter heads. What crazy tales have you been telling in school?"

"That must have been Semele. Yedlar made up that tale."

"I think you mentioned her before. It set me to thinking. If you ever want to invite her here…" She snapped her fingers and the wall rippled. It suddenly was hung with a dozen faces, most of them frozen in mid-snarl. Three of the decapitated heads were still dripping holographic blood.

"This is crazy."

"Diana's girls are kind of savage. This would certainly please her."

• • •

Astaroth was full, the shadows of three other moons slowly moving dots on her clouds. He opened his book, touched the question mark and wrote: loving a bad girl.

The page flickered and then showed the answer in ornate script:

The three sat down with a calabash of palm wine.

"I once loved a decidedly bad girl," Delubas the Bold said. "She was a harpy and her talons racked my back until my skin hung in tatters. We copulated in her filthy nest, which was made of bones and skulls." He touched his ear. "See? She bit my earlobe right off and spat out my golden earring." A fond smile lit up his face. "That was the best sex I ever had!"

Gunnar closed the book. This wasn't the kind of answer he was looking for.

Chapter IX

From *Restricted Worlds, the Observations of a Star-Trotting Vagabond* by Yuri Hopkins, writing for the *Alastor Herald*, monthly magazine, now with Mirricyllai-approved horoscope.

The Bright Way is the official city religion of Blue Scimitar, a syncretic grab-bag of philosophies and eccentric pantheons, featuring goddesses and demons from all over the Gaean Reach. The believers take Mirri's name in vain and swear by Apollo's beard. Mirri is their Stella Maris, who protects the sailors and fishermen and can still any storm.

Most Scimitarians also believe wholeheartedly in garden gnomes that walk during the Dark Eye-blink and will fulfill any wish if you catch them in mid-stride with a net woven of your own hair.

The most curious avatar, without doubt, is Saint Dismas the Good Thief who had been crucified next to Yeshua, Diana's Brother Who Died Twice.

—⁂—

There were no seasons on Phaedra and a Great Year lasted almost ninety standard years. Accordingly, the Phaedrans made up their own cycles.

The school year climaxed during Gunnar's eleventh month there, with the Ball of Saint Dismas.

Smaller children found clockwork fish in the gold-painted basket of the Yule-bear, while their older brothers and sisters folded paper butterflies or threw lilies from their windows. The two nights before the Ball were filled with furtive whistles and sighs, flitting shadows.

. . .

"Saint Dismas?" Lavoine said. "Me at the ball of the Good Thief?" She laughed and it was almost a caw. "Do you see me slow dancing in rose-red tulle, with three bows in my hair? Ha, where I walk the daisies shrivel! The butterflies scream and flee!"

"I gather that is a 'no'?"

"It is." She strode away and didn't even look back over her shoulder. She was sure he would be standing there like a kicked puppy, his shoulders slumping.

This was deeply stupid. She's the Monkey King's Daughter: she can't stand sentiment or anybody looking vulnerable.

Gunnar straightened his back, lifted his chin. *There are more fish in the River, as Justine said. And girls like me. At least Anne did, even if she said I still had to work on my kissing.*

He found Semele in the park behind the Pillar of Good Cheer, her compound bow raised. She pulled the bowstring taut and it sang a high C when she let go.

He waited until she put her weapon down.

"You are shooting invisible arrows?"

"Any fool can put an arrow through a circling vulture, Gunnar. A true Daughter of Diana doesn't need to see her prey tumbling down to know her arrow flew true."

"I get it." And he did. "It's like repeating an act with your eyes closed or in a dream. Only then is it pure. Only then you don't need a reward or a confirmation."

She smiled at him and he saw one of her front teeth was crooked. It made her authentic. This was the self-confidence of a Daughter of Diana: take me as I am. I won't change for you.

"I saw you ogling me," she said. "Thinking me prey, like a skittish hind with huge, alarmed doe eyes. That your arrow would pierce me." She touched the blue butterfly on her brow. "This tells the world that I vowed to remain pure. That no man would defile me." She spoke like the heroine in an ancient play and it suited her.

"I know. Diana is the virgin goddess. I'm no Actaeon to be torn apart by my own hunting dogs."

"I see you did your research." It was impossible to determine if she was pleased or if she thought him a pedant, trying to impress a girl with his knowledge. She clacked her tongue. "Well, yes."

He frowned. "Yes, what?"

"Yes, I will go with you to the Saint Dismas dance. You may hold my hand; you may even embrace me, but no kissing."

"Otherwise you'll turn into a pumpkin?"

"Worse. The goddess will be displeased." She put a hand on his shoulder. "I like you even if you keep sniffing after that bitch. I wear the blue butterfly now but that isn't forever. Virginity is a young girls' game and I'll tear my butterfly off and throw it in the River the moment I start my Walk with the Galleons."

There it was again. The Galleons. Walking with the Galleons. But it was no use to ask. He knew that by now.

"I'll be there," he vowed. "Holding your hand the moment you take the first step."

"Only Diana knows the future." She lifted her left hand, drew a circle with a rather sharp nail on his brow. He stood stock-still, willing himself not to flinch. She stepped back as if to admire her handy-work.

"I have marked you. Marked you like a tree for the woodsman to cut down. Right now you think me the second best choice."

"No, no! I..."

"Pierced his heart, Diana," she sang out.

"Cut out his liver, Artemis. This proud stag is mine, Lady Moon!"

The circle on Gunnar's forehead throbbed and the words repeated themselves in a high silvery voice.

Great, the small part of him that wasn't panicking thought, *another practicing witch. How the hell do I choose them?*

The dread faded: it no longer felt as if he had an icicle rammed up his spine. But the voice hadn't been imaginary.

"Some people say that we virgins take honor too seriously," Semele said and suddenly she giggled. "You should have seen your face! There is no magic! Spells are pure balderdash." She shook her head. "That voodoo girl sure hooked her claws in your brain. Wake up!"

She doesn't know. She doesn't know the goddess heard her prayer.

"And if I took you in my arms and kissed you right now?"

"Then my butterfly would shrivel and fall off. All the girls of the convent would laugh at me and call me 'Eagerling'. One without a trace of self-control. I would hate you forever."

"But I saw you kissing another girl."

"That was just a dear friend. A sister-hunter. Diana doesn't mind."

Semele reached down and the arrow she put on the bow was real enough this time. She turned and it pointed right at his heart. "Now leave me. I'll see you in three days for the dance. I haven't noticed any butterfly landing on my windowsill yet."

"But I don't know where you live!"

"You will no doubt find out."

Chapter X

From *Restricted Worlds, the Observations of a Star-Trotting Vagabond* by Yuri Hopkins, writing for the *Alastor Herald*, monthly magazine, now with Mirricyllai-approved horoscope.

Ezulia: Alastor 2956 was settled by an orthodox voodoo sect. One of their major deities, Baron Samedi, had once been the African chieftain Ghede, famed for his cruelty.

Centuries after his death, his shade was lured back from the 'wide yam-field where white elephants roam', by a ritual involving rum and burning cane sugar as well as the blood of half a dozen victims.

Several thousand years of worship and sacrifices made him one of the most powerful gods, capable of taking over the body of any believer.

The counsel of houngans, the high priests, decided to experiment: if the pale shades of the dead could be made into gods, how much more effective might an AI then be? A being that started out with a more than human intelligence?

Ezulia is a burnt out cinder now and third on the list of Restricted Planets. I wasn't even allowed to orbit the planet. The Whelm deported the few survivors to places all over the cluster.

—⚏—

alk with the Galleons. I'll tear my butterfly off and throw it in the River the moment I start to Walk with the Galleons. Suddenly Gunnar couldn't stand not knowing for another second. But how did this "Your uncle will tell"-business work? Just stepping up to a likely adult probably wouldn't do.

Wait. It is just knowledge. There is one place where they hold a copy of the Bibliotheque, a repository that is kept just below the Turing-limit and will answer any reasonable question.

The ferry took him to the floating dome of Alastor Centrality in the bay. Gunnar had often seen the cupola from the tip of Cape Juniper, gleaming in the sunset. *I should visit the Center,* he had more than once thought. *Sometime soon.*

The edges of the dome were coated with frictionless glass to keep noxious Riverlings away. Higher up, a hedge of razor wire coiled, an invention almost as old as stone axes and fire.

Gunnar was the only passenger.

"All off!" the ferryman cried when the bow touched the pier. He eyed Gunnar: "This is your first visit, boy? Your parents are wise to send you. Here is the knowledge of the whole Alastor Cluster to be found. The wise words of twenty-nine Connatics! Much better than any local college where they'll only fill your ears with tired superstition."

"Yes," Gunnar said. "I have to consult the Bibliotheque. Homework, yes. Where exactly is it?"

"Straight on. Through that gate with the roaring lions."

The dome proved as deserted as the deck of the ferry. Gunnar had imagined a teeming crowd, hundreds of students and frowning savants. He found an empty hall instead, and three dozen pillars of swirling light: probably the library nodes.

A man stepped from a niche, smiled. "You have a question, Gunnar?"

"Sure, but perhaps I should start with how do you know my name?"

"Well, my daughter has often mentioned you. You and her other friend Yedlar."

Gunnar stared at the bland face, the guileless blue eyes. This man could have been a rose gardener or a confectioner who built castles from fondant and marzipan.

"You are Lavoine's father?" He felt a letdown, a draining of life force and the world suddenly seemed dreary and gray. *Such an ordinary father. It must have been the mother who gave Lavoine those fierce fox-genes, her dark magic.*

"She told you that I'm the Cursar, I hope?"

And the bland, nondescript face became a perfect disguise instead. This man could walk the streets of Blue Scimitar and his face would be forgotten the moment he turned a corner.

He's the Cursar, the planetary governor. He can call the Whelm down, order the death of a thousand rebels. Gunnar's father had been an admiral of the Whelm, a swift and deadly sword, but it was the Cursar who wielded that sword in the Connatic's name.

"Yes, she said that. Lavoine did."

To love the Cursar's Daughter. It sounded almost like a tale, something the comrades in Gunnar's endless book would tell. *And him standing here as a kind of humble librarian, listening to the questions of his subjects, learning what they really thought and wanted. Just like the Connatic.*

"But you had a question?"

He tried to still his tumbling thoughts. "Uh, yes. Well, I'm not from here, as Lavoine probably told you. I don't know the simplest things. When you turn sixteen you Walk with the Galleons. I haven't the slightest idea what that means.

" 'Go ask your uncle,' the people here say. I don't have an uncle here, only three aunts. My mother's brothers all live in other cities. I've never met them."

"I see. A problem that is easily solved." The Cursar strolled to one of the pillars of scintillating light. "Let's ask the Bibliotheque. There must have been quite a number of visitors who aren't averse to explaining strange foreign customs."

He touched the pillar and said: "Walk with the Galleons."

Text scrolled down. In the ancient times even watches and egg-timers had been able to speak: mankind would never make that mistake again.

"Fools try to people the sky with gods and demons, crying: 'There surely must be more!' This while the Gaean Reach is filled with mysteries, many of them dark and awful.

"Take the Galleons of Phaedra. Immense ships sail down a mighty river, never mooring, like a convoy of Flying Dutchmen. Who steers them? What immortal sailors climb their masts?

"All our human tech fails at their approach, and even lenses refuse to augment the human eye. No picture was ever taken, and the Connatic has ordered the Galleons off limits for all, on pain of death. Monitors follow the Galleons on horseback and shoot any criminal who enters the water.

"The colonists of Phaedra have an interesting coming of age ritual called Walking with the Galleons.

"On his or her sixteenth birthday a boy or girl leaves the ancestral home and follows a Galleon on foot. These pilgrims circumnavigate the whole of Phaedra, never staying more than a day in a single place. When the 'walkers' return, they are as cosmopolitan as any star-trotter, each city along the way being a world in itself.

"Not all travelers return, sadly. Between the cities lie stretches of primeval wilderness, with wild boars and tribes of augmented chimpanzees who consider humans the tastiest of monkeys.

"The boys and girls carry poisoned throwing knives and crossbows. That isn't always enough. A knife may have a cracked poison reservoir, a quarrel can miss, and you have only one chance when an enraged boar charges you.

"Those who don't complete this pilgrimage, become objects of scorn. They are called 'half-hadjis' and they usually end up as streetsweepers or bird-catchers."

The text faded, disappeared.

"Does that answer your question?" the Cursar asked.

"Quite sufficiently. There are details but I don't think they are that secret."

"Talk softly," the Cursar said, "and carry a big ironwood cudgel when you go. That works in any wilderness." He shook Gunnar's hand. "Always nice to meet friends of my daughter. Lavoine doesn't make friends easily, you know."

Gunnar didn't take a swift-bahn bubble car home, but walked all the way. His heart sang.

Two girls to love. Lavoine had the newly acquired glamour of being the daughter of the most powerful and dangerous man on Phaedra, but Semele had promised to tear off her butterfly for him. Even if he had to wait at least a year.

There was that drinking-song Lamoraal and Yemde da Lagrimas had sung when they tried to drink the cannibal king of Heimburgh under the table.

> Two sisters I've loved,
> Take another skull,
> And fill it with sizzling mead.
> One was as fair as spring,
> Clothed in sprigs right green.
> Take another skull,
> And fill it with sizzling mead.
> The other was dark of soul
> And sleek as a cat,
> With a thousand tricks.

It fitted perfectly, and Lamoraal didn't have to choose. He got both of them in the end.

Though the fair one cursed him, and ever after, each silver sesterce that Lamoraal earned or stole, turned into a copper piece of the lowest denomination the moment the cock crowed. And her sister sent the Dreadful Hare That Coughs in the Night after Lamoraal…

No, perhaps it was safer to choose one of them before things became really serious. He was no Lamoraal after all.

"Show me, Justine," Gunnar pleaded the moment she stepped through the door. "Please," he added. The floor of the living room was littered with crumpled paper butterflies. "I printed a step by step manual but my butterflies refuse to flap their wings. And there isn't a word about how to steer them to the right window."

"Give me a piece of paper. It isn't anything a girl should know but my brothers weren't exactly patient or dexterous and I had to fold their butterflies. Otherwise they would have gone to their graves as virgins." Justine took the glittering paper, folded it several times, her fingers moving too fast to follow. "It is for your little witch? She'll trample your butterfly and spit on it."

"Probably. But it isn't for her. And anyhow, this is something all the other boys can do. I don't want to stand out as a främling. As a clumsy-fingered Garnet."

"A clumsy-fingered Garnet! Ah, you are assimilating! Fitting in!" She opened her hand and the white butterfly flapped around the chandelier of sea-glass, shot out of the window.

"What's wrong with fitting in? You brought me here. You told me I was born a Blue Scimitarian."

"Touché. Now, I'll show it once more. This time slow enough that even a clumsy-fingered Garnet can follow it. It is like the origami on Yem Ulani, yes? All mountains and valleys and a sixfold trapeze twist in the end to power her." She looked out the window. "The lumens aren't dimming for the night yet. You still have hours. Fold a dozen before you go. There isn't any good way to aim them. They flutter where they want."

"Mirri curse me! I just realized I haven't the slightest idea where she lives…"

"No need to call on the goddess. Second Glass-blower street, number seventeen." She spread her hands. "I hope you don't consider me a busybody?"

"You are. I don't mind."

The Esplanade was hung with lumens: soft lights that drifted to and fro in the breeze, slowly changing color. Other boys strode along the strip of fused rock, their faces firm with determination or their lower lips trembling. This night they would either return with lilies clutched in their hands, or utterly devastated when their intended love plucked the butterfly of a rival from the air.

He passed the Golden Catfish. There was the sound of music utterly ancient, from a time that humans hadn't even reached the moon.

He had visited the tavern once with his mother, when the Go for Broke Jazz Band was playing.

The grizzled veterans shook their heads.

"We were all in love with you, Justine," the ukulele player with the knitted hat had said. "And look at you now! A full-grown son! But you are as pretty as ever."

"Prettier," his companion said.

It had all been very embarrassing.

• • •

He crossed the enormous Prater Rughalt square with the decapitated statues of the Three Directors, and then ascended the two hundred and six steps of the Leonissa Stairs, each step inlaid with nacre and imported amber. The First Glass-blower street, the Second, and now number seventeen...

He looked up and there was only one open window. Pale legs dangled in the shifting light of a lumen but the face of the girl remained in shadow, impossible to be sure. There was a certain amount of risk: if it was one of her sisters who sat there and caught his butterfly he would be obliged to take her to the ball.

No matter! Any sister of Semele was bound to be beautiful.

Gunnar wound his first butterfly, launched it into the air. A boy was allowed six butterflies: one more and he became absurd.

Diana must have smiled upon him because the butterfly went straight up and passed close to the window. An arm moved fast as a striking snake and caught the butterfly. A moment later a lily fluttered down.

"Semele?" he said.

"The one and only." She pulled her legs up and closed the window.

That was all, but it was enough. No, perfect. *She has agreed. We'll be dancing at the ball.*

On the night of Saint Dismas, Gunnar hired a rickshaw with the same runner who had welcomed them the first time.

After a drive that seemed over in an eye blink, he stepped from the rickshaw and rang her bell, his heart thumping in his throat. *A hundred ways to spoil it. To show myself as the foolish främling I am.*

The door opened instantly and there she stood: a maid Marian, clad in green velvet. She wore Greek sandals, the silver cords wrapped around her tanned legs. No bow, but three elegant throwing knives hung from an ornate girdle.

"You look..." He shook his head. "I have no words. Like a warrior princess from my endless book."

"High praise indeed." She took his arm and climbed into the rickshaw.

The runner shook his head. "You out-worlders, you are as bad as Garnets. Stealing all our most beautiful girls..."

• • •

The Hustler Hedbomas College for Young People was lit up like a carousel, glowing bunting hung in the trees and gay music was playing. A single cross rose from the center of the square with an effigy of the burgomeister Arnhold Calomar as the Good Thief affixed to it. It was all in fun. He was as corrupt as his predecessors, taking bribes from everybody who stepped across the threshold of his office, but the swift-bahn ran on time and the poor were well-fed and clothed. Arnhold was a scoundrel but he was *their* scoundrel.

The usual band of high-hill fiddlers mounted the platform: men with waxed mustaches and women who wore ornate headdresses and little else. One of the girls could have been Anne's sister.

The pupils started out dancing in two rows, one of boys, one of girls. Soon they swirled together, hooked arms with their partners.

Semele's eyes shone, her hair swirled. When the third song started, *Bats in Flight*, she put her arms around his middle, pressed her body against him and Gunnar needed all his self-discipline to refrain from kissing those wondrous lips.

She was wearing perfume, he noticed, something clean and subtle, like the smell of blue gentians. Or perhaps it was her own girl-scent.

The number ended and they walked over to the bowl of cider.

"Hey, Gunnar. Isn't this great?" Yedlar stood just behind him, Lavoine on his arm. She was wearing a gown of rose-red tulle and her hair spread in dozens of braids, each with its own butterfly-shaped bow.

She's toying with me. With me and Yedlar, using us. And we have no more to say than a sock-puppet. But knowing this did not help. *She's just too beautiful. The Cursar's daughter.*

Semele tugged at his arm and he followed her.

"You were staring!" she hissed. "Your mouth falling open and panting like a dog. Do you want to creep back to her? She'll probably dump your friend, dance the rest of the night with you. Anything to make trouble. To spoil everybody's happiness!"

"I'm standing here," Gunnar protested, "with you!" but Semele was just too angry.

"Take me home," she said. "Right now. That is the least you can do."

Chapter XI

From *Restricted Worlds, the Observations of a Star-Trotting Vagabond* by Yuri Hopkins, writing for the *Alastor Herald*, monthly magazine, now with Mirricyllai-approved horoscope.

Chevalier was never officially colonized. The Great and Illustrious Union of LARP players from Numenes chose an empty world far in the outback for their Seventieth Lustrum. The Death of Billy the Kid had been announced as the theme, with Old Earth's Wild West as general background.

The Union bought an obsolete troop transport and two thousand players boarded with their families. Some were clad as desperadoes, with long leather coats and six-guns, others as Chinese railroad workers. A hundred marshals sat polishing their stars; ladies of easy virtue walked the corridors clad in crinoline and lace or almost nothing at all. In the hold, mules bayed, horses snorted.

Entering the system after a three month journey, they passed two gas giants and the captain named them Zanegrey and Alamo.

A double planet heaved into view: one a rocky ball, the other a western wet dream with wide prairies and red deserts.

A herd of native mustangs suggested the name of their playing field: Chevalier, after the French word for 'horse'. That those mustangs had six legs and the heads of scarabs, didn't really matter. One shouldn't look a gift horse in the mouth and they *had* hooves and manes.

The festivities took all of two weeks.

Time to go home. The village they had built would become a proper ghost town, with the gallows still standing, the doors of the saloon clapping in the breeze.

The star drive lifted the ship half a meter from the ground and then expired.

The players had bought the ship quite cheaply. "Something for the hobbyist," the seller had said. "You'll probably have to tinker a bit. Replace some spools."

Now, those men and women were the crème de la crème of the re-enactors: they could sew their own clothes, tan the hide of any animal, forge plows and swords from bog iron.

But none of them could even repair a toaster.

Some fifty years later a scout-boat landed in the center of Billy Town, intent on bringing them all the comforts of civilization and reuniting them with the rest of the Cluster.

They hanged the pilot from the highest tree, leaving him for the crows which weren't exactly crows.

The Chevalierans quite liked what they had become for real: desperadoes and farmers, black-smiths and ladies who were no better than they should be.

—m—

"Is the dance already finished?" Justine asked. "I thought it lasted until the morning?" She put her brush down, pushed aside the vase she had been glazing with copper oxide. "Uh-oh. Such a long face. You two quarreled?"

"Lavoine turned up after all. With Yedlar. And Semele said I stared at her. That I preferred Lavoine to her."

"And did you?"

Gunnar had never lied to his mother. "Yes. But no longer than a heartbeat. She was so…female. The way I had never pictured her."

"Well, I don't see any scratched-out eyes."

"Semele…she's too civilized." He sighed. "And now she hates me."

"It is a problem. With any other girl, falling on your knees and covering her face with a dozen kisses might have helped. That's not an option with a huntress."

"No, it isn't. I blew it."

• • •

Back in his bedroom, he opened his endless book, wrote 'huntress' and 'love'.

> "My huntress," Delubas the Bold said, "she was such a little minx! How she loved loving. She came back from a hunt, her hands dripping with dragon blood and she cried: 'Dear, dear Delubas. I burn, I ache. Pull down your…' "

Gunnar slammed the book shut and considered pushing it in the slot of the garbage-burner. These rogues clearly didn't understand the first thing about a huntress.

Gunnar almost missed the second gong the next day, and the classroom was full, no absences at all. The only place left was next to Lavoine.

Semele must be sitting in the back row and he didn't dare to turn around while he felt all the eyes on him. The girls would be sniggering, whispering in each other's ears and pointing. *Star boy took a huntress to the ball. How stupid can you get? She stormed off. Perhaps he tried to kiss her?*

Lavoine reached for his hand, squeezed and then let go. It was a signal that he was unable to interpret. *Sorry? You are my real boyfriend now? Yedlar was just a mistake?*

"She let me feel her breasts," Yedlar told him at recess, "and kissed me twice. And then, this morning she didn't even allow me to sit next to her." He spread his hands. "And now?"

"We go on the same way. Nothing has changed."

Already the ball and his meeting with Semele seemed like a fading dream. Seeing her in the park, impossibly competent, breathtakingly complete. "I'll tear off my butterfly for you." The walk in the dark to her home. Sitting in the rickshaw he had hired. How grown-up he had felt! A man! And Semele his woman!

Lavoine strolled in their direction, slurping a can of lassi through a glass straw.

"Say, let's meet at Gunnar's house. At sunset. There is a new spell I want to try. Cape Juniper has the best view of the River."

She turned around, not waiting for an answer.

"A spell," Yedlar said. "She never showed us any magic. Only spoke about it."

"Now don't you dare to give up," Justine said.

"It's no use," Gunnar said. "I tried to apologize after school. She just walked away and didn't want to look me in the eyes."

"So she hates you? Hate is an emotion. Hate is a good start. At least Semele still notices you."

Gunnar rose, put his bowl in the cleaner. "Sorry. I have to run. I promised to meet someone at sunset."

"I can guess who. Well, I won't bother you. I have an assignment of my own."

"Dancing with that flower-monk again?"

"He's as nimble as a mountain goat and knows all the right things to whisper in a woman's ear."

The last sunlight faded from the sky, leaving only Astaroth and a single maroon cloud.

"You know veves?" Lavoine asked.

"Sure," Gunnar said. "The magic circles voodoo priests draw to summon gods and demons. One of my father's sergeants was a voodoo man, a houngan even. He told me they were made out of Old Earth symbols, names of gods, commands in languages nobody spoke anymore."

"Yes, words and commands. And you don't have to know what they mean. Only that they work." There was a pause. "You two remember master Ooka showing us the letters and words that the River writes? If we used them in a veve, who knows what could happen?"

Who knows what could happen? Gunnar was an army brat and he had a healthy respect for weapons, for anything that could go off with too enthusiastic a bang. This sounded suspiciously like starting your camp fire with sticks of dynamite.

Spells were real: after Semele's invocation of Diana he felt certain of that. And *these* symbols were probably much more potent than a handful of badly translated Latin words. The Elder Civilization had been monstrously powerful, carelessly carving continents and raising mountain chains, moving whole suns.

Yet he felt a sudden surge of curiosity, the joy of doing something quite dangerous. Living on the edge, like a crab, precariously clutching a rock in the breakers.

"But why now? He told us months ago."

"For a spell, you have to wait for an auspicious moment, as the houngans say. Well, it doesn't get any more auspicious than now." She pointed. A Galleon was plowing through the evening mists, its mother-of-pearl sails glowing. The sound of bellowing walruses rolled across the water and a dozen mist-horns answered.

Chapter XII

From *Restricted Worlds, the Observations of a Star-Trotting Vagabond* by Yuri Hopkins, writing for the *Alastor Herald*, monthly magazine, now with Mirricyllai-approved horoscope.

Meeting my first Monitor was disconcerting to say the least. First there was the sudden extinguishing of the lumens along the Esplanade, the dark racing from the warehouses all the way up to the hillside villas.

A moment later my communicator shut down with a plaintive beep.

"So," a voice just behind me said, "you are a främling."

I turned around. The woman was clad in a dove-gray uniform and wore a porcelain mask so thin you could almost see her real face. "We don't like strangers much here, especially not with a holy ship sailing past."

I had heard about that strange and lethal corps. The Monitors followed the Galleons down the River, looking for heretics. Other sources said that they didn't follow the Galleons but were quite ordinary people who donned their masks the moment a Galleon was sighted and took their crossbows from behind a vase of dried sun-flowers or from the bottom of a chest of yellowed gala uniforms.

She looked me up and down, fingered her crossbow.

"I could shoot you. This kind of arrow dissolves the whole body and leaves only the head. We put that on a stake as a tidbit for the crows." She shook her head. "No, too much work. I have to walk all the way to the Fields of Galleon-deniers. Just go back to your room, främling, and don't come out before the Galleon is well gone."

—⚊—

avoine tugged a faber from her purse, turned the ungainly switch of the 3D printer. Threads of titanium-doped panzer-glass emerged, looped. They turned solid the moment they hit the air. Panzer-glass was nine times stronger than steel and had all the hardness of diamond without the brittleness.

"I used the whole river as a model," Lavoine explained. "All of their symbols. You don't have to know what a word means for it to work."

Work. The word triggered a sudden understanding.

"A veve. It is a circuit! Like the chip in a computer."

The glowing lines emerged faster. They grew more intricate, almost hairy as a thousand side branches and streams were added. A shudder, and the whole banner curled around and bit its own tail.

"Yes, a circuit. I never thought of a spell as a circuit but I think you are right."

"It is Elder tech. You don't know…"

"Without a battery, a circuit is just a knotted wire. Let's do it right." She took a fusion battery from her purse, tore the plastic seal off.

"Isn't that a bit strong?" Gunnar said. A heavy duty battery could lift a whole villa and put it down a thousand kilometers away. His stomach clenched, became a painful knot. *Perhaps I should take it away from her?*

"Don't be a shiver-mouse."

The leads clamped themselves on the glittering hoop and a green indicator started to glow. The hoop was drawing power.

Gunnar looked at the hillside: the Galleon was trailing a wake of darkness as the lamps of the city were extinguished one after another. He estimated the distance: two minutes at most and then the battery would shut down, become as inert as a slab of lead.

"Nothing," Lavoine sighed after half a minute, and Gunnar breathed easier. *It's a dud. There's no reason why it would work. A handmade circuit, without calibration. It's like throwing sticks into the air and hoping they will spell out one of the wise sayings of the First Connatic.*

"Don't give up yet," Yedlar urged. "Perhaps it takes some time. To, well, warm up? Or wait: turn the battery on and off. That often does the trick."

The pupils of his eyes were wide with attention, his teeth clenched. He clearly believed in Lavoine's spell.

She moved the switch back and forth, then snatched her hand back from the loop.

"Something is happening now."

Blue and green sparks were creeping along the threads, tracing the circuit. They glowed brighter, became a dazzling emerald.

The loop shriveled like a burned thread of wool, crumpled.

"Mirri!" Lavoine cursed. "Well, at least we tried. And something happened. Those sparks..."

"Look..." Yedlar whispered. There was awe in his voice. Awe and fear. He pointed to the Galleon. On the sails the double snake glowed, first blue, then green, settling to a red field shot through with viridian.

A furtive movement high above him. Gunnar tore his gaze away from the sails, looked up: the same symbol pulsed on Astaroth, filling most of the disk. It died down at the same moment it winked out on the sails.

Yedlar, whose parents were orthodox Animists, breathed "Holy Crow, we did it!"

Mental alarms were going off in Gunnar's brain and he didn't feel a trace of triumph, not even wonder.

"We did something deeply stupid. I bet hundreds of people saw it. And if it was only this single ship the Monitors will be scouring the shore. Arresting anyone they meet."

A Monitor would shoot first at the slightest suspicion. There would be no revival: being shot by the Monitors made you automatically guilty.

And yes, there rose the three-toned cry of a siren from the hills. Someone must have hit the 'Avalanche' button. It was taken up in a hundred places until the whole city seemed to wail its fear.

"To my house," Gunnar said. "It is the closest and Justine isn't home. She's out, dancing with that flower-monk. When asked, we say we stayed in my room the entire evening, playing. Yes, playing The King in Yellow." *No, that won't work. I told Justine I would meet Lavoine to look at the setting sun. That would be from the Cape of course, not from behind a window. I'll have to tell her the truth.*

It turned out even worse: Justine's little skimmer hung in the clamps. The monk must have canceled their date.

Justine stood in the open door of the kitchen where she would have seen them running all the way down from the watchtower.

"Any idea what the ruckus is about? The screen showed the Monitors clearing the whole Esplanade, arresting anybody in sight. And they are doing the same on the other side of the River." She looked him straight in the eyes. "I see that you do. Come inside. Go up to Gunnar's room. All three of you. You were here the last hour…"

"Yes, playing The King in Yellow," Gunnar said. "We…"

"Don't tell me anything. I can't blab to the Monitors what I don't know."

The doorbell warbled a quarter of an hour later.

A man and a woman stood on the porch. They didn't have to show their ID-coins: the porcelain masks and the lifted crossbows with their glass quarrels were identification enough.

"There was disturbance, as you probably know," the woman said. Her voice was almost a whisper and you had to lean forward to hear her. "This house now, it is very close to the river and it happened just as the Galleon sailed past your watchtower."

She swiveled her head and Gunnar could almost see the cross-hairs in her eyes. "You and your children are the only ones at home? No husband?"

"My husband was Admiral Kallenbach. The mad Hierarch blew him up."

The woman looked at her colleague. "No husband, she says. Check that."

The man pushed past them, ran up the stairs, his weapon raised.

"We were playing The King in Yellow in Gunnar's room," Lavoine said. "Until we heard the sirens."

Please keep your mouth shut, Gunnar tried to telepath at her. A witch should be able to read thoughts if they were that frantic. *Shut up! Shut up!* Once you started talking it was very hard to stop. Name and rank, never tell them anything more. And just keeping your mouth shut is even better.

"I often play that that game myself," the woman said. "Who were you? Your avatar?" It was clearly a trick question, of course, and anybody who didn't know the game would now start to stammer.

"Cassilda, sera. She's my favorite."

They had been playing the game feverishly, Gunnar informing them of characteristics of the protagonists and the nine playing modes, the surroundings, the diverse monsters of the bottomless lake. You learned astonishingly fast when your life depended on it.

"We started out rowing on the Lake of Hali," Yedlar added, and Gunnar could see the woman's suspicion ebbing.

"Nobody else at home!" the other Monitor called down.

"Stand against the wall," the woman ordered, and she stared at him. Gunnar knew she was memorizing their faces, the nine cardinal proportions that identified any face. She would still be able to recognize them if they ran past her in a panicked crowd twenty years hence.

Taking a picture was of course impossible right now, with the Galleon still close. Even the sirens had had to be started by hand and were powered by tanks of compressed air.

"Good." She stepped back. That was all. They left, not even bothering to close the door behind them.

Gunnar's mother folded her arms, looked down at them, stern as a justiciar. "Now tell me everything."

Chapter XIII

From *Sayings of the First Connatic*:

How I would like to say: "I sleep well at night because I know the Connatic is watching over me!"

—m—

"Your probe didn't see anything?" the Connatic mused. The globe of Phaedra still rotated, pushing city after city into the daylight.

"I'll explain." Admiral Patriska Uzbar touched her left earring and now a picture of Astaroth, Phaedra's primary, appeared. The two copulating snakes filled most of the disk. "This is a sketch, a composite of the pictures hundreds of witnesses made. About ten thousand saw the naming symbol of the Elders appear on the sails of the Galleon, but only some were looking straight up at Astaroth."

"No photographs?"

"Impossible to take any. From space, the Galleons show up as flecks of mist and even binoculars refuse to focus. Nobody has ever seen a Galleon from up close."

"And the alarm? The Code Purple Three? If you say that no instrument can see the Galleons?"

"There was a radio pulse from the Galleon, aimed at Astaroth."

"Like an alarm going off," the Connatic said. "Worrisome. And it means they left something on Astaroth as well." He pictured leviathans swimming in the depths of the lava-seas. Wise and cruel as the sea-dragons of Chinese legends. No, that was just a fancy. Reality always turned out to be much worse than your imaginings.

"We should send someone," Esclavade said. "No, no, certainly not you, ser! We can't afford to lose our leader when at any moment there may be monsters jumping out from behind the hedges. But the Whelm should certainly be ready. Perhaps we should have men down there in case the whole situation blows up in our face?"

"I already thought of that," the Admiral said. "I found an officer who has been stationed on Phaedra before. He even asked for leave recently. To go there."

"How convenient. And the reason?"

"Matters of the heart," the Admiral said. "Which is the most compelling of reasons. No one will suspect him."

"Suspect him?"

"Well, this fiddling with Elder tech isn't exactly a child's game. There must be an organization behind it. I did a scan of Phaedran cults and came up with the Deep Warriors. They argue that we have grown soft as mushrooms and are no more than lowing cattle. That we need a worthy opponent."

Esclavade frowned while he consulted the room's data-bank. "Got them. This looks more like the ravings of armchair generals playing with wooden soldiers. Philosophers who don't know the right end of a projac."

"You're probably right. But you don't need to be a trained commando to do something dangerous and deeply stupid." She touched the earring again. "Now attend. This is the man we will be sending down to Phaedra."

A face appeared. It seemed rather severe to the Connatic, the head shaved except for a single lock of hair, the eyes slanted. He looked tight-lipped but perhaps that was only at the moment the picture was taken? There were laughing-wrinkles around his eyes.

"Li Huang-ho. He was stationed on Phaedra. Together with the late Admiral Kallenbach. Both men fell in love with a certain Justine. She married Kallenbach, but I suspect Huang-ho never stopped loving her."

"I see. Convenient for us."

"Huang-ho became the adjutant of the Admiral. One might think that would lead to awkward situations, but they remained best friends. He was the one to inform the widow when the Admiral was killed."

The Connatic looked at his secretary and there was a wordless exchange.

"Grant him leave," the Connatic finally said. "No, better, put him in Alastor Centrality as a liaison for the Whelm. The Cursar asked for one, Esclavade just told me. The Cursar asked several times. Until now there was no reason to send one."

Admiral Uzbar moved her fingers, typing on an invisible keyboard, then clutched the air to pull blocks of information down which only she could see.

"What rank, ser?"

"Something high. Ah ... Field Marshal by special appointment of the Connatic? If he needs to call down the Whelm, I want them to listen to him."

"There is no such rank in the Whelm."

"There is now."

Chapter XIV

From *Techno-secrets and those who keep them.*

All forever batteries are made and charged on Hasdrubal, Alastor 936, by the Wigbolt clan. The oval batteries deliver a steady current of 237 Volts by 45 Hertz and none of those batteries has run out yet. Opening them doesn't cause them to explode, but just leaves them inert.

There are rumors that the forever batteries are Elder tech, and that the Wigbolts discovered an automated factory in their territory. Hasdrubal is a decidedly low-tech world and the Wigbolt clansmen would still be illuminating their yurts with oil lamps but for those batteries, so perhaps there is something to the rumor?

Three times, starmenters tried to raid the capital tent city: on each occasion their ships turned into blobs of glowing metal the moment they entered the atmosphere.

Maybe the Wigbolts are techno wizards like the savants from Nue Mars, or perhaps they have found more Elder tech than just the forever battery...

Walking down to school under the starry sky, Gunnar knew that something fundamental had changed. The air felt charged with unease. People kept staring to the east, even long after the Galleon had passed around the bend in the river. All the street-lamps were burning but it felt precarious now: as if the power might fail again at any moment, the forever batteries becoming inert.

There wasn't a single Monitor in sight because their authority ended the moment a Galleon was gone, but they had taken their prisoners with them. Some would probably return in the next two days, without a single memory of their interrogation. Others would end up as food for the mantas, unceremoniously tossed into the River. Monitors didn't believe in taking chances.

Just outside the school hedge he saw Semele talking with a friend, a girl who also wore a butterfly. She must be a senior girl because hers glowed with a tint that was closer to green than blue. They embraced, kissed. It didn't look very sisterly at all and Gunnar flinched.

Semele looked up and their gazes crossed. Gunnar stood frozen, as if he was a butterfly himself that had just been stabbed through the heart with a silver needle.

Semele lifted her left hand and the lantern made her nails glitter and once again he felt her touch on his brow, heard her whispered spell:

"Pierced his heart, Diana.

Cut out his liver, Artemis.

This proud stag is mine, Lady Moon!"

He stepped forward and it was like wading through thick syrup, through freezing mud: "Semele…"

"Do I know you?" There was a smile that wasn't a smile exactly. *She's still furious. She hasn't forgiven me.*

"No," he sighed. "I don't think so."

Master Ooka wasn't alone: a man stood next to his lectern, stiff as a statue.

"Ser Larimac would like to have a word with you," master Ooka said. "He's an officer of the Benevolences, who…"

The man stepped forward, lifted a hand. "No, let's call a scorpion a scorpion and not a fluffy bunny. We Monitors aren't benevolent in any way. We guard this world against monsters and we have to be monsters ourselves. Utterly ruthless.

"Right now, with the Galleon ten, twenty kilometers distant, I don't have any authority. If I did as much as touch a citizen with a goose-feather, any justiciar could arrest me. But don't titter or think yourself safe. Soon a new Galleon will pass and our memories are long."

"Nobody here would doubt that, ser," master Ooka said. He didn't sound servile.

"Good. Right. I'll come right to the slimy kernel of this rotting peach. The Galleons are sacred, sublime in their journey. Yet at sunset something set them off. By now, everybody has heard of the Elder Sign appearing on the sails and on Astaroth itself. We consulted the Bibliotheque and it has only happened two times before in our entire history.

"Once, immediately after the first landing, when the explorers tried to board a Galleon. The Elder sign rippled across the sails and all nine men instantly liquefied, with only their skeletons remaining.

"They weren't the only victims: every member of their families died at the same moment, up to the ninth grade of kinship. Ruby skeletons. Some of them were hundreds of light-years distant."

"They didn't tell us that," master Ooka muttered.

"So I inform you now. The second time, a whole city vanished. It vanished so completely that even the memory was gone.

"We only rediscovered it recently, on duplicate maps of the early settlements on Old Earth itself. There is an account, however, of the Elder Sign appearing on a Galleon. The first time the sign was only visible for half a second; the second time all of two seconds." He nodded. "Yes. I see that you understand, dear citizens. Last night it remained visible for three whole seconds and perhaps even longer. We are still waiting for something terrible to happen." He folded his arms. "There are twenty-six cities along the river as far as I know. Perhaps there were a hundred, or a hundred and fifty before the sign flashed? Perhaps they scrubbed our memories?"

There followed a silence deep enough to hear the night-gulls gurgle.

"On each occasion there was some kind of interference with the Galleons. Human interference. I want you all to think back. Did you notice anything unusual? Did any of your friends brag that they knew the secret of the Galleons? That they would ride on them?" A pause. "Signal them?"

They know. They know what we did. He's only playing with us.

Lavoine lifted her hand. "Ser? Signal them how?"

She's crazy. When a lion is stalking you, you have to keep very, very still and hope he forgets you.

"You tell me, sera."

"Well, there was that sign on the sails. If you want to communicate, you start with repeating someone's words. We learned that in xeno-lingua class and first contact protocols." She spread her hands. "So perhaps someone sent them the Elder Sign? And they replied with the same symbol?"

The Monitor stared at her, clacked his tongue.

"Mirri help me! We never thought of that. It was a conversation, not just an alarm going off." He turned to master Ooka. "You are to be com-plimented. The spirit of inquiry is very much alive in your classroom." He saluted Lavoine. "Thank you, young lady. If you ever want to join our corps…We need dedication as well as supple minds."

He turned about, marched from the classroom without a further word.

"Well…" master Ooka said. "A bit hard to concentrate on second-ary quantum derivatives right now. You are dismissed. Go home!" He waved his hands. "Chop chop! Go play under the stars."

Outside, the night was enormous around him, with every footstep shockingly loud. Gunnar halted and tried to calm his wildly beating heart. *That stupid brat. Teasing a mad dog. As good as saying that she did it. No, stop. It worked. We are the last they'll suspect now.* He took a deep breath. *Relax. Look around.*

The Fontinella Wisp curled above the hills, streamers of red and golden suns, runaway stars that had been ejected from the Alastor Cluster.

Above Astaroth's poles, auroras and blue sprites danced. Those five moving dots trailing ghost-light must be incoming star ships. Four turned to the left, making for the orbital transit station. Phaedra was a Restricted World: no star ships were allowed to land. The fifth star flew on, emitted a green pulse before retreating slowly.

They must just have launched a shuttle. He took his macroscope from his pouch and locked it on the fifth dot. Even at a magnification of half a million it remained a hazy oval but the long keel identified it as a Cuchullan class super-dreadnought. When he was seven Gunnar had built a model. The Whelm owned only three of those monsters, warships powered by three dozen star drives, enabling them to traverse the entire cluster in a single day.

I wonder what was urgent enough to use one of their mightiest warships just to drop someone off. Gunnar was very much afraid he knew the reason. A violet flash made him blink: the ship had gone into whisk and would already be light-years away.

"Gunnar."

Right now, Semele was the last person he wanted to see. Not with his whole body still feeling shaky, his brain a quivering jelly.

"Yes?"

"She did it, yes?" Semele said. "Lavoine signaled the Galleon."

"Don't talk crazy. If a Monitor hears you…"

"I see. You were there." That deeply strange and upsetting smile flickered across her lips again. "Don't worry. Your secret is safe with me." It sounded like a peace offering but she instantly spoiled it by adding: "The Monitors would kill our whole group. Just to be safe."

He found Justine upstairs, bending over her furnace. Behind the diamond pane, her vase was cooling to a deep, angry red, the glaze from far Fisk crystallizing into a snowflake pattern.

"There was a Monitor in our class," he told Justine. "Asking if we had seen anything suspicious."

"And?"

"Nobody could help him."

He didn't want to tell her about Lavoine's crazy grandstanding, the risk she had taken. Justine already considered Lavoine a bad influence, the kind of girlfriend a mother would dearly love to strangle or feed to the sunfishes before she became her daughter-in-law.

Justine was completely right about Lavoine, of course, but that didn't change anything. Gunnar still wanted her. If he closed his eyes he saw her face, her braids dancing with every lithe step. Lavoine darted like some fighting fish, impossible to predict what direction she would choose next. While Semele… He shook his head, trying to dislodge the images.

"Have you ever loved two men at the same time, Justine?"

"Wrong question. I've been in lust with as many as three men at the same time. In love? No, love is something more exclusive. More obsessional. You can't sleep. You keep looking at your communicator until your eyes burn. You hear it ring even when it doesn't ring. And in Blue Scimitar, you are supposed to be monogamous. Because of the Fatima, I guess. Her second law dictates: 'No man may have more than a single wife, and that goes both ways'."

"Still, there are all those songs about loving two women."

"That was on Chevalier. There you had nine men for every woman. It's like fantasizing about suckling pig and strawberry shortcake when there is a famine, and you're happy to eat fried cockroaches and stink-berries. Not a good role model." She stopped. "Sorry. I think I heard the gong."

The doorbell rang again.

"Yes!"

"You were expecting someone?"

"Sure!" Justine fairly flew down the stairs.

No doubt it is that flower-monk again. I really hope Yannis doesn't become a fixture. A sentence rose up from that ancient Earth play that master Ooka had them perform last semester: "Methinks that man smiles too much, Milord."

He heard voices downstairs. Justine's high and excited, almost girlish. The other voice was too deep, too serious for the flower-monk.

"I insist," Justine said. "We have more rooms than we can ever use. Of course you can stay here."

"Well, I kind of hoped that you would say that."

Gunnar recognized the voice and when he slowly went down the stairs it was almost a replay of the worst moment of his life: Justine standing in the embrace of Li Huang-ho. But this time it was just the opposite: Huang-ho's face was glowing, a smile almost too big for his mouth, his eyes shining.

He has never stopped loving her, Gunnar thought and it sounded almost like a song from Chevalier, but this time it wasn't a lie.

He raised a hand and felt a smile tugging at his own lips. Such a big lump in his throat. "Hi, Huang-ho. Welcome. I hope you don't want me to call you 'Stepfather'?"

"That would be a bit premature."

"But not too premature!" Justine said and giggled.

"Come." Huang-ho beckoned him and when their old house-friend laid his arm across Gunnar's shoulders and hugged him, it felt exactly right. Like a sorely missed family member finally returning home.

Chapter XV

From *Love the one you're with*, sung by The Desperadoes, Chevalier: Alastor 1642

> If the woman you love,
> Closes her door in your face
> And calls your mustang
> A hobbling nag,
> Well, brother, I guess
> You'd better
> Love the one you're with.

—m—

"Love the one you're with." For once a Chevalier song gave sound advice. It also didn't help that the door of his mother's bedroom was still closed after five hours, and that he heard them laughing all the time. They weren't having sex, only a Havflorden-beast from Alastor 1717 had such stamina, but they were having *fun*. Which was even worse, somehow.

Gunnar put the song on pause and the horses froze in mid-gallop. He reached for his communicator and gestured Lavoine's number. The communicator of a Whelm soldier would be voice-activated, remembered thousands of numbers and could even speak in an emergency. A civilian phone knew its own number and that was it.

"Are you doing something?" he asked when her face appeared.

"Yedlar is here. With me."

Love the one you're with. But then you have to be with her for a start. And it doesn't help if she's with your best friend right now. "Did you two have dinner already?"

Yedlar's face appeared next to Lavoine's. "You are welcome if you bring some decent food." He indicated two steaming bowls which were clearly untouched.

"My mother," Lavoine said, "she believes in gumbo." She scowled. "A cast-iron pot that has stood bubbling for generations. I purely hate it! It always tastes the same no matter what she throws in."

"Right. No problem. Where are you? At Yedlar's house?"

"No, at mine," Lavoine said. "It is…"

"I know. The Cursar's villa. I met your father."

The look of consternation on her face was all he could have asked for. He raised his hand, broke the connection.

The Cursar's residence wasn't one of those fashionable soap-bubbles on a stalk. He had gone for the antique César Manrique look: A low villa hugging the landscape, the roof covered with cacti and most rooms underground.

There was the shimmer of a damping field ten meters up, and the walls had that sheen only an army brat would recognize: collapsed matter, no more than a micron thick.

This villa could survive any explosion short of a three megaton hit, and the damping field would take care of one of those. In a damping field any fusion reaction petered out before it could start up.

A girl some years his senior opened the door. She was an impossibly sophisticated creature: long platinum blonde hair, eyes as gray and glossy as a storm-tossed sea. She wore a single tattooed veve on her brow: an elegant cross between a spider web and the biohazard sign.

This is what a Cursar's daughter should look like. Suddenly Lavoine seemed childish, a posturing little girl.

"Hi, I'm Ezulia," she said. "You've come for my sister, I guess." Her voice was a contralto, with an exotic accent impossible to place.

Ezulia? Her mother must have been one of the rare survivors from the Voodoo world.

"She's with another friend. Probably making out. You'll have to wait until it is polite to walk in."

"I doubt that. Lavoine isn't that kind of girl."

"Ah, you have her pegged! She's a teaser. The little bitch won't let any boy kiss her." She pursed her lips. "While I…" Her hand went down, touched the amulet at her throat. It made him notice her breasts, which was probably just what she intended. A balladeer from Chevalier would have called them 'domes of delight' and her lips 'red as cherries' even if Ezulia's weren't red at all but a matte pink.

The Cursar seemed such a nice guy, but his whole family is poison.

She looked him up and down. "Wait! You're the army boy. The admiral's son." There was wonder in her voice, a kind of grudging admiration. Gunnar had seen the effect before: the warrior mystique. It would probably be quite useful when he grew a bit older but right now it only made him blush and feel like an impostor. He straightened his shoulders, lifted his chin. "Where do I go?"

"Down the stairs. Third door."

He could feel her gaze in his neck all the way down.

"Ha, there you are," Lavoine said. "I heard you talking. My sister? She's such a flirt, but she never delivers."

Just like you. "I did bring some braised eel and watercress."

"Good," Yedlar said. "We were talking, me and Lavoine. About how we should go on."

"Go on?"

"Well," Lavoine said. "The spell worked. Kind of. But we'll have to fine-tune it."

He stared at them, unable to believe his ears.

"Now, if only we had some artifact. A fragment of a Galleon?"

"You're mad. The Monitors almost caught us and you want to try again?" He put the heating box with braised eel down on the little table next to Lavoine's aquarium of decorative jellyfish. "Have a nice meal. I'm out of here."

The older sister was still standing in the hall. Clearly waiting for him.

"I heard you shouting down there. Something didn't work out?"

"You could say that." He felt furious, almost berserker-angry as his mother would call it, and willing to try anything. Even to kiss Ezulia, which she would probably allow. Kissing and more.

She looked up at him and there was that classic half a head's difference in height.

No. He did want her, no doubt, but he didn't like her the slightest bit. 'My woman, she's a little bit of a devil and a little bit of a saint,' the Desperadoes would no doubt sing about this sister. Except that she probably was all devil. Kissing her would probably embroil him in a spot of trench warfare between the sisters, with himself as the principal victim.

He walked past her, said "See you," and closed the door behind him.

He entered the glass cabin of the swift-bahn and sat down. The route first took him downhill to the Esplanade, past the trees where night-moths with glowing wings clustered and lovers sat around fire bowls, roasting mushrooms. Then the rotting wharves in front of the Porcineyl Palace, the warehouses, the space-port.

His anger slowly evaporated. He was the only fool here. Lavoine was what she was and would never change. Let Yedlar have her and good riddance. *I hope she'll dump him soon, and that Yedlar will find someone nicer. He's my friend after all.*

Chapter XVI

From *Restricted Worlds, the Observations of a Star-Trotting Vagabond* by Yuri Hopkins, writing for the *Alastor Herald*, monthly magazine, now with Mirricyllai-approved horoscope.

Next, the fisherman took me up the hill, made me kneel behind a hedge.

"Now," he whispered, "look through this very convenient hole. Aren't they a balm for sore eyes?"

Girls were dancing and swirling in front of a temple, supple as dervishes. Most of them seemed quite young and fresh as flowers. All wore blue butterflies on their brows.

"Why, exactly, are we kneeling behind a hedge?" I inquired.

"Well, the acolytes and priestesses, they are all like sisters. And older sisters are worse than brothers here. They take chastity quite seriously. They would argue that our gaze is like tearing the gowns off their little sisters, like fondling their newly budding breasts." He licked his lips.

"They would probably be right. What temple is this anyway? There is a tree growing through the roof and I see a dozen vultures sitting on the lintel. They look kind of expectant."

"The temple of Diana. Why?"

"Are you completely out of your mind? Do you know what the priestesses do when they catch you spying on them?"

"I know the tiresome tale. This is different. They aren't exactly taking their clothes off to bathe in a forest pool."

I scuttled back on hands and feet and only rose when I stood on the road again. I looked over my shoulder: the fisherman was still gazing through the hole in the hedge, but I guessed the show was over for him. There was a feathered arrow standing upright between his shoulder blades.

"You like young girls?" A priestess stepped towards me from the shadow of a laurel tree, reached for a second arrow.

"I like girls but I prefer them a bit older, sera. More mature. Like you."

"Sorry, I'm already spoken for. But you may tell me how beautiful I am."

I wasn't out of the woods quite yet. A molester of little girls, until I could prove otherwise.

"Well." How dry my lips suddenly felt! "Your eyes are like, er, yes!

> dreaming emeralds,
> Plucked from the deep dark sea.
> I could ski forever
> Along the perfect slopes
> Of your snow-white breasts."

She smiled. "Go on."

No one has ever called me a poet. Happily, this charming lady had a tin ear and she let me go after the seventh stanza.

Gunnar heard voices from the kitchen the moment he opened the door, and halted. It would be embarrassing to find them embracing or kissing.

"...report directly to the Connatic," Huang-ho said. "But that rank is kind of secret. Only for emergencies. Right now I'm an Inspector Extraordinary. Which means no one can order me around and I'm allowed to poke my nose into anyone's business, even the Cursar's."

"Hey?" Gunnar said and knocked on the half open door. "I'm home."

They weren't embracing but sitting at the kitchen table. Huang-ho had his hand on a Whelm-grade communicator, a slab of polished titanium which could probably do anything short of tying his shoelaces, and that as well, probably.

"I was telling Justine about my own job. I'm to investigate the anomaly. The signs on the Galleon and Astaroth itself."

Great. Now we have the Connatic's bloodhound sniffing around in our own home. "There was something about your new job?"

"The Connatic, or I think it was Admiral Uzbar, made me Field Marshal. Which is as high as you can rise. If the Connatic is the Supreme Commander, then I'm the officer just below him."

"I heard that part," Gunnar confessed. "Only if there is an emergency."

"Yes. Now that isn't something we should ever speak about. Not even by mistake."

"Huang-ho has to mind-lock you," Justine added. "He'll do the same to me."

"Right. No problem." Gunnar had been mind-locked before, once on Midlour where touching your nose or lips could get your head chopped off. It was like instilling a reflex to avoid something.

He put his hand on the communicator. There came no sensation at all, no voices speaking or flashing lights like the first time.

"That was it?"

"Say 'Field Marshal'."

Gunnar tried to, but the word flitted away before it could reach his tongue, then became a nonsense word. Gibberish.

"It worked."

"I'm new here and you aren't," Huang-ho said. "Please help me. Keep your eyes wide open, your ears pricked up. Tell me any rumor you hear, no matter how absurd."

Like Lavoine formulating a new spell to catch the attention of the Galleons? "I will."

"I heard…" his mother said. "Well, the Deep Warriors, they have said we should do something about the Galleons. That this is our world and that they're only animals. Nothing holy about them."

Good. Throw him off our scent.

"The Deep Warriors. Admiral Uzbar also mentioned that name."

Sleep remained elusive: a hundred thoughts and regrets kept swirling through Gunnar's tired brain. He rolled off his mattress, put on his boots and went outside.

In the distance he could see the lamps of the city on the other side of the river, like dancing ocher fireflies.

The fire-bowl was still glowing and he saw the dark shape of Huang-ho outlined against the white wall of the villa.

He remembered another night, sitting with Huang-ho in front of a fire-bowl. Chevalier's sister-world, Kabbalah, painted a half-moon in the sky, almost as big as Astaroth. They had been talking about names.

"Why do you have such a strange one? Huang-ho, it sounds like made-up name."

"My mother was a staunch believer in Mirricyllai, just like your mother. She gave me the name of one of Earth's mightiest rivers: the Huang-ho. The rivers are Mirri's children and she loves and protects them."

"Huang-ho," Gunnar had repeated. "And Gunnar? That's just a name? Nothing more than a couple of letters?"

"Gunnar is an Old Earth name, Justine once told me. It means 'brave and bold warrior'. Not bad for the son of a grand-admiral."

"What if I don't want to enlist in the Whelm? If I don't want to become a soldier?"

Huang-ho had laughed. "Then you'll be a brave and bold shepherd, the bane of dire wolves! Or a bold and brave accountant."

The memory faded and he was back on Phaedra.

"Couldn't sleep?" Gunnar asked.

"Too many questions and no answers at all." Huang-ho spread his hands. "I hoped all that would stop when I was back with your mother."

"Love never solves anything," Gunnar said, and to his chagrin he recognized it as a quote from Chevalier. Still, this felt right. Man-talk. "Now, Huang-ho, if you want someone to love you, what…"

Huang-ho shook his head. "Never become abstract in matters of the heart. Say her name."

"Semele. She wears a blue butterfly. Here it means that she has sworn never to kiss a boy until she starts her Walk with the Galleons."

"And she doesn't notice you?"

"She's quite aware of me and hates me. She kissed a girl-friend. Right in front of me."

He told him about the park, her spell and the fiasco at St. Dismas' ball.

"A woman scorned," Huang-ho said.

"I know. I know! But I didn't scorn her. It was just a moment."

"She thinks otherwise. You have to win her back. Start at the bottom. Become part of her world."

"Paste a blue butterfly on my brow?"

"That is possible?"

"No, Diana is a girls' game."

"There must be something else she does after school?"

"She runs. Cross-country, marathons and relay races."

"Then run with her."

"I can't. I'm hopeless. I can lift weights, throw a ball and hit the hoop running, seven times out of ten. I tried cross-country running and twisted an ankle the first time. Anyhow, after half a kilometer I get stitches in my side. Red specks dance in front of my eyes."

"The usual well-known symptoms. Keep running and they will go away. The second wind."

"You're a runner?" Gunnar didn't wait for an answer. "Can I run with you the next time? So I'm not the last to arrive when I try a triathlon with her?"

"Splendid idea." Huang-ho jumped up. "Shall we start? No time like the present."

The stitches, the laboring heart, the desperate gasping for air like a fish out of the water: it was all as he remembered, but he kept on running. And there came a moment that it went smoother. The pain never really went away but it ceased to matter.

"That hill-top," Huang-ho pointed, "and then we return to the villa."

Gunnar fell down on his mattress, heavy as a sodden sandbag. His legs were covered with scratches and the soles of his feet burned. There must be blood-filled blisters, but he would attend to them tomorrow.

He closed his eyes and instantly started dreaming.

To his dismay, it was about Lavoine. She stood on the tip of Cape Juniper and wrote the Elder sigil in the air, blue flames issuing from her fingertips.

The Galleons rounded the bend of the River: a dozen of them, and they tugged a flood wave behind them.

It was a wall of dark, churning water that reached all the way to the hilltops and was erasing block after block of Blue Scimitar.

"Stop that!" he tried to scream, but his voice came out a mouse-squeak and she kept gesturing, the wave rising higher and higher.

He woke up with a gurgling scream, and of course it was still dark outside, the dawn of the Great Day at least thirty hours away.

Chapter XVII

From *Lonely Planet Guide to the Alastor Cluster*:

The third colony ship arrived after a sixty year flight with its twin star drives stuttering. They were refugees from the Third Caliphate, which they considered far too slack in matters of religion.

The Mujaheddin of the Blue Scimitar had sworn to find a place "where their sons could bow down low in peace to the Thrice Reborn Suleiman." 'In peace' meaning that they would be free to chop off the head of any heretic and drop ungrateful daughters in the quicksand, clad in a festive leaden gown.

Well, even the best laid plans…Fatima the Bold chopped off the head of the Thrice Reborn Suleiman the moment he set foot on Phaedra's soil, with his very own blue scimitar.

She lifted the still blinking head by its hair and showed it to the people. "No ungrateful daughter will ever be dropped in the quicksand again, or left for the hyenas!" she declared. And thus it has been ever after.

—ᴍ—

Gunnar saw Huang-ho kneeling in the creeping gorse at the tip of Cape Juniper. A dozen hovering lumens made the shadows dance. Three blue-clad technicians waved long-handled detectors through the air, consulted their communicators.

"That doesn't look good," Justine said. "Perhaps we should come clean?"

"A bit late for that."

"It isn't easy, keeping a secret from your lover."

He eyed her. "You two are lovers?"

"Of course. If this had been another world than Phaedra, another city even, I would probably have taken them both as husbands."

"Ah. But you said that loving two women…"

"It is different for girls."

Sometimes it became kind of embarrassing, their policy of always speaking the truth to each other, never holding back. Still, having a new home every few months, with strange and often repulsive customs, it had been the only way to keep sane.

His mother hissed. "The one to the right, he has found something." She turned to Gunnar. "What's there to be found?"

"Lavoine's veve. She made one in the shape of the River. All those Elder hieroglyphs, and then she powered it up. It burned, but something might be left. I told you!"

"Get your macroscope."

A magnification of fifteen was enough to discover that they were in deep trouble. The head-technician was plucking strand after strand of blackened spider web from the heather. Only fragments were left of the hoop, but it would probably be enough to recognize the River, to reconstruct what Lavoine had been attempting.

Ten minutes later an air-car dropped down from the sky, with the Whelm's hornet insignia on the side.

Justine's communicator buzzed.

"We have found something," came Huang-ho's voice, "and I'm taking it up. When I arrived, I left a patrol-ship and a small force at the transit station. Our forensic lab there is centuries ahead of anything in Blue Scimitar."

"Will I see you at dinner?" Justine asked.

"Probably. It's rather straightforward. Someone constructed a kind of antenna, trying to hail the Galleon."

"Antenna?"

"Ser Hubert recognized several Elder symbols. Think of it as trying to get a circuit to resonate. Or even more primitive: stamping on a bridge until you hit the natural frequency."

"Wait. You mean marching soldiers bringing a bridge down?"

"Exactly. And thinking of a fallen bridge, perhaps our terrorist was not trying to communicate? Perhaps he wanted to attack the Galleon, shake it apart."

Gunnar suddenly knew Huang-ho was right. Lavoine hadn't wanted to communicate at all. It had been an assault, or at the very least, a challenge.

"A dead end," Huang-ho said. "It burned something fierce. Not a trace of DNA left."

Justine topped up his wine-glass. "And you looked around for other traces?"

"Oh, enough DNA. Yours and Gunnar's. We identified two of his friends and a hundred other Blue Scimitarians. Cape Juniper is public land and a favorite spot to watch the sunrise. A pity."

"And the Deep Warriors?" Justine asked.

Don't push it, please.

"Nothing. Either they are extremely well-organized and hidden, or they are such a small and inconsequential cult that no constabulary has started a dossier."

Four more runs with Huang-ho and Gunnar felt almost competent. The stitches in his side never went away completely and there was a third wind after the second, he discovered to his chagrin. Still, he could now run on and on under the stars and when he stumbled he almost always found his stride again without falling headfirst into the sedge.

They stopped at the top of the hill, looked out over the night city. It was the morning of one of the Small Days. The lumens were growing stronger until, walking the Esplanade, it almost seemed to be day, except for the still dark sky.

"Do you think I'm ready?" he asked Huang-ho.

"You won't finish last at least." He folded his arms. "Now, let's talk tactics."

"Tactics?"

"Don't run next to her. Don't compete with her. Ever. The way you described her, Semele is a proud girl. Despite some rather romantic and uninformed stories, defeating a huntress will not make her love you. It will only make her angry."

"She already hates me. She despises me."

"Well, she can hate you more. Give it your best. She's certain to notice you. Just don't finish last. She would see you as an overconfident fool, then. One who should have known better than to compete with his betters."

Entering the classroom, Gunnar saw that master Ooka stood alone behind the desk: no Monitor. Still, he'd better sit down next to Lavoine: changing places would give the wrong signal. To whom, he wasn't exactly sure, but the Whelm Manual for the Accomplished Soldier stated that an operative shouldn't change his routine when under suspicion. Nothing drew the attention of the secret police as quickly as skittish behavior.

It wasn't Huang-ho he feared, but the Monitors. The man who had visited their classroom hadn't inspected any of the other groups.

No doubt the Monitors were needed, but it came awfully close to using rabid wolves as guard-dogs.

Master Ooka was sketching a purifying plug for a water bottle on the glow-board.

"Sooner than you think, you'll be taking your Long Walk. Think of parched lips, your tongue a flap of leather. The only water you see bubbling past is colored a poisonous green.

"'O Mirri,' you call, 'what a fool I've been! If only I had listened to our wise teacher Ooka. Now my only choice is to die of thirst or of poison!'"

The class tittered: a Yoranda-clown wasn't half as funny as their teacher miming ultimate distress, his eyes almost rolling from their sockets, his tongue flapping.

"But you get a second chance. Right now! Repeat after me: pick the hollow stem of an evergreen, insert a strip of stone-wort and drop a copper half-ozol into your bottle.

"Your water will start to glow, then to bubble. Wait half an hour for it to cool and the poison to precipitate.

"Sip through your straw to kill the last of the flesh-eating bacteria. It will still taste awful and give you stomach cramps, but now you'll see the light of a new Great Day."

Lavoine touched Gunnar's left foot.

"The next time," she whispered, "the next time we'll do it right. Then they will really notice us."

"Not again! There won't be a next time. If the Monitors notice us at the Cape, they won't ask us what we are doing there. They'll just start pulling fingernails."

"You are afraid to live."

He had thought himself immune to the scorn in her eyes, the way her lips curled up in a kind of un-kiss, like a princess's lips would recoil when she was forced to kiss a toad. "You want to be safe." She said 'safe' as if that was the dirtiest word that existed, and the horrible thing was that it worked. That suddenly 'safe' seemed a coward's choice.

She's manipulating me. Using loaded words. It is like a spell.

Knowing that didn't help a bit. Gunnar had been a professional expat all his life, a chameleon by necessity, always looking for the safe thing to say, the right way to act.

Try to be brave for once, that was what Lavoine was saying, the button she was pushing. Don't be a good obedient soldier, an underling. You are a man! You have the right to be stupid, to be reckless.

"How?" he heard himself say.

"It must be something more ambitious. Not just calling a single Galleon. Something big enough for them to notice."

She doesn't have any idea. She's just boasting.

"So, you aren't thirsty anymore," Master Ooka continued. "But now you hear a rumbling growl from the bushes. And do you have a weapon? A nice sharp knife or a bow?

" 'O sweet Mirri,' you wail, 'what a fool I've been! If only I had listened to our wise teacher Ooka.' "

Outside, the first gray of the slow sunrise was outlining the mountain tops. His communicator buzzed.

"There is a cross-country run starting in half an hour," Huang-ho said. "You are wearing the right shoes?"

Gunnar looked down. He had forgotten to change to sandals after their morning sprint around the cape. "Yes?"

"The High Meadows. It's only a five kilometer run, but her name is on the list. I put yours there as well."

"But I'm not ready! I'll end up last!"

"You'll run like a hare with a dozen foxes snapping at its fluffy white tail. You won't have a choice. Before the start, the arbiter will call out the names of all contestants. He'll read your name, and if you aren't there to answer, you'll have lost before you took a single step." He chuckled. "You don't have to thank me."

Mirri be praised, at least Semele didn't board the same cabin on the swift-bahn. He wouldn't have known where to look, what to say to her. *Why aren't there any war games about how to act in these kinds of situations? Wasn't this the same as a campaign? With hidden snipers, pitfalls around every corner?*

Most of the cabins switched to another line, moving to the right and left. The lit streets with their false daylight fell behind until his cabin was the only one going up. He drifted past fields of night-blooming suthervall with their grazing mouflons. A shepherd lifted his staff with the obligatory glow-globe and Gunnar waved back.

"High Meadows," a recorded voice called. "End of the line. Please disembark and close the door behind you."

It was cold outside, with a frigid breeze blowing straight down from the ice field.

Well, I'll be running up a sweat soon enough.

The only light came from Astaroth's waning half-moon, and Gunnar saw the contestants already lined up. He broke into a run.

The faces were pale ovals and it was impossible to see which belonged to Semele. Perhaps the third one from the left?

"Hessen, Marek?"

"Present!"

"Justinesson, Gunnar?"

"Here!" He saw a girl jerk her head, look in his direction. *Well, now she knows. I'm in for it.*

The arbiter raised his hand and the mechanical swallow flapped up into the sky, exploded in a shower of glowing sparks. The signal. He threw himself forward.

Ten, twelve steps and the dark and stars enveloped him, the breeze in his face which soon ceased to be cold. *Don't look to the right. If you see her you'll stumble. Just be your legs, your feet.*

Gunnar imagined himself a ram-scoop star ship: gulping down the hydrogen, ejecting it in a Cerenkov-blue fusion flame.

The stitches in his side started after the second kilometer and he gasped for breath. *Run on. It is only pain.* And yes, there came the Second Wind, his body switching to an anaerobic burn and filling his blood with endorphins.

Now only the running remained. No Gunnar, no contest, no girl to impress. He crossed a field of thistles and the thorns clawed his skin right through his trousers. It only made him run faster: with this run- ner's high, any sensation only heightened his joy.

He was running somewhere in the middle of the contestants and that was right. *I won't be a straggler. I won't be the last.*

In the distance lights showed: the pulsing double line of the finish. "Now it is time to go all out," a voice said in his head. It was high and silvery and not human at all.

Diana. The Huntress herself. She wants me to win. Or perhaps not. Perhaps she aims to have me burst a blood-vessel in my brain, fall down in a heart-attack.

That silvery laugh again, which wasn't an answer at all.

He ran, Gunnar was the hare and the fox, the fastest man alive. Just legs and pounding feet. The line passed in a dazzling flash and he stumbled, rolled through the heather.

When he pushed himself up, Semele looked down at him.

"Not bad," she said. "Not bad at all. You came in fifth."

"And you?"

"Second," another girl said. "So stupid! She should have been the winner but she kept looking sideways. At you." There was envy in her voice and pure malice. "That's one girl who won't be wearing her butterfly much longer."

"Stop it, Yen!" Semele clenched her fists, then strode away.

Gunnar was still on his runner's high, where all things are clear and luminous.

He looked at the girl. "You love her, don't you?"

"You're a man. A rutting animal. You don't know anything about love!" She ran away, trailing a sob.

"How did it go?" Huang-ho asked. His face glowed just above Gunnar's communicator.

"Hard to say. Not bad, was her comment."

"And then?"

"Nothing really. There was another girl who called her boy-crazy and Semele strode away. Angry or embarrassed."

"A girl's best friends are seldom your allies. They want to keep her for themselves."

"I think this girl is even worse. She also loves Semele." He stared at the screen. "Wipe that smirk from your face! This isn't funny!"

"Sorry. See you at dinner time."

Chapter XVIII

How sweet
To sail down the River!
The meanders of
Your journey
Endlessly
Writing
And rewriting
The Great Hymn.
A happy animal,
Thoughtless and free.
Who needs brains
And clever schemes
With all your enemies
Dead and defeated?

— Elder inscription on the surface of a neutron star.

The Connatic might be universally loved, or at least respected, but with a population of five trillion you always get the inevitable madmen. The zealots who heard demons, or worse, angels whispering in their ears that the Connatic was Ahriman or the Antichrist.

Accordingly, the protective screen around the Connatic was rather extensive and intercepted 6.3 assassins a day. Some of those watchdog systems came close to Turing grade: not even a microbe could waft in the direction of Oman Ursht or it was known and labeled.

When the Connatic woke up in the middle of the night and saw a shadow standing at the foot-end of his bed, he knew his visitor must be something extraordinary. Something more than human.

He blinked thrice and the web the master technicians had laid across his retina activated. The room became clear as day but that didn't help much. The face of the intruder proved to be no more than a mask of quicksilver, the eyes blue sparks and the nose a stub. The sigil on his brow was unmistakable, though.

"So you are one of them?" the Connatic said.

"Of those you call the Elder race? No, not at all. They stand high above me. I'm no more than a —" the Connatic felt insubstantial fingers stroking the convolutions of his brain, soft as the wings of a moon-moth, plucking the right words from his memory "— a golem, a manikin. Something they made for a specific function. Wait, I see the history of ancient China in your memory. Those pictures fit my makers the best.

"Think of me as the most humble of guards, one who is stationed miles away from the Forbidden City proper and has never even seen the gates of the palace where the Emperor slumbers. I'm the first line of defense, to keep vermin away, or anything that might disturb the sleep of my masters and wake them up."

"And we wouldn't want that? Them waking up?"

"Well, you have tunneled into their holy places, gnawed their most precious gobelins like cockroaches. They would be aghast to discover you. You hate cockroaches: they would consider you a thousand times more unclean and move to exterminate you."

"We found out about the Grand Rainbow. That they are trophy suns."

"Yes, once my masters were the most fearsome warriors you can imagine. Conquerors whose greatest joy was the dismay of their victims. How entertaining to skin a captive alive, pluck out eyes and feelers!

"Think of one of your barbarian warriors. A Tamerlane, a Genghis Khan. But in the end my makers matured, or perhaps they just grew tired? Like one of those ancient warlords they started to yearn for the simple life: a bamboo hut, next to a murmuring brook, to spend the endless afternoons of their immortality painting characters and misty mountains. In that stage they created the Azure Parade around the dazzling blue star Ajhura: one living world for every sun they had stolen."

"I get the picture."

"But even that was too active. Next, they scaled down their intelligence and ferocity until they became as simple and content as the beasts of the fields. But deep down they remained predators. Attack them and they will instantly transform into the savage warriors of a hundred thousand years ago."

"I see. You came because of Phaedra?"

"Yes. Some fool meddled with the Galleons and that woke me. It doesn't take much because I'm only the first line of defense. The sound of a breaking stick, a touch on a spider web. Make sure it goes no further than that."

"What happened, exactly, on Phaedra?" the Connatic asked. "Are you allowed to tell me?"

"There is one thing that all gods frown upon: infidel lips intoning a holy prayer."

"Yes?"

"The meanders of the River, they are hieroglyphs spelling out their whole history, their greatest triumphs, their deepest secrets. Someone built a circuit in the River's shape and it called out that prayer. Very loud and rather garbled. If it had been any clearer the Galleons would be wide awake now."

"I see. Any idea who built that circuit?"

The guardian snorted. "You humans all look the same to me. Could you locate the ant that bit you a week ago in a teeming ant heap?" He pursed his lips. "But there is one thing the gods hate even more. Hearing their names used in vain."

"We sent a man down to Phaedra. He's most competent: Li Huang-ho will find those idiots. Stop them."

"I hope so. For your sake."

"You don't agree?"

"A wise ruler knows how to delegate. An even wiser one might decide that a more hands-on approach is appropriate." A smile that was almost human curved the silver lips. "I slept, but only in the way of the hare, with one eye open. I saw you flit from world to world and you amused me. Your tiny tales are fingernail paintings but still nice. I would miss them."

The guardian stepped back and melted into the wall. It was only then, belatedly, that the alarms started to warble.

Chapter XIX

From *Restricted Worlds, the Observations of a Star-Trotting Vagabond* by Yuri Hopkins, writing for the *Alastor Herald*, monthly magazine, now with Mirricyllai-approved horoscope.

According to the ancient legend, King Arthur would wake in times of trouble and take up his sword to save Albion once again.

Blue Scimitar has something better. Every generation will have its secret Fatima, who might be growing lilies or herding giant kiwis all her life, but when there is a true emergency, she will step from the shadows and pluck the Blue Scimitar from Mirri's raised arm.

It was a Fatima who sailed the flagship of the Three Directors into the harbor and threw three heads on the quay, right in front of the trembling citizens.

"These were the heads of the snake," she cried. "Now kill me the rest of the body!"

By nightfall not a single pirate was alive along the whole length of the River.

When I walked down the souvenir stalls of the Esplanade, I noticed that no single face on the statuettes was the same. There were Fatimas with red curls and Fatimas with pointed noses, Fatimas as pale as buttermilk, or blacker than obsidian.

"Giving her a standard face would be sacrilege," a carver explained. "Any girl can become our fierce Fatima. Even a bat-herder's daughter."

—⅏—

"Assemble in the atrium," the voice of the rector rumbled from the speakers above master Ooka's lectern. "Right now. This is, ah, quite important. An emergency, yes."

The rector was a figurehead, respected by none of the teachers and more some kind of mascot than a feared leader, but he sounded panicked, his voice strident.

"Leave all your stuff on the table," master Ooka ordered.

The atrium quickly filled, sounding like a cross between an aviary and a panicked herd of long-horns. The rector stood on the platform, waving his hands. Next to him, on the chair usually reserved for a visiting lecturer, waited a stranger who, even while sitting down, towered over the rector. The man wore a uniform Gunnar couldn't place: a sky-blue satin tunic embroidered with stylized moon-fish and squid, boots of tanned sharkskin. His red face remained strangely indistinct, as if Gunnar were seeing him through a pane of moving water.

"The Sahjib of the Guild of Fishermen and Eel-keepers," Lavoine said. "I saw him talking to my father in the morning."

Master Ooka jumped onto the platform, went to stand next to the visitor, and clapped his hands. Silence instantly descended.

"I see that everybody is present." He snapped his fingers and the visitor rose from his chair. The soles of his boots didn't quite touch the ground but hovered at least ten centimeters from the floor.

"I'm not really here," the Sahjib said. "Right now, my recording will be speaking in a hundred classrooms and offices. In every factory of Blue Scimitar. I trust that my colleagues in the other cities will be doing the same." He reached up and pulled a picture down out of thin air. "This is our harbor, half an hour after our fishing fleet should have returned with their catch. As you can see there are only half of the usual boats. The other half foundered, pulled down into the depths by tentacles, rammed by dolphins. And all the fish have been altered, mutated, even those on the farms. There isn't a single one left without three tails and poison coursing through its body." He sighed. "In one stroke we lost half of our food supply. We still have the highland grain and the algae. No one will get hungry but our meals might become kind of bland. And the River itself: putting a toe in the water will cost you that toe." He gestured again and several fish swam past in the projection.

"Notice that all the Earth fish are now three-tailed, and even the stickleback bears poisonous needle teeth."

A fat bass turned around, lunged and swallowed the underwater camera drone.

"I don't think this is coincidence. The Galleons were provoked and they struck back. As is their right."

The projection faded and the chair was empty.

The pupils sat frozen, their faces pale. And then the clamor started. Some of the girls and at least three boys were sobbing. *O Mirri, one of them was Hunre, the fisherman's boy who had taken him to the ocher city*…Hunre looked wildly around, his eyes rolling. He then jumped up and ran from the hall.

Master Ooka raised his hand and once again it worked. He seemed formidable: a wise warrior from the time of the Three Directors.

"Don't wail like a herd of shufflers! Suddenly we are living in interesting times, as the ancient Chinese would say. But we are of proud warrior stock! We won't panic. Every age has the leaders it needs. Right now, a Fatima will be awakening." His gaze swept the hall like the beams of a lighthouse. "She might be any of you girls. But don't wait for her to lead you, to order you around. Think how you would act if you were the Fatima."

Gunnar turned his head: Semele sat upright, her eyes glittering with a cold resolve. *If there is a Fatima, it should be her.*

"A Fatima," he heard Lavoine say. "And any girl could be her. How interesting."

"Let's walk down to the pier," Yedlar said to Gunnar when they left the classroom. "I want to see those killer fish with my own eyes." He shrugged. "Some people are easily panicked."

"Hunre," Gunnar said. "He ran away and I think his boat…"

"Good idea," Semele said and took her bow from her locker. She never closed her locker: only a suicidal fool would mess with the bow of a temple girl. "Perfect idea. Go down to the water. I never shot a monster." She looked at Gunnar. "Did you ever catch a monster fish? One who has just eaten the father of your favorite niece?"

"I…" There was only one answer. "I'll come with you."

Suddenly most of the class was running down to the mole, Semele and Lavoine in front.

Where had Lavoine gotten that harpoon? It looked like a museum piece: a bone spearhead with wicked barbs. Wait, she tugged at the end and the harpoon grew half a meter longer.

The East mole swept far into the River, three dozen bamboo piers where the fishing boats usually moored. Quite a few of those slots remained empty.

The very smell of the River had altered, Gunnar noticed: no longer bracing and clean, but sour and sickly sweet at the same time.

The whole River is changing, the Elders are elderforming the whole moon once again, making sure those pesky humans can't live here anymore.

The tea houses were deserted, the terraces empty and most of the chairs still upside down. After the announcement, the few early patrons must have fled in a panic.

Gunnar couldn't blame them. The River lapped at the pier, only meters distant from the tables, and everything that swam or drifted in those waters had turned lethal. Even the smallest fish would bear hollow cobra teeth, and every jellyfish would be trailing tentacles with Portuguese Man-o'-war grade poison.

"And now?" Lavoine said. They stood at the iron railing on the very end of the mole. Above them, the banner of Blue Scimitar snapped: a sword held in a decidedly feminine hand.

"You have that harpoon," Semele said. "See that sunfish there? The priests call it holy, a servant of the Galleons. Let us see the color of its blood."

The two girls seemed to have melded, turned into a pair of amazons, no, something more elemental and no longer quite human, and that was wrong, horribly wrong.

Let us see the color of its blood. It sounded stilted, like something the heroine of a decidedly third-rate play might screech to her soldiers.

"Don't throw!" A voice called. "He's ours. He ate my parents!"

A fishing boat was passing the head of the mole. Hunre was

standing in the bow, holding a mortar he must have stolen from the Mountaineers' Depot at Flamine Square. It wasn't a weapon per se but the dexax-tipped rockets could vaporize an avalanche or bring a sky-scraper down. Next to him stood a little girl, holding a projac. Probably a sister.

High tech. All ships on the River were sailing boats, completely low tech by decree of the Connatic, not even allowing a communicator or an electric torch. The sloop lay way too high in the water, Gunnar saw to his horror, with only the tip of the keel touching the surface. Repulsors were worse than mere tech; they were as high tech as a space-drive and would draw all the monsters from miles around.

The little girl raised a fist and cried: "I am the Fatima! I am the avenger!" She didn't sound heroic, only very young and afraid. She sighted on the sunfish, pulled the trigger of the projac.

The fishing boat vanished. Only bubbles rose from the whirlpool it had left behind.

Gunnar stood frozen. Had he really seen a maw huge enough to swallow a complete seven meter long sloop?

Whelm reflexes learned in kindergarten made him snatch Lavoine's arm. "Back! Don't throw. It'll only make them notice you!"

Something rose from the waters, a tower of writhing, rainbow-scaled flesh with far too many eyes. It looked down on them and held that pose.

They ran.

Gunnar kept to the rear. Another Whelm reflex: a soldier covers the retreat of fleeing civilians. Not that he carried any weapons except for his fists.

Only when he felt the basalt of the quay thudding beneath his feet did he dare to look back. No trace of the monster, but of the lighthouse at the end of the mole, only a stump was left.

"Holy Mirri," Yedlar whispered. "Would you believe that? That was a salmon."

"Not anymore," Semele said. She put the glass arrow she was still holding back into her quiver. "I was such a fool. I almost got all of you killed!"

"I wasn't following anybody," Lavoine declared. "I was only doing what a Fatima would do."

"Your Fatima is a fool then!" Semele retorted, and the argument might have gone farther if the justiciars hadn't arrived right then and arrested them all.

The holding cell of the Justiciary was nothing like a medieval dungeon. It had no less than three toilets and rather soft benches, no doubt meant for drunks to sleep away their delirium. Still, it was rather crowded with most of the class huddled on the floor.

An hour passed, then another, and after three hours Gunnar lost count.

The lights dimmed and the window turned a deep blue: it must be around eight o'clock.

Gordimar of the North Hill Lobarithes walked to the front, clutched the panzer-glass bars that formed the door. "You can't just hold us here! I want to call my lawyer."

The single guard looked up from his endless book.

"Really? You did something bad enough to need a lawyer?"

"I..."

The guard gestured and the bars started to vibrate, colored an alarming blue. Gordimar jumped back, his fingers trailing a string of electric sparks. Several pupils catcalled or giggled: Gordimar wasn't well liked.

"Any others who want to call their lawyers?" the guard asked. "No?"

Around midnight the first parents arrived.

"I won't call you stupid," Justine said. "This goes way beyond stupid. You were just warned that the River was filled with monsters that devoured half the fleet and you went running to the waterside." She shook her head, sighed.

"The girls, they were running in front. Semele and Lavoine."

It sounded lame and it was as close to a lie as not to matter. He had felt the exhilaration of doing something forbidden and deeply stupid. *As if I were a naughty boy, trying to impress the girls.*

"It was stupid," Gunnar said. "Sorry."

"Well," Huang-ho said, "nobody was eaten." Which wasn't true at all but Gunnar didn't correct him.

• • •

Gunnar woke half a dozen times, his heart thumping, a scream just behind his lips. Each time he was in the middle of running down the pier, the monster-fish coiled above him like a patient cobra. Time after time the sloop drifted to its doom, the keel trailing a swirl of bubbles.

He threw off his quilt, walked to the window and depolarized the glass.

The sky shone a deep blue: this was still the sunny part of the Great Day. To the south, the Three Clowns grinned but their smiles now seemed more like sneers. Which was probably right: according to the Bibliotheque they had once been monsters, on par with the Demon Princes in Gunnar's *My First Book of Heroes and Rascals.*

Gunnar felt a sudden wave of homesickness. Not for any world in particular, but for all of them: the endless pampas of Chevalier, the suns dancing and dipping behind the mountains of Marune, the palace of the Connatic a black outline against the glorious sunset…

On Nuovo Palermo, girls had looked up at him with glittering eyes. Any one of them had probably been willing to kiss him, sleep with him. But those girls had nephews and uncles watching their every move. Nephews with machetes and catapults that fired venom-coated icicles.

No, Phaedra was better. Those beautiful Palermo girls would become as fat as their mothers the moment they had snagged a man.

He gestured to the window to make the darkness return and tugged the quilt all the way up to his chin.

Chapter XX

From *Restricted Worlds, the Observations of a Star-Trotting Vagabond* by Yuri Hopkins, writing for the *Alastor Herald*, monthly magazine, now with Mirricyllai-approved horoscope.

For thirty-seven years, slaves and indentured workers hacked and polished the gneiss cliff overhanging the center of Blue Scimitar. Slowly, the countenances of the Three Directors emerged: Uztan with his pugnacious forward-jutting chin and his left cauliflower ear; Hiram Ostermin's three-pronged beard; Lenoke's afro headdress as bulbous as a badly trimmed ornamental shrub.

When the Fatima broke their power and rolled the originals of those heads across the quay, Blue Scimitar faced a problem. Blowing up those heads might well bring the whole cliff down. Leaving them wasn't an option: it would be like having the face of your tormentor tattooed on your eyeballs. And they might inspire later generations to deeds equally dark.

That night, Mirricyllai appeared to the Fatima and told her: "Look at their faces. Don't they make you think of Lefar, Lefar and Elephant, the three Fools of the Commedia Brava? Who would ever fear them or revere them?"

—

The whole crew of the recently freed stone-carvers instantly volunteered, their ranks swollen by anyone who could wield a hammer or a pickaxe.

In the next week, fat lips, curved in an imbecilic grin, replaced Uztan's scowl and an enormous wind chime was hung from his left earlobe. Twenty meters tall robins nested in Lenoke's hair. All three evildoers had sported formidable noses: they were carved down to round knobs and painted a bright red.

—

Climbing the zigzagging stairs to the Faces I found the steps infested with painted fools: gawky boys wearing Lenoke's nest wig, with little mechanical birds shrilly tweeting; girls with their faces painted fool-pale and wearing false lips. All were trying to sell me something: a festive mask or three-fools-rings, or a perfume that would make my girlfriend giggle.

A boy stepped up next to me and said: "Pay me ten ozols, främling, and I guarantee you safe passage all the way to the Eyrie. I won't try to sell you a single thing and won't allow anyone to try the same."

I eyed his athletic body, the face that would make small boys cry, and agreed.

The view from one of Lenoke's upper nests proved excellent: I could see all the way to Garnet across the Greater Bamboo Forest.

"This is a high place," my guide declared. "The highest. But see how low the balustrade is here. Right easy to stumble and fall!" He held out a hand that could crush a coconut. "Ten ozols is cheap for your life."

Clearly the Fatima's scheme hadn't worked: even clowns could turn bad. But, as the First Connatic had said: "Life is sweet and no price too high to keep it." I paid him and he even agreed to guard me on the way down.

"Let us part as friends," I said to him when we passed the ticket office in front of the stairs. "Let us embrace."

"Why not?" the big lout laughed. "If that is what främlings do."

In my hotel room I counted the money in the billfold I had rolled while embracing him. He must have had a lucrative day: it came to more than two hundred ozols.

—ɯ—

"Have you ever traveled to the other side of the world?" Huang-ho asked. Daylight had finally returned and there were paradise-vultures circling above the villa, their plumage resplendent. "It is quite a lot colder there without Astaroth's warmth. All the mountains are covered with snow and the River runs with ice floes."

"Never had the chance," Gunnar said. "There are no trains or shipping lines here it seems. The air cars are powered by the grid and can't leave Blue Scimitar. No one is allowed to fly above the River anyway. The line-boat takes five hours to sail to Garnet."

"Well, as an inspector I claimed my own flitter from the Cursar's car pool. We'll fly straight across the pole: Slate Hulle lies on the other side of the world, and there is someone I want to speak there. Quite urgently."

"Whom?"

"The Ildmar of the Deep Warriors. Their leader."

"So you found them."

"Certainly, and I think Justine was right. This is a man who is looking for trouble." Huang-ho touched his communicator and a face appeared.

The man had to be in his eighties, still young and vigorous, and good for another forty years at least. His eyes were the right kind for a warmonger, for a prophet: deep, sunken, burning with conviction.

Even in this grainy video Gunnar felt the charisma, the carefully channeled hate. *This is a man who despises us all. Who sees us as barely human.*

The voice came on and it was a deep voice, majestic. A voice you desperately wanted to believe.

"If you don't run with the wolves," the man declared, "you must be one of the sheep."

The track stopped, started to loop again.

"This is the only sound recording we could find. The rest is just slogans on walls or posts on the common channel. Our Suleiman Khan, he's kind of elusive. Leaving fewer footprints than a snow-ghost."

"But you located him?"

"The Monitors did, but the next Galleon is some nine days distant. No authority, eh. They called me in."

• • •

Huang-ho's flitter turned out to be a scratched bubble of panzer-glass, lifted by the biggest repulsor plate Gunnar had ever seen. Two old-fashioned air scoops would accelerate it to a pedestrian Mach two. It was like riding a diligence or a hot air balloon but it would get them there. Probably.

The River dwindled behind them, became a thread and sank behind the foothills. The mountains loomed, range after range. Sometimes a green valley blinked on and off for a moment, like a seam of emeralds.

"Nobody lives down there?" Huang-ho asked.

"Some bat-herds. They ride their giant bats and milk them for an essence that is prized as a drug on some of the god-worlds. It makes you hallucinate.

"Yedlar, he tried it once and told me that he was walking through a garden with jeweled trees, with a big golden face in the sky shouting gibberish. It went on for hours and he became very bored."

"Well, that is one thing I won't try then. There's nothing wrong with a twist of soma or a nice pipe of opium if you want to relax."

"Say, Huang-ho, why exactly did you take me on this expedition? Why not a trained justiciar or even a Monitor?"

"They would want to arrest a criminal and I'm not even sure Suleiman Khan is one. And arresting him would cause the rest of them to go underground instantly. While you, you know the Phaedrans by now. You have been here for almost a year."

"Sorry. I won't be able to tell you anything about those... what did you call them? Those Hullians. Every city is different and each cherishes its difference. I haven't even visited Garnet and that's the next city downstream."

"Well, perhaps I like having you with me?" Huang-ho spread his hands. "I saw you grow up. My knee was your mustang and I gave you your first drone. When you two went away, it was like..."

"I understand," Gunnar said. "I really do. You were always part of the family and now you are again." And because they were men, and more importantly, soldiers of the Whelm, that was all they would ever have to say about it.

• • •

The city of Slate Hulle lay in the daylight, just like Blue Scimitar, but the River looked very different on the other side: gray and cold and no orchards blooming along the banks, but black dendrons and yellow lichen that grew man-high. Most of all, the sky looked unfinished: Gunnar kept searching in vain for the disk of Astaroth.

The city slowly resolved while they descended: a hundred identical squares around a single five-sided parade field with a gilded tower.

Gunnar raised his macroscope: every house looked exactly the same: mansard roofs covered with slate roof tiles, tiny, circular windows. Portholes really.

This must be one of those deeply egalitarian cities, Gunnar decided, with nobody owning a single ozol more than his neighbor. He felt a stab of apprehension. These societies were the worst: being different, no matter in what way, would instantly brand you a criminal.

"I'll put us down in front of that tower," Huang-ho announced. "There doesn't seem to be an airfield."

Three justiciars came marching to the flitter the moment Huang-ho opened the door.

"Främlings," the first one said with a high, breathless voice, "we don't like främlings here in our peaceful city." His uniform was matt black, with a gold braid on the shoulders, and he carried a projac of an unknown type. It looked quite efficient, however.

"We'll have to arrest you," another announced with a certain glee. "Setting down on holy ground."

"You can try." Huang-ho took his ID coin from his pouch, touched it to his forehead. The stylized hornet of the Whelm appeared, doubled and redoubled until the insects formed a golden, buzzing swarm. "I am an inspector of the Whelm. I can make the sky fall on your head." He raised a fist. "Defy me and you defy the Connatic himself!"

No more play-acting was needed: they were already kneeling. Their officer had thrown his projac away as if it had turned into a hornet.

"Good. Right. I have come to arrest a wrongdoer. A criminal."

"Of course we'll help you," the officer said. "He must be a främling, recently arrived. Otherwise his neighbors would have alerted us. All know the importance of harmony here."

"Get up, ser. We know his face. We have his address." Huang-ho looked around. "I notice there are no street signs?"

"All citizens learn the map in kindergarten. That is enough. Nothing ever changes. We are living in the Perfect City, what you would call Utopia."

"We need a city map then. I didn't attend your kindergarten. And I need that map right now."

Five minutes later one of the underlings came running with a flapping map the size of a tablecloth. The corners were torn, Gunnar saw, and the map itself was bordered with dancing teddy bears and butterflies. It must have come straight from the wall of a nearby crèche.

Huang-ho must have more than one augmentation because a single look was enough to memorize the entire map.

"Got it. Now don't you try to follow us. This is Whelm business. Those who interfere do so to their sorrow."

They crossed a city park with fountains that only dribbled. There wasn't a single tree or flower to be seen, only reindeer moss and gravel gardens with rounded rocks.

Next came a long lane flanked by heroic statues. Some depicted savants consulting scrolls, others represented warriors raising swords, or masons building a wall.

"They all have the same face," Gunnar said.

"Yes. They show the founder of this city, Rodhart de Baston. He was rather talented as you can see. The Perfect Male. As his wife was the Perfect Female. All citizens try to emulate them." He pointed. "There, in the distance. You see her."

And yes, they soon walked past the towering statue of a rather formidable looking woman. Gunnar eyed her out-thrust chin, the frowning brow: a termagant, a dragon lady and certainly not the kind of woman one wanted for a mother.

"Here." They stood in front of a three-story apartment building with the usual porthole windows. Huang-ho pushed the door open. "Room number 23. That must be on the next landing. They start the numbering here at the ground floor."

"I think we found the right place," Gunnar said and waved to a faded graffiti slogan on the wall of the stairwell.

"...of the sheep," was still visible but the rest had been scrubbed off vigorously enough that the underlying concrete showed.

"Ah, yes. If you don't run with the wolves, you must be one of the sheep."

The stink of mold and mouse droppings made Gunnar gag and it became stronger with every step. Some of the long light-strips flickered, and that was the first time he had seen such a thing. The Perfect City clearly didn't consider maintenance a top priority.

The door was a slab of scratched aluminum.

"No nameplate nor a bell to ring," Huang-ho said. He tried the door-knob but the handle just turned freely.

"Hey," he called. "Let us in!"

He waited to the count of ten and then pounded on the door. It sounded like a sledgehammer. *He must be wearing riot gloves.*

"Go away," came a faint voice.

"Open up! I'm an officer of the Whelm."

"Go away."

"This is becoming tedious." Huang-ho took a step back and glued a glittering blob of putty onto the doorknob. "Better step back."

"In the games an officer just pulls his projac and melts the lock."

"That is an excellent way to weld the whole door immovably to the frame. You need a tank then to ram it open." He gestured. "Now step back. The explosion should only smash inward and no farther than thirty centimeters, but sometimes you get shards flying around."

A hiss, immediately followed by a sound too loud to hear, as if a hundred thunderbolts hit right in front of Gunnar, a flash that turned the whole world a searing white and then nothing. Not even darkness.

Chapter XXI

From *Interview with master-healer Lodewicke,* First Blue Scimitar Gazette.

"Half an hour after death, that is about the limit. If we have you in a gel tank by then, we can probably save you. Two months later you are as good as new. If you are wealthy enough, mind you, and if your brain is still intact. Saving your life is free, but being pretty or handsome again is going to cost you.

"But don't come in with some corpse found days later in a swamp with its feet in a bucket of concrete. Beyond that half hour, you are spoiled meat."

—⁂—

"This should do it, ser. Can you hear me, boy?"

Gunnar tried to move his tongue. It nestled like a fat slug in a mouth lined with sandpaper.

"Yes," he croaked.

"Adolpho be praised! Now try to open your eyes."

Adolpho be praised. It must be Huang-ho who was speaking. Adolpho was his personal birth-saint whose icon he always wore on a string of jade beads. No doubt he had been counting those beads, while sitting next to Gunnar's bed.

"I...I'm trying, but...It seems I've forgotten how to open my eyes."

"You opened them. Ser, have another look at his optic nerves?"

"Certainly. Yes, I see what is wrong. The connections didn't fuse."

A blob of light bloomed in the darkness.

"Something is coming, Huang-ho."

It resolved into a face. No, not a face. A mask, with glowing lenses for eyes.

"Your face!" Gunnar didn't ask what had happened. There had been an explosion, obviously.

"I stood right in front of the door when it detonated," Huang-ho replied. "The whole door was a three centimeter thick cake of dexax, sandwiched between sheets of aluminum. It went off when I blew the lock."

The man behind Huang-ho, who wore the red and green face paint of a master-healer, added: "It ripped off your friend's whole face, and most of his skin. Burned part of his skull to charcoal." The healer nodded. "It will take another week or two before he can flirt with the ladies again. He was wearing his uniform and his gloves and that combination is almost bombproof. Only broke three ribs and no other bones.

"Now you, that was worse! All the bones in your body were splintered, your heart crushed. But your head was in his, well, call it the blast shadow. Just a bit of lost skin and we had to grow a new eye. The other one was salvageable."

"I have just informed Justine," Huang-ho said. "She should be here in five minutes."

Gunnar lifted his arm and his fingertips touched a vase with a preserved rose. It bounced away, light as a soap bubble.

"Where are we, in Mirri's name?"

"The transit station. There is a regiment of Whelm commandos stationed here and I kept contact with them when I went to arrest Suleiman Khan." His mask produced a hideous grimace which was probably intended as a smile. "One of the small perks of being an Inspector. When they lost my signal, they instantly launched a patrol boat. High burn all the way down, and then a fusion burst to stop. They probably broke every window in Hulle. They arrived just in time and every boat carries a gel tank for casualties."

"How long have I been here?"

"Seven days."

"Ah, that wasn't very long."

"Seven Great Days."

Mirri help me, more than two months.

"Did you, did the Whelm get him? Suleiman Khan? Or the Deep Warriors?"

"I was in a coma the first five days and the Monitors took it upon themselves to arrest members of the Deep Warriors. They caught hundreds in the first sweep, then arrested two thousand more. There are twenty-six Galleons floating down the River, and where they pass, all civilian rights are suspended. The Monitors become the absolute law."

Being the son of an admiral, Gunnar knew how precarious crowd-control was, every population a potential mob. "But they are no better than vigilantes!"

"It's even worse. Without electrical power, they couldn't use any advanced apparatus: no lie-detectors, no mind-mappers. They made people confess, even if they weren't part of any conspiracy at all."

It was almost a textbook situation: looking for traitors was a sure-fire way to create them. If there hadn't been any real Deep Warriors except for Suleiman Khan, there would be now.

The door opened and Justine shouldered the master-healer aside, knelt next to Gunnar's bed. "You're back!" Her gaze flitted aside to Huang-ho. "Is he?"

"I can talk," Gunnar assured her. "I can even grumble."

"Good. Your girl has been pestering me. Asking about your health thrice a day." She pursed her lips. "You must have impressed her."

Gunnar couldn't very well ask "Which girl?"

"I have told her you are awake." Her communicator started to buzz. "Well, here she is."

It was one of those perfect Heisenberg moments, a dead-or-alive cat-in-the-box moment. If it was Lavoine he would probably end up a starmenter, or at least very sorry in the end, but life certainly wouldn't be boring. While Semele was still an enigma, fierce and sweet like the tangy honey the glacier-hornets gathered in the high meadows and defended with their lives.

He put his thumb on the contact button. "Yes?"

Semele's face was as beautiful as a cameo of cream-stone and equally unreadable. "You are alive. Good. But this changes nothing."

Her face winked out.

"Ay…" Huang-ho said, "talk about abrupt."

"Well, at least she confessed she was glad you are alive," Justine said. "That is a start."

Gunnar threw his hands up in the air. "Why does it all have to be complicated?"

Justine didn't say anything like "Welcome to the real world." Her sly smile was almost as bad.

It felt strange to walk once more down the gangboard of the shuttle: the starling egg blue morning sky, the tree-toads singing. Almost a repeat of his arrival.

They took the swift-bahn to the Cape, and the windows seemed more scratched than ever, the plush of the seats so mangy that Mirri's face was no more than a blob.

There was a sweet, almost cloying smell in the air when they ambled to the villa. The gorse had come into bloom while he lay convalescing in the transit station. Thousands of yellow butterflies hovered above the fields, a sparkling golden haze.

Lavoine and Yedlar stepped from the porch. They were holding hands. *Good. At least that was sorted out.* Still, he felt a stab of chagrin. *She could have waited. She should have waited.*

When Gunnar was five, the Crèche-father had pounded the ninety-three possible emotions into his head. Useless mind states, like: I'm just a poor little boy. Please love me. Or: nobody knows that I'm a secret prince, stolen from his cradle. Naming them robbed those parasitic memes of most of their mind-sapping power.

Ah, this was a quite clear-cut case of the 'Veteran coming home.' His best friend has married the girl, who had promised to wait. His old job is gone, or even worse, has become obsolete.

Once named, the chagrin vanished. *Let him have her.*

He hobbled in their direction, his legs still unsteady after two months of weightlessness.

Gunnar spread his arms. "It's great to see you guys!" And it was. *We can still be friends.* Wasn't that what an ex-lover was supposed to say? Well, perhaps that would even work.

They remained until little nightfall, when the lumens faded to red and only the house-lights were left.

They spoke of nothing important and that was perfect. Only

— 117 —

school-talk: that Yolisse had been sent to the rector when she arrived giggling from a dose of happy-weed and couldn't stop laughing.

That master Ooka had been dumped by dame Genova, the xeno-linguistics teacher, and was seen dancing down the Esplanade the very same night, with one of the Hulverman girls.

"A much better wife for him," Lavoine declared. "Better-looking than Genova, too, and she laughs at his jokes. What more can a man ask?"

Gunnar's communicator started to buzz as he watched them board the swift-bahn. Semele's butterfly icon glowed but the camera remained off.

"You are home," she said. "Can you run?"

"Not right now. My bones are still knitting and…"

"There is a Riverside cross-country, the next Dark Eye-blink. Nothing very strenuous, and this isn't about winning."

"I think I can make it."

The Dark Eye-blink: three hours under a dark sky, the disk of Astaroth filled with writhing Rorschach letters. Lovers were supposed to read their future there, sitting at the riverside. But running in the mid-day dark would be more appropriate with a huntress.

"See you then." The butterfly blinked off.

At least she was willing to talk to him, and she even joined him the next morning as they waited for the school-horn to sound.

"You fought a monster and were almost killed," Semele said. It felt like an opening gambit.

Don't spoil it. It was as if he were looking at himself from a distance. Marveling. *I must have become a Scimitarian. Gone native, except that I was born here.* On Chevalier, a father would take his son to a brothel the day he turned fifteen. If he were a native of Ciromaj: Alastor 671, with ten girls to every boy, Gunnar would already be married, probably twice.

He had been consulting the Bibliotheque on the transit station, researching Phaedra's mating patterns.

The legend of Fatima had distorted the usual systems. Here, a man was seldom the one who took the initiative, not with the central role model for a girl being the warrior-princess.

"Better scrap that 'almost'. It took them half an hour before they had my heart beating again."

"Still, that is a thing Diana likes in a man. Hunting the monsters in the woods. Even if they take a human shape and the forest is a city."

Gunnar frowned. "That means I can sit next to you?" Translated in the terms of her chivalrous, mythic world: *Lady, may I wear your colors to the tourney?*

"Well, everyone can sit where they like. But I won't snort and change places, if that's what you mean."

Sitting in the back of the classroom next to Semele felt passingly strange: on his first day here, master Ooka had placed him and Lavoine in the front row, and that hadn't been changed since.

Other things clearly had.

"I saw half of the boys with that scimitar insignia on their school uniform, Semele. An upside-down scimitar inside the Elder Sign. Some girls wear the same symbol as an earring. What does it mean?"

"It is the emblem of the Deep Warriors. They wear it just to spite the Monitors. It also means that they spit on Fatima. Look at the hand holding the sword: it's a hairy troll's paw. Male. 'High time a man took charge,' they mutter. 'It was a mistake to cut off the head of the Thrice Reborn Suleiman.' "

"I bet they tear those emblems off the moment they see a Galleon rounding the bend of the River."

Semele snorted. "Those stupid Monitors! Arresting all those people. Before they started, there weren't any Deep Warriors."

"Well, their leader blew us up. I ..."

"I wonder. Look, I saw his face, Gunnar. The great and mighty Suleiman Khan. It was on all the screens, a River-wide alert. Only it didn't look like a real face to me. It was too perfect. Exactly what a warrior-prophet should look like. And the voice: such resonance. A god-voice. Humans don't sound like that."

She's right. I must tell Huang-ho.

He waved to the teacher, rose. "I have to leave. Family matters!"

"You know best. But I'm still expecting your essay on Garnet wedding customs tomorrow."

Chapter XXII

From *From Appendix to The Art of War, revised edition*:

"He's too clever for his own good," an Old Earth saying goes. It is tribal wisdom and how true! The average genius often proves to be a quite irascible fellow, devoid of the civilized graces. He considers himself a castaway, living on an island solely populated by chattering monkeys.

Still, there are moments when a genius-level solution is needed. Think of a Go-master pondering his next seventeen moves, or a strategos commanding a thousand star ships.

A Daughter of Diana starts out firing an invisible arrow at an invisible target. When she hits the center a hundred times out of a hundred, the abbess orders her to discard her bow.

The mental discipline allows a Daughter to enter her trance at will, bootstrapping her intelligence to the 170 IQ level.

For a short time only. Her solutions are always wildly inventive, but as with higher mathematics, there is no guarantee they are congruent with any real-life situation.

Huang-ho answered his communicator at the first buzz.

"I know why we couldn't locate Suleiman Khan," Gunnar blurted. "He doesn't exist. Someone built a false persona. The voice we heard, it probably was a recording. Nobody crouched behind that door or told us to go away."

"I know."

"You *knew* and didn't tell me?"

"I was notified only five minutes ago. The survey-results of that flat got mislaid somehow and I wasn't exactly at my best, with parts of my brain still regrowing. They scanned for DNA and there hadn't been a living person in that room for months."

"A trap, ser," Semele said over Gunnar's shoulder. "Set especially for you. You are somebody high in the Whelm, yes? Sent to investigate the business with the Galleons? The symbols and the fish?"

"You have a hunter's mind. I must speak with you. Bring you up to date and then make sure you won't mention anything to strangers."

"I have heard about mind-locks."

"I got one, too," Gunnar said. "It is just to protect us."

They met on the terrace of Gideon's, at the end of the third pier. The sign still showed a smiling lobster, something that most certainly was not on the menu anymore.

Most of the tables remained vacant, and it was easy to understand why. The River still wafted that sickly-sweet smell across the city, and the stump of the lighthouse was a potent reminder as well.

Some Earth-life had been filtering back from downstream: single tailed eels, edible crabs. The last monster salmon had been sighted three weeks ago. Still, there wasn't a single sail to be seen on the River.

If you wanted to cross the River you had to take an ostrich-drawn cart all the way to Garnet or Green-stone and board a ferry there.

Huang-ho still wore his healing mask, but Semele took it in her stride. Perhaps because it fitted her worldview? A warrior with a silver mask was a staple in myths.

"How long till you can take that mask off?" she asked.

"Almost there." The mask grinned. "It will be a shock, seeing skin again when I look in a mirror. This here —" he rapped his signet ring against his metal brow "— it feels like my true face by now."

"Perhaps it always was?" Semele said. She leaned forward. "But right, tell us what the Whelm found out about him."

"Well, as recently as three years ago, no Suleiman Khan existed. The first mention of the Deep Warriors was inserted into the index of the Phaedra room on Numenes. When Admiral Uzbar went looking for terrorists foolish enough to meddle with the Galleons, the Deep

Warriors and Suleiman instantly popped up. Better documented than anything I found on Phaedra herself."

"They wanted us to find the Deep Warriors," Gunnar said.

"Scapegoats," Semele nodded. "People to hide behind."

"There weren't any real Deep Warriors," Huang-ho continued, "just a club of some grumbling old men. But there are now. They are springing up like poisonous toadstools. The burgomeister asked the Cursar to give the Monitors free reign, to make them legitimate even when there's no Galleon passing." He threw up his hands. "Such foolishness! That would turn half the city into Deep Warriors before the next Nightfall!" The mask smoothed. "Someone wants to wake up the Galleons. To make them react. The new monsters and the fish changing isn't enough for him and ..."

Semele lifted a hand. "Or her. Women can be as ambitious as men. Not many empresses earned titles like the Merciful or the Good."

"Point well taken. He or she wants chaos. War. And the risks don't matter. He feels quite strongly about ..." He spread his hands. "If only we knew his ambitions! Or even if he's here on Phaedra."

"Say, that man you two tried to arrest? Who told you where he lived?"

"The Monitors. An anonymous call, but it showed the mask and crossbow of a ..." He shook his head. "Anybody can use that call sign. Monitors are secretive. I didn't think anything of that."

"It was them, then. And you must have been getting close for them to show their hand so blatantly."

Gunnar felt completely left out, no more than a spectator. The Whelm had a word for people like Huang-ho or his father: 'strategos'. People who were like Go-masters, always looking at least three dozen moves ahead before they moved a stone. Semele was clearly carved from the same precious jade.

"Is she an outsider, a främling?" Semele said. "You said the trail was first laid on Numenes, in the Phaedra room. But that might be misdirection." She closed her eyes, raised both hands, made a circle with thumb and index finger, then reached for an invisible bow and arrow. "Tell me, Diana. Hunt with me the Bristly Boar of the Truth."

She froze, stood as still, Gunnar thought, as a marble statue in a forest clearing. The picture was crystal clear. He saw a marble Semele statue, her bow raised, lichen growing on her left arm, a fallen nest at her feet with a single bright blue egg. In the Alastor Cluster there were a thousand mental focus systems, ways to stoke up your brain until it flamed like a flare star. This must be one of them.

"They live here," Semele said, and Gunnar heard a silvery voice echoing her words. *The goddess, she's speaking with Semele's voice.* "Right here in Blue Scimitar. They have to be nearby to catch the reins of the runaway Horse of War. To right the ancient wrong."

"They?" Huang-ho whispered, clearly unwilling to break her trance.

"Three women, one man." Semele opened her eyes. "That is all I know."

"One shouldn't get greedy, asking a goddess for advice," Huang-ho nodded.

So Huang-ho also heard that silver voice. Good to know it is real. That I'm not just hearing voices like an ordinary crazy with a serotonin imbalance.

But then Semele gave a perfectly logical breakdown of the steps that led her to those conclusions.

She doesn't know! She didn't hear Diana's voice, just like the first time. Or perhaps it is unbearable if you are a strategos, a deeply logical player, to have the winning moves whispered into your ear?

"Do you think they will try again, Semele?"

"Very soon. They almost got through to the Galleon, but it only reacted in a reflex. Like swatting a mosquito and then dozing off again. That talk about seeking a worthy enemy wasn't misdirection. It is something they feel very strongly." Semele pursed her lips. "I think Gunnar and I shouldn't miss the rest of the classes. Do you have that mind-lock gizmo on you?"

That was the moment that Gunnar could have raised his hand and said: "Wait! There is something I must tell you. The both of you."

But he didn't.

Chapter XXIII

From *Restricted Worlds, the Observations of a Star-Trotting Vagabond* by Yuri Hopkins, writing for the *Alastor Herald*, monthly magazine, now with Mirricyllai-approved horoscope.

The Order of Seventh Day Skeptics teaches that the Cluster goddesses are quite real: escaped AIs who have somehow found the holy grail of stabilization and now hide behind a divine mask.

When I visited Mirricyllai's cathedral, I was properly impressed, but didn't feel the immanence described by other pilgrims, the sense of a supernatural presence.

Perhaps I shouldn't have declined the candle the novice tried to sell me at the entrance? The sniffer in my communicator alerted me to the presence of half a dozen hallucinogens in the wax, and ten ozols for a small tea-light seemed rather steep. Still, visions, whether supernatural or chemically induced, are the way the higher beings communicate with their believers.

Inside, the glass work proved exquisite, even better than the collection of the Great Museum in Itwitar itself: octahedrons and intricate spirals, orreries of mythical solar systems.

Mirri's sisters resided in side alcoves, fashioned from clear glass, all coloring deriving from cleverly placed grids and Fresnel lenses.

The goddess herself had been carved from a single block of rose-quartz and inset with precious stones. Her tiara alone, pale star-stones in a filigree of orichalkos, would be worth a Director's ransom.

She held the Blue Scimitar high, like The Lady of the Lake offering Excalibur to King Arthur. Only here it would be a girl who would take that weapon from her hand to become Phaedra's Fatima with all the glory and the privileges that implied. It wouldn't be an act to undertake lightly: a false Fatima would be struck dead the moment she touched the hilt of the sword.

Right then, a girl pushed past me: her hair a tangle of raven curls, and rushed up the ladder that reached all the way to Mirricyllai's sword-hand.

She stood swaying on the last rung, shrieked: "I am the true Fatima!" and touched the sword. Ball-lightning instantly jumped from Mirricyllai's other hand and burned the girl to a crisp, with only the blackened skeleton left standing for three, four heart-beats before it crumpled and rattled down the ladder.

One of the fused vertebrae rolled to the tip of my left boot. I knelt down and pocketed this unique souvenir.

Three priestesses appeared just then, pushing brooms and sluicing the blackened stones with pails of sudsy water. This occurrence was clearly not as unique as I had first assumed.

From *MEMO, for the Field Marshal's eyes only*:

The Fatima is chosen in times of extreme troubles by a secret ballot. Only the women are allowed to vote, for obvious reasons.

When the Fatima is chosen, by a 67 percent majority, she walks to the Cathedral and takes the Blue Scimitar from Mirricyllai's hand. The statue's left arm contains a sixteen terawatt fusion battery: if a false Fatima touches the scimitar, she is instantly incinerated. This system works well, at least for the Scimitarians, and her death is universally seen as an act of the goddess.

—ɯ—

Returning home, Gunnar found Justine donning her best Mirriday outfit: a blue mantle with a hologram overlay of rushing waters, a yellow fisherman's hat of oiled sailcloth, webbed wading-shoes. "I'm visiting the cathedral," she said. "Do you want to come along?"

"Sorry, I'm not that religious," he began, but suddenly it seemed the right idea. He still felt dirty: he could use some forgiveness. Not telling things to the ones you love was as bad as an outright lie. Still, goddesses were in the business of absolution. They drank guilt like a fine liquor.

"I'll come. The Cathedral, that's the big tower with the sword?"

"I can't guarantee that Mirri is holding the authentic Blue Scimitar, but as long as most people believe that it is…" She shrugged. "That is the way symbols and magic work."

The glass tower scintillated and shone with ten thousand facets. At the same time it seemed very sturdy and delicate to Gunnar.

They took their boots off, walked through an arch of bottle-green glass and emerged in a hall made of mirrors and swirling rainbows.

To the right and left rose statues of the twenty-two lesser goddesses of the Cluster: Samra of the Winged Sandals, Hespia Who Walks in Twilight, the single pale blue star of the Unterwerlt set in her diadem. And there, Semele's Diana of Ephesus, with her many breasts and her bow.

Mirricyllai formed the centerpiece, three times as tall as her sisters.

No doubt the situation would be reversed in another sector of the Cluster. Gunnar hastily squashed the thought. It wasn't polite and perhaps even dangerous. The goddesses weren't exactly known for their broad-mindedness.

Justine halted in front of the statue, looked up to the face of the giantess.

"I'm not here to pray for something, or even to ask your advice. You already granted me all I asked for." She put two wax figurines in the bowl at Mirri's feet. Sparks jumped from her fingertips and the wicks of the two candles caught fire.

"My offerings," Justine said. "My heartfelt thanks, Heavenly Sister."

"The candles," Gunnar said, "you gave them our faces?"

"I prayed every morning for your survival when I heard that you and Huang-ho had been killed," Justine said. She bared a wrist: it was covered with scars and some of these looked quite recent. "Offered her my own lifeblood in exchange."

Two flames hung above the candles: they shone like stars in outer space, unwavering. Gunnar saw the flames creep down, swiftly consuming the wax.

There was a stillness in the air, a suspension of time. *The goddess sees all of eternity at once, and a century for her lasts no longer than a single beat of a mosquito wing,* the liturgy said. Right now, Gunnar *believed.* It had been his mother's prayers and Mirri's intervention that had saved him and his stepfather, not the healer, not those clever Whelm machines. Such a number of things that could have gone wrong: starting with the arrival of the patrol-boat just one minute too late to preserve them in the gel-tank. "You would have been spoiled meat," as the healer had told him, "only fit for the carps."

He looked into Mirri's eyes and they came alive, as if some cosmic switch had been thrown. He felt her gaze, her awful presence. There was no motherly love in that mix, no trace of protectiveness. *She saved me because she can still use me, because I'm an essential thread in the gobelin of the universe that she's weaving.* It didn't feel like his own thought, more like a divine voice-over, an offhand comment.

Gunnar stood frozen, like a mouse caught in a cobra's gaze. The presence slowly receded, became a memory, leaving only a rose-quartz and onyx statue clad in a lapis lazuli cloak.

Gunnar looked down and saw that the figurines were completely consumed. Only the blackened wicks were left.

"Right," his mother said. "She accepted my offering." Justine tugged at Gunnar's arm. "Let's go. This is no place to tarry."

She also must have felt the presence of the goddess. Never a comfortable thing.

"There is something else," Justine said. "When I heard that both of you had survived, I realized that one should not put off the really important things."

"You are talking about Huang-ho?"

"I have been selfish. It is a lot easier in Blue Scimitar for a man if he can call himself a husband."

Chapter XXIV

From *The Wise Sayings of the First Connatic*:

No one promised you would see your grandchildren dancing among the daisies.

―〰―

The Connatic was standing on his favorite balcony, looking out over a landscape that had grown almost as familiar as Numenes' ocean, when he became aware of another presence.

He turned around: the face was still a quicksilver mask, with only the eyes alive.

"You. How are things on Phaedra?" He spread his hands. "It is hard to get an overview. There is such a thing as standing too close."

"Badly, and it's going to get worse soon."

"I see. I'll contact my Field Marshall."

"He's doing what he can. But like me, he's neither allowed to, nor capable of interacting with the Elders. The moment they become aware of you humans, all games are over, all curtains pulled shut on your nice, tiny stages."

The Connatic took a deep breath. *This is just another crisis. There have been more than I can count and the Cluster is still orbiting the Galaxy. The suns still shine down on three thousand prosperous planets.* "What do you want me to do? That I'm not already doing, I mean?"

"Send an evacuation fleet and park it just beyond the outermost gas-giant. Perhaps you can save some of Phaedra's inhabitants when the Galleons wake up. If so, lower the ships on their fusion drives at least twenty miles from the River."

"No star drive?"

"Do nothing to suggest that you are an interstellar species. That would really make them sit up. As inhabitants of a single solar system, you are just fauna, animals. An interstellar drive makes you rivals." He frowned, a movement that sent ripples across his whole face. "I read that you have told Esclavade and Admiral Uzbar about me. See to it that it goes no further."

"I'll alert the Admiral," the Connatic said but the balcony was empty once again.

Admiral Patriska Uzbar had dreamed of this: a worthy enemy. Not just a police action to curb the enthusiasm of some crazy cult, no half-an-ozol dictator. The screen showed her the assembled fleet: an arrow of pulsating dots, and each dot a battalion. The assembled firepower was enough to detonate a sun, burn planets clean to the bedrock. And if the Connatic was right, this fleet was as effective as a couple of water pistols or a packet of wet firecrackers.

I could have become a horse-woman, she thought, *trotting past the cottages of our tenants and waving to the good-wives, or sitting down in the parlor, sipping a cup of tea with my sisters.* Suddenly it didn't seem to be the horrible option it had before. *He handed me the mightiest fleet in our history and I'll be facing a court-martial if I fire a single shot.*

She turned to her screen. "The destination is the gas-giant Lucifer, in the system of Phaedra, Alastor 824. We arrive in deep stealth and assume an orbit in the shadow of the gas-giant. You have the coordinates. Hook up to your flagship. We depart at 17:49 exactly."

The most recent base of Bela Gazzardo, arguably the Cluster's most famous starmenter, lay in a ravine bisecting one of those sunless worlds in deep space. It drifted close to the point where the freighters bound for Sarvanelle and Gironai had to emerge to make the next jump.

There were no real days in deep space but Gazzardo perversely held on to the time of his home-planet: it was now eight in the morning on Chevalier, the world he despised the most in the whole universe. He owned five wives who considered themselves fortunate to have him as a husband, and he would never jump around in any line-dance again, trying to catch the eye of a pig-faced milk-maid.

When he boarded a ship, he shot any man out of hand whilst wearing a cowboy hat. Any women wearing crinoline fared even worse. Three of their kind had refused the white courting rose of the gawky boy the starmenter had once been, and laughed in his face.

An alarm sounded and the face of his bosun appeared. "We're getting a hell of a big pulse. Something will be arriving in less than ten minutes. Something fat and lumbering."

The signal was indeed rather strong: a freighter loaded with transuranics or a hold filled with collapsed matter?

"Raise all ships. We'll barricade the exit point."

When Patriska Uzbar's screen lit up, she saw a face any Whelm soldier would instantly recognize.

"To the freighter. Ramp down your drive and stand by to be boarded. This is your lucky day! If you survive, you'll be able to boast for the rest of your life that Bela Gazzardo himself captured you."

A smile crept across Patriska's face and made her almost pretty for a moment. "I think not." She turned her thumbs up, thus connecting to all her commanders. "Fire at will."

The first ship to emerge was a gold-plated state yacht, the kind magnates ride to impress the lesser folk. It even had a figurehead, some lady with a splendid bosom, holding a...flaming sword? He frowned. And her helmet had the shape of a hornet.

"Disengage!" he screamed. There were others who used splendor to shock and awe, to overwhelm. And no magnate would have two Thribolt projectors mounted next to the spine of his star drive. The Whelm just wouldn't allow it, and would instantly mark him a starmenter.

The next ship to appear was a Michiel de Ruyter class dreadnought and that was the last thing Gazzardo ever saw.

Chapter XXV

From *Restricted Worlds, the Observations of a Star-Trotting Vagabond* by Yuri Hopkins, writing for the *Alastor Herald*, monthly magazine, now with Mirricyllai-approved horoscope.

"Well," said the Whelm officer I had met at the Three Naked Nymphs, "you are a journalist, no?"

I assured him this was the case.

"Would you like to see a typical Blue Scimitar wedding?"

"Sure. There will be dancing, and witches telling the virgin bride how many sons she will bear?"

"She isn't exactly virgin, but yes. Diana's priestesses will shoot three apples off the head of the bridegroom, and if he flinches he might be skewered." He nodded. "The bride, she instructs her maids in self-defense, and they want to make sure the groom is worthy of her."

———

When I arrived at the wedding three days later, it was the officer who was sitting on the lower throne. A target was painted on his brow.

"You might have told me it was your own wedding," I said. "For the bride I bought a katana inscribed with MAY YOUR ENEMY'S LIFE BE SHORT, and the groom gets a single-shot pirate's gun from the weapon shop. You know, the one with The Right to Buy Weapons is the Right to be Free."

"Good choice, ser," a boy said. "My mother *loves* knives."

———

The knife act was spectacular, with the bride-to-be throwing the first knife. The high-priestess walked in, wearing a burning skirt, and told the bride she would bear a hundred daughters who would be fierce as wolverines. Then there was the dance of Nineteen Veiled Ostriches, who were ridden by monkeys in red capes.

The high-priestess clapped her hands and the wine-fountains started to bubble. Half a dozen stuffed boars were brought in, and we went on to toast to the happy couple.

Afterward it all became a bit hazy but I woke up in bed with the high-priestess I had met before in front of the temple. "They warned me all främlings are as horny as jumping hares. Nice to see they were right." She kissed me, put my hands where they were the most useful. "Once more?"

"Of course," I said.

—⟨⟨⟨—

The sky shone the deepest possible blue and Gunnar found it hard to believe that soon the twilight would race up from the east.

He recognized Semele from a distance, clad in the forest-green and arterial red of a temple acolyte. She hadn't been present at the wedding: the high-priestess had only come with the girls from her star-team, who were all much older than Semele.

She wasn't alone, however. At least a dozen similarly clad girls stood at the starting line.

So it won't be a private affair after all. They will glare at me. Spit at my feet. A man-beast, come to seduce their virgin sister. One in particular.

He had found out her name, hacking the list of temple acolytes. Larissa. It always paid to know the name of your enemy. Names were magic.

He straightened his back, lengthened his stride: arriving all humble and apologetic wouldn't win him points with these viragoes.

"Sey, Semele. Sey, Larissa." *Sey* being the formal greeting a warrior gives a rival just before combat.

Semele nodded, smiled back at him. "It's a cross-country run. Nothing very strenuous. Just until the Eye-blink fades."

Mirri help me. Three hours. And most of them are girls. They're the better long distance runners.

"Men always burn out fast," Larissa said, echoing his fear. "No staying power. No stamina." She still looked wan, a permanent frown between her eyebrows that hadn't been there the last time.

The River devoured her parents. He felt a stab of pity. *And now I've come to steal her lover.*

The darkness came marching on across the mountaintops, turning their gleaming ice-fields to dull slate. The tree-toads fell silent and even the rustling of the leaves stilled. Mist coiled from the River, streamed out across the field.

Strange. Gunnar didn't remember that happening on the other occasions. At his first Dark Eye-blink he had been standing with his mother at the end of the mole, and the River had been clear — so clear they had seen the landing lights snap on in the mountains above the ocher city.

"Ready?" the arbiter asked, and raised his projac. The gun would launch a fireball, just like at the first run. Hovering, the fireball started out as a red dove flapping its wings, then a green eagle, and it finally exploded in a shower of blue feathers. That was the moment to start sprinting.

Gunnar detected a movement behind him. Silent as ghosts, Monitors were emerging from the mist. They rode pale horses as sleek and spare as greyhounds. Mist and Monitors. That meant...

"Now!" the arbiter called: the electric dove flew up into the sky and almost immediately went out.

No one ran because the eerie choir of a Galleon now drifted in from the River: notes as clean as silver claws on a carillon of icicles.

A hiss, then two more. Above the Galleon, fireworks bloomed, sketching the Elder sign in strokes half a kilometer long. Once, twice, thrice.

From the Galleon rose a howl, a screech of inhuman outrage and then the sign was echoed on every single sail.

Around the Galleon the water slowly stilled, became a black mirror. For the first time in the one and a half thousand years that humans had lived on Phaedra, a Galleon had halted.

"He did it!" Larissa screamed and pointed at Gunnar. "I saw him launch those flares and attack the Galleon!"

Chapter XXVI

From *Restricted Worlds, the Observations of a Star-Trotting Vagabond* by Yuri Hopkins, writing for the *Alastor Herald*, monthly magazine, now with Mirricyllai-approved horoscope.

A Cursar is always chosen from one of the high families, with roots deep in the planet's history. He shouldn't be a cretin, but intelligence isn't the most important factor. Breeding is. The current planetary governor can trace his bloodline to the first Fatima, and he married the last surviving houngan from the voo-doo world, which effectively made her Queen of Ezulia. That is enough royalty to please even the most exacting Blue Scimitarian.

—

Husbard Lylliasson answered his own communicator and instantly consented to let me interview him.

"I'm an avid reader of your columns. The view of a främling is quite refreshing! No gilding a stink-flower or tiptoeing-around, eh? Your description of the Monitor was right to the point."

—

I met the Cursar's wife and his two charming daughters a week later: Ezulia and Lavoine, both quite formidable females who somehow dominated the whole room.

Ezulia was pure glamour, one of those fabled goddesses that promised you the night of your life but would leave you a wrin-kled mummy in the morning light, all your blood and life force sucked from your veins.

Arch Lavoine would whisper in your ear and the next moment you would find yourself on a stolen space yacht with her, out to rob an idol in a haunted temple of its left emerald eye.

If only I had been forty years younger! No, even twenty would have sufficed. But now I knew them for what they really were: poisonous demon-spiders in the shape of a girl.

I pointed to the life-size portrait above the fireside: a scowling man, turbaned and with a three-pointed beard, brandishing a blue scimitar. "And who might that formidable warrior be?"

"Well," the Cursar said, "he's a kind of black sheep in the family. Still, we are rather fond of him. Suleiman the Thrice Reborn."

"Family? But I thought the First Fatima was your ancestress?"

"Fatima was his favorite niece."

The Cursar's wife spoke up for the first time. "Any pantheon needs its demons even more than its saints. We offer honey and rum to Legba. Tears and tree-toad blood to Lord Suleiman."

"He's a god? A god of what?"

"Of rancor. Of revenge long delayed."

—⚉—

The holding cell of the Justiciary had been crowded the first time; now there weren't even decent standing places left. The Monitors kept bringing in new miscreants, and although most citizens knew better than to protest, there was a non-stop din. The pheromonal stink of fear burned in Gunnar's nostrils.

"They called me a Galleon-denier," a butcher complained, "and I didn't even wear a Deep Warrior badge!"

"The moment I get out of this," a glam-tailor with pointed slippers and a feather-crown swore, "it'll be the first thing I'll sew on my jacket! I'll parade down the Esplanade calling: 'Piss on the Galleons! Piss on the Elders! The Suleiman is right!'"

Gunnar touched his arm. "I have been away for some time. The Suleiman?"

"He told us that the Monitors and the Galleons are our enemies! That Phaedra belongs to *us*! That Fatima is the real traitor, siding with the Galleons and the Monitors." The tailor spread his hands and in his eyes smoldered the fire of a very recent convert. "He's of the ancient stock. He is the old Suleiman reborn!"

"They should torpedo the next Galleon that appears!" added a girl who openly wore the Suleiman-badge.

"Well, the Galleon halted here," a priest of Mirri said, "and it isn't going away any time soon. Thanks to you idiotic warriors!" And that was the start of a riot.

Gunnar woke up with a pounding headache. A stun-shot from a police projac set on 'neural' would have left no more than a rested feeling, but projacs were far too high tech to work in the neighborhood of a Galleon. It must have been sleeping gas, the stuff the bat-herds used to pacify a rabid riding animal.

He wasn't in the holding cell anymore but in an office with the egg-shell-white walls of a bombproof shelter. On the wall hung a portrait of Mirri next to a picture of the First Connatic holding a Hussade stick and the casque and tunic of a Numenes Rover. Both were animated: a waterfall cascading from Mirri's raised hand, the Connatic butting an adversary into the last tank and reaching up for the Sheirl's golden ring.

"Back again, I see."

A fat Monitor looked down on him. Two more stood at the entrance and must just have entered because the smallest one was closing the door. The usually translucent porcelain gave them a kind of anonymity that was more threatening than any true mask could have been: you could almost recognize a neighbor from seven houses over, or the girl who sold pickled sea-anemones in front of your favorite shrine, but you just couldn't be sure.

The visitors' masks appeared to be quite new, not scratched and dull like the mask of Gunnar's jailer. Their uniforms also looked unused and could have been just spun by a 3D printer.

"Up!" his jailer ordered. "The captain and his aide here, they want to ask you some questions."

The rank of captain was quite arbitrary, Gunnar knew. The Monitors were self-organizing: those who showed the most 'abernet', that cold and precise zeal and unquestioning reverence for the Galleons, were automatically seen as leaders and obeyed.

These two fairly radiated 'abernet', leaning forward, their hands half raised as if ready to throttle any Galleon-denier.

Dread gripped Gunnar's bowels. These two looked as dangerous as wild hyenas, hungry and eager for the kill. But then, belatedly, he noticed the bow of the smaller Monitor: it wasn't made of panzer-glass. It was a compound-bow, layers of glass-fiber alternating with horn, ivory and ironwood. The kind of bow Diana's acolytes carried.

"Go with them, boy," the first Monitor said. "Tell them everything if you don't want to end up with your head on a stake."

"Thanks," Gunnar said when they descended the marble stairs in front of the Justiciary. "I don't think the Monitors really believed it was me who had stopped that Galleon, but they sure don't believe in leaving loose ends."

"Sorry," Semele said. "Larissa..."

"Not your fault."

"We'll meet Justine at the Eastern forest gate," Huang-ho explained. "She'll bring our communicators and my projac."

Of course: carrying an energy weapon or a communicator would instantly brand them as impostors. No Monitor would carry anything high tech which wouldn't work close to the Galleons.

"Wait," Gunnar said. "Those uniforms and bows. How did you ever print them, Huang? All fabbers should have stopped working the moment the Galleon appeared."

"Had them for weeks. I believe in taking precautions, and the masks and uniforms are one size fits all." He steered Gunnar into the shelter of a porch. "Walking a prisoner through half the city is rather risky." He opened his pouch. "I have a mask here. Your own uniform."

"Now walk like your father," Semele said, and Gunnar didn't correct her on that 'father'. Huang-ho had always been an integral part of the family, as important as a Blue Scimitar uncle. "Big strides and ready to jump. Smelling the stink of heresy on every street corner."

How scarily easy it was to feel like a Monitor once you donned the mask! Every unmasked face instantly became the face of a potential enemy. The weight of the bow in your hand made you yearn to use it. And then there were the sails of the stranded Galleon, billowing above the roofs without the ship moving a single inch. They gave the impression of headlong speed. Perhaps they were now turning the whole moon, making her rotate faster and faster?

"We'll have to cross the Prater Rughalt Square. It is the only way to the forest gate."

"Is that a problem?"

"Well. The Suleiman is holding his speech there. And half the city will be there to applaud the new Fatima."

"We have a new Fatima?" Gunnar was Scimitarian enough by now to feel a surge of joy. All their troubles were over. The Fatima would lead them, save them.

"O, yes, we have one," Semele said. "The worst possible Fatima." She paused and it wasn't for effect, only that she clearly couldn't bring herself to speak that name. "Lavoine."

The Prater Rughalt Square was huge. It had been designed to hold most of the citizenry at the Midyear Fest, once every forty-five years.

Gunnar noticed the sound of the crowd from streets away: even louder than the hubbub at a Hussade game, yet strangely different. There was a kind of hesitancy to it, as if the crowd wasn't sure if they should applaud or jeer.

They turned the last corner, and saw that the always empty square was filled to capacity. It was a deeply unsettling sight, because every single person seemed to stand apart from all the others. Like a cloud of atoms, all with exactly the same negative charge.

Monitors stood with their crossbows raised, next to red justiciars with riot sticks, magnates clad in mountain silk, young mothers with their babies cowed to stillness.

Gunnar's eyes were as sharp as gene-surgery could make them: Lavoine stood on the platform where the burgomeister normally opened the opera season, leaning on a sword.

"It is the real one," Huang-ho said, "in case you were wondering. She plucked it from Mirri's hand after the Galleon halted. Normally, the hidden battery would have burned her to a crisp, with her not even being nominated..."

"I see." With the power off, any girl was free to take the Scimitar.

The Cursar stepped forward and spread his arms. He was wearing a turban, the desert mantle with the water-recycling hump from the historical Third Caliphate dramas.

"I give you...the true Fatima! The Scimitar has chosen her."

Lavoine raised her arm, held the sword high.

The applause was deafening, half a million mouths screaming their assent. Gunnar had to clamp his jaws shut to keep from joining in.

Lavoine put the sword down, stood waiting, and silence descended; a silence so profound that only the shrill cries of the swallows were left.

"Oh yes," Lavoine said. "I thank you, my dear followers. But now I bring you news even more joyful!" She beckoned to her father who joined her. "After all these centuries, your rightful Suleiman has returned. Yes, here he is: the Four Times Reborn Suleiman!"

Her final act was a masterstroke. She took the Elder sign with the inverted scimitar from a pocket, pinned it on her breast. Now the Fatima and the Suleiman were inseparably joined. Joined against the Elder Galleons.

"I don't understand," Gunnar said, while they walked through a city that felt almost abandoned. "The Cursar was already the most powerful man on Phaedra. What did he gain? Except the enmity of the Monitors? With all high tech on hold they are the most dangerous warriors left."

"He's the Cursar," Huang-ho said, "but only the Cursar. Not the god he wants to be. Not the Reborn Suleiman. And there are his wife and his daughters. They want a god, too. I bet they pushed him into it. Fed his vanity."

"He didn't think it through. All voodoo gods started out dead."

"We make our own gods and goddesses," Lavoine had explained. "You start out with a dead hero, one who has been very successful or dire so they won't forget him for generations. A burner of cities, one who skins orphans alive!

"We bring him back to life by dripping our own blood on his grave, plying him with clumps of honey and sugar, and rum. We dream of him until he walks out of our dreams and sits in the True World once again. A hundred, a thousand times more powerful. A god."

"They want him as a god," Gunnar said. "But first he has to be dead."

"He'll see that differently," Semele said, "the Cursar. He'll be dead but immortal."

There was a wistful undertone in her voice that Gunnar didn't like at all.

"We are going to…where exactly?"

"The next city," Huang-ho said. "I have to warn the Whelm. The Galleon is blanketing the whole radio-spectrum and the Whelm macroscopes will only see mist. They haven't the slightest idea what is happening here."

"Good," Semele said. "And then the Whelm will descend with a hundred ships, a thousand ships, and arrest the Cursar!"

"There is the Galleon. If a star ship tries to descend, the repulsor plates will short out, and it will fall down from twenty miles up." He shook his head. "No, I'll signal them as soon as we are outside the range of the Galleon."

"And if we find a Galleon anchored at Garnet, also?" Gunnar asked.

"Then we'll formulate a new plan. A battle plan seldom survives contact with the enemy longer than five minutes."

Chapter XXVII

From *Restricted Worlds, the Observations of a Star-Trotting Vagabond* by Yuri Hopkins, writing for the *Alastor Herald*, monthly magazine, now with Mirricyllai-approved horoscope.

Yalantin, Alastor 98, heads the list of Restricted Planets. Not a single spaceship that landed there ever left again. The longest radio contact lasted all of three minutes and ended with an exclamation, followed by: "You're never going to believe who is walking to my airlock now! Not in a thousand years."

The pilot of the other ship had his macroscope focused on the landing place: even analysis in a dozen wavelengths beyond and below the human range only showed an empty field of lichen, not even a butterfly fluttering past.

—

I orbited the world twice: it showed a mottled ocher surface, with three shallow equatorial seas. No trace of the country-sized mandala or the cultivated fields the other explorers had mentioned.

"You!" the ultra-phone barked, "are you landing or not? That would make you number seventeen on this watch."

"Who are you?"

"The Whelm. I did something quite stupid, otherwise they would never have stationed me here. You landing would at least be something."

"Sorry, I'm not going to oblige you. But I have the most recent recording of Clad in Scarlet. With Gertrude O'Hara."

"That would certainly help."

—m—

Hand a hero — or even worse, a heroine of the Red Sonya kind — a flaming sword and tell her not to use it. Next, watch her slowly go mad with frustration. Burning out that starmenter's nest had helped, but only momentarily.

"No way to get that sharper? Not a single clever algorithm?" Admiral Uzbar threw up her hands. "We can orbit a world and take a snapshot of a despot's face from a million miles distance and count the hairs of her eyelashes."

"That is only high tech, sera," the science officer said. "Human high tech." The science officer was a traditionalist: his ears cropped to a point, his hair an ink-black cap.

On the screen, the mountain chains and the polar caps of Phaedra were quite sharp. You could zoom in until you could see a swallow dart past, or count the pebbles on the shore of a glacier lake. The River and all twenty-six cities remained hidden by shimmering loops of mist. The mist was threaded by the kind of un-color you got when you tried to look with your own blind spot. It was impossible to gaze longer than two or three seconds at the live picture.

"No messages of any kind from the surface?" she asked.

"The whole radio-spectrum has fallen silent around Phaedra. We can't even hear the snap and crackle of polar light anymore."

The single patrol ship and the crew of the transit station had been evacuated the moment the planet fell silent. Evacuated in the most circumspect way: using light sails and a nuclear drive usually only used for maneuvering. It would be weeks before they arrived at the gas giant.

"And I'm not allowed to move any closer," the Admiral lamented. "Playing hide and seek!"

"Well, yes, ma'am," the science officer said. "It is like playing hide and seek, sure. But with a ravenous grizzly bear, and us no more than toddlers armed with wooden swords."

They remained scrupulously polite while on watch but she prized his candor, which never crossed the line into impertinence. Even your lover of ten years should know his place.

"Keep looking. Keep listening."

Chapter XXVIII

From *Restricted Worlds, the Observations of a Star-Trotting Vagabond* by Yuri Hopkins, writing for the *Alastor Herald*, monthly magazine, now with Mirricyllai-approved horoscope.

"This is the last time I serve you a hard-boiled gator egg and a latte macchiato, ser," the boy behind the breakfast buffet said.

"I'm sorry to hear that. Were my tips too stingy?"

"You won't hear me complain! Far from it. But tomorrow I'm starting my Long Walk. Following the Galleons." He hesitated a moment. "Would you like to come along, ser? Not the whole way, of course, but to Garnet only. The next city."

It was clear that I wasn't any longer the uncouth främling, after three weeks in the hotel. That I had been courting and bedding his niece was probably also part of it.

In the eyes of most Scimitarians Ayla was sickly pale, and thin as a rake to boot. Here the most popular women were voluptuous, if seldom fat, with skin the color of chocolate.

I grew up on Yethro, and the girls of my youth walked pale as snowdrops and were as slender as reeds. Making love to Ayla felt like bedding the Yethro Spring Queen.

"I'll come," I said. "What should I bring? Mosquito-proof clothes, my projac?"

He laughed. "A bullet- and claw-proof coat would be better. A projac won't fire while we are keeping pace with a Galleon. No, buy a crossbow with a hundred quarrels, and a brace of spring-loaded poison knives."

—

The swift-bahn ended at a wall of rustling green: swaying

bamboo trees with parasitic flowers the size of cartwheels. On the River, the sails of a Galleon had just appeared as promised.

An ironwood gate of five meters height formed the entrance to the forest: it was clearly intended to keep the denizens of the wood in, not the visitors out.

A viridian gloom surrounded us the moment we passed the threshold. With every step, the ground gurgled beneath our boots.

He raised a hand, looked around. "Wait," he whispered and that was the last word he ever said.

I chopped off the sting of the giant scorpion clinging to his back with my machete. There was no time to wind my crossbow and I finished the monster off with a dozen hand-held quarrels.

———

"Only half of the walkers return." Ayla shrugged. "Not your fault." She pulled me closer. "I haven't started my own Walk yet. Care to accompany me?"

S emele's face turned leaf-green the moment they entered the forest. Moving patches of sunlight slid across her arms.

"Great effect," Gunnar said. "Smart body-paint?"

"No, chromophores. Built-in camouflage, like the skin of a squid. My great-grandmother came from a jungle world and the gene is kind of dominant." She nodded. "I usually keep it on neutral. Why make the less talented jealous?"

Great genetics for our kids to have. Gunnar pushed the thought away. She was walking with him but she was still wearing that damnable butterfly, still boy-proof.

The Long Road paralleled the River, a black and green glass ribbon of fused earth. Seedlings had cracked the surface from below, and they had to detour around hissing water-willows and false cherry-trees with their deadly fruit.

Huang-ho and Justine went in front, both armed with crossbows and panzer-glass machetes.

Semele was next, with Gunnar forming the rearguard.

"You don't have to look anxiously over your shoulder every third step," Semele said. "I bet you read that article by that *Alastor Herald* journalist. You know, the so-called star-trotting vagabond."

"I did," Gunnar confessed.

"Giant scorpions are actually quite rare. He was just aiming for sex and sensation. To give an armchair traveler on Numenes a pleasant shudder.

"Listen: during the initiation we camped for a full *week* in the forest and didn't lose a *single* girl. Well, we had to amputate Miskra's left leg when she got bitten, but that was easily regrown once we got back."

"I see." Still, the green gloom to his right seemed filled with a thousand rustles and gurgles, the eerie calls of noxious insects. "I wasn't afraid. More looking around eagerly, hoping to spot that eight-legged anaconda master Ooka told us about."

"You'll see one before we reach Garnet. That is a promise." She turned around, touched her brow. The butterfly flapped its wings once, twice and then vanished.

"Well," she said, "this is the Walk after all. Even if we are walking away from our Galleon and hoping to find an empty River at the other side." She raised an eyebrow. "What are you waiting for?"

"We'll watch your back," Huang-ho called from the front. "Just go for it."

"But don't take too long," Justine added. "I heard something big pacing us for the last ten minutes."

Embracing the most desirable girl in the universe while you are anticipating a giant scorpion stabbing your neck, or the ground opening up in the maw of swamp-grabber: call it a unique experience. *Focus!* he told himself. *Another soldier is watching your back.*

Semele was taller than Anne of Green Gables and quite a lot taller than Lavoine, but she was clearly experienced. *Kissing all those girlfriends,* Gunnar thought and he didn't feel a shred of jealousy. *She's kissing me now.*

Semele was pleasantly curved but most of that was sleek muscle. *An athlete, a warrior maid. She'll fit right into the Whelm.*

She stepped back. "If we take off our clothes now, we'll be covered by bloodsuckers in a heartbeat." Her smile was dazzling but she remained a huntress, eminently practical.

A quarter of the way in, Huang-ho raised his communicator, stabbed the power button. The screen remained stubbornly blank. "How far does the influence of that damnable Galleon reach? If only..." He gazed at the River, shook his head.

"If only, what?" Justine asked.

"It doesn't matter."

Justine didn't insist, but Gunnar felt the sudden tension between them. *She has asked before and he has probably answered that there are subjects he isn't allowed to talk about. That ended it. Justine won't act like a spoiled civilian. She's Whelm. She understands all about the need to know.*

Little night arrived, but here in the middle of the jungle it had no effect. There were no windows to turn dark, no lumens to switch to counter-phase to absorb the light from the sky. Bedding down without a tent of smart, claw-proof fabric would be suicidal, even with half of them standing guard.

Gunnar had already used up three quarters of his quarrels. Semele only a third because she seldom missed. Good as she was, Huang-ho was clearly the better shot: he *never* missed.

Gunnar didn't notice most of Huang's targets. A many-legged snake sliding down from a branch was the first sign Huang-ho had used his bow. And later there had been that shark-monkey he shot in mid-leap: only a hand-length away from Semele's back.

It made Gunnar feel quite clumsy. *I should train more. Huang-ho is a true warrior, almost as good as one of those monks in The Incredible Legend of the Shaolin Brothers.*

The strange thing was that he didn't remember Huang-ho ever competing in any of the ship games. He was competent: when he and Gunnar's father were throwing shuriken, Huang-ho hit the darting hawk as often as did the Admiral. Which wasn't all that often. When Justine competed with them, she always ended up with the highest score. *A kind of misplaced politeness? Not willing to shame his superior? No. All had always been above board and straight between the two friends.*

"He's good," Semele said when a needle-bird tumbled from a tree-top, just before she slapped her barbed arrow into the groove. "Your father."

"Actually, he's my stepfather."

"You don't act like it. You love him."

Which was quite true. The face of his father had been fading for some time: Justine also had never hung his portrait on the wall. "The dead are gone," she told Gunnar. "He boarded his last ship and I know Mirri will keep him quite busy. Why bother him?"

"You went with us," he said to Semele. "You left your parents."

"They can take care of themselves." She laid a hand on his shoulder, squeezed. "I chose you."

"I need you more than they need you?"

"My mother can hit an owl's eye at sixty paces. My father runs seventy miles without getting winded. You are quite competent. For a boy."

When Gunnar stumbled for the third time, Huang-ho made him halt. "No need to tear a muscle." He opened his hand. "Take this. There is nothing smart or high-tech in this pill. Just chemicals."

The pill was the standard 'keep-going' pill from a Whelm medicine kit. There was only one thing wrong with it: Gunnar had seen the contents of Huang-ho's pouch. There had been a roll of mono-filament, a magazine of quarrels and nothing else. Certainly no medicine kit.

Some sleight of hand. He must have kept a single pill somewhere in his coat pockets.

The pill, whatever its provenance, did its familiar magic: Gunnar's gaze instantly cleared, his stride lengthened until he seemed to fly along the path.

A last stretch, and in the distance a gate loomed among the thick bamboo trunks. Gunnar ran the last twenty meters, shouldered the gate open.

The city of Garnet sparkled in the sunlight, and it was like stepping into a sultan's treasure room. All houses were faceted jewels, with translucent walls of artificial garnet and ruby, each house bearing a bell tower with a massive wind gong. Close to the harbor, almost at the end of the mole, a Galleon drifted.

Huang-ho cursed, raised his communicator.

"It's no use," Justine said. "I already tried mine. Not even a hiss."

"I have to know if it is like this everywhere," Huang-ho muttered. He seemed to talk to himself and he looked confused, deeply troubled. "I have to ask. Even if it isn't allowed. I have to."

He walked stiff-legged to the River. It seemed to Gunnar that his stepfather was pushing against a howling wind or wading through a knee-deep snowdrift.

Huang-ho knelt down on a small beach, put his left hand in the water.

"All twenty-six of them, Adolpho help me. And they are almost awake. Already phase three."

When he rose, he found Semele's crossbow centered on his brow: a shot that couldn't miss.

"You are not from here, are you?" Gunnar's lover said. "A främling's främling. Not human at all, and most certainly not Huang-ho."

He spread his hands. "I can explain."

"You were him," Justine said and now there were two cross-bows raised. "Ninety-nine percent Huang-ho and for a while that was enough. Only tiny details to worry about, and you always told me you weren't allowed to talk about them."

"He comes from them," Semele said and jerked her head to the River. "Something the Galleons made."

"True."

Justine stepped closer, her finger hooked around the trigger. "Huang-ho, is he still alive? Or did you kill him when you stole his face, his memory?"

"He's still very much alive. Dreaming. He's dreaming our life. It was the true Huang-ho who spoke with you, his lips you kissed. When he wakes up he'll remember everything."

Semele stood stock-still and Gunnar saw her lips move in the Diana-prayer, entering the trance. Huang-ho didn't avert his eyes, looked right back.

Semele breathed out, blinked.

"He's telling the truth."

"Huang-ho would have been dead by now," the Huang-ho double said. "The Cursar offered me a glass of liquor at my arrival. Mountain Dew he called it. Only later I realized it would have killed any human norm body. Slowly, over a period of two weeks and leaving no traces. But my metabolism isn't exactly human."

"And now?"

"I'm still mostly Huang-ho. I'm the Field Marshal and I have to warn the Whelm. Tell them what to do."

"And my husband?" Justine said.

"He's in the mountains. We'll go to wake him and then take a ship up to the Whelm."

"My Huang-ho?" Justine asked. "He's seeing, dreaming this right now?"

"Such is the case."

Chapter XXIX

From: *Interview with Admiral Uzbar*, free fashion magazine of the *Alastor Herald*:

Admiral Uzbar: "The Whelm is all about warrior mystique, to overawe your enemy with your splendor. A dagger, its handle inset with emeralds seems all the sharper, a gold-plated projac more deadly."

Question: "I saw you wearing a watered-silk evening gown at the reception of Grand Marouf Benedict, a bracelet of green gold. That, too, is part of the Whelm uniform?"

Admiral Uzbar: "Well, my gown is bulletproof and my bracelet can project a dozen useful illusions, like twenty Bright Haven berserkers storming in, brandishing razor whips."

—⁂—

The first Garnet they met, raised his left hand and intoned: "Hail to Suleiman! May He and the Fatima live forever!" It sounded like a challenge. "You are not from here. Främlings."

Huang-ho gently shook his head, an indulgent smile on his lips. "No, my friend. We all are subjects of Suleiman. All brothers and sisters of the Fatima. There are no främlings here."

"True. But why aren't you wearing their emblem then?"

"We just came in from the forest. We didn't want to risk dirtying them." He reached into his pouch, pulled out three emblems. They were twice the size of the man's and clearly made of more precious materials than 3D-printed plastic. "The Suleiman sent us on a survey. To inspect his realm. With no vehicle able to fly, we had to go on foot."

The man frowned. He was clearly still suspicious. "But how do you report to Him then?"

"In the oldest, time-tested way. Justine, show him our cage with carrier pigeons."

Which she duly did.

Traveling with a magician had its perks, Gunnar decided. Would this new Huang-ho be able to conjure a banquet out of thin air when they rolled out a blanket?

"Where are you going, if I may ask?"

"There should be an abandoned monastery in the mountains. With a great view of the city." He nodded to Semele. "We can't take any pictures of course, but my daughter here is a great water-colorist. She draws most charming flowers and adorable bluebirds."

"She draws most charming flowers and adorable bluebirds," Semele grumbled the moment the man was out of earshot. "A great water-colorist! I've never been so insulted!"

"I had to improvise. Sorry."

Garnet turned out to be much smaller than Blue Scimitar: a brisk walk of about two hours brought them outside the city limits.

Stony fields stretched under a misty sky with four sun dogs surrounding Syrthene.

When Huang-ho thumbed on his communicator, the screen instantly lit up: they must be out of the reach of the Galleon. He scanned the wavelengths, but the only result was a test pattern and the call screen of the weather satellites.

"Not much use. I wanted to signal the patrol boat or the transit station but I see now that the boat is gone and the station abandoned. Using an ultra-phone is too dangerous, with the Galleons almost awake."

"Dangerous?" Semele asked. "What would happen if they wake up?"

"They would kill you. Kill you all. Which would be a pity."

He reached up and a glowing oblong appeared from thin air. A turn of his left thumb in a direction that hurt Gunnar's eyes, and the sleeping body of the real Huang-ho drifted down, settled on a bank of grit.

"When he wakes up, you'll board the spaceship. He'll know what to do. I dumped as much of my memory into his brain as would fit. Mostly instructions for how to get there. What to say and do."

"Wait!" Gunnar called. "What spaceship?"

"This one. Me."

He unfolded, that was the only right word for it. He unfolded like an origami flower and became something else.

Gunnar eyed the six meter wide soap bubble: it seemed quite fragile, not space-worthy at all. He saw throbbing veins and a tiny heart in the walls. It was still a living body.

"We'll fly through space in *this*?"

"It's only good for three hours," Huang-ho said. "But that should be enough. It is quite a bit slower than the usual star drive but it won't alert the Galleons. Lily-white Elder tech."

The voice was coming from *behind* Gunnar. He turned around: Huang-ho was sitting up, and this Huang-ho wore the uniform and triple hornet sleeves of a high Whelm officer.

"I won't act like a dunce and ask if I'm still dreaming. I clearly am not."

Justine stared at him, gulped. "Do you remember everything? Do you remember *us*?"

"What happens when the elephant comes walking down your belly?"

Justine colored. "Yes, you remember everything." She threw herself into his arms.

The ship rose like a soap bubble. Swaying, the walls expanding and shrinking alarmingly.

"That's only to circulate the oxygen," Huang-ho reassured them. "They don't use ventilators here and the trip is too short to use air-scrubbers."

Garnet shrank beneath them, the buildings becoming heaps of jewels. At the height of seven miles, the whole River valley turned into a misty ribbon, shot through with nacre.

It felt like escaping, no, worse, fleeing. *I'll be back. I'm doing it for you.* He pictured his city: filled with mist, in the grip of the Suleiman and the false Fatima. *I made it my home and now everything is spoiled. No, this*

*is different. The first rule of the Whelm: never storm a fortified hill. Retreat
to fight another day.*

The last of the atmosphere was left behind and the stars came out. A
surge to the left and now even Astaroth started to shrink fast. It became
a fat dot with Phaedra and the other moons no more than points.

"Illegal contact with the perfect masters," a voice spoke right inside
Gunnar's head. It wasn't in any language he had ever heard but at the
same time perfectly understandable. A picture flickered through his
brain: Huang-ho's double dipping his hand into the River to find out
what was happening in the other cities.

"Rogue guard of the lowest order detected," the same voice continued. Gunnar got an impression of massive power and intelligence, but
no sentience at all. No trace of the "I am" or the "This is me, unique and
unlike any of the others" feedback loop.

The others sat frozen, listening like rabbits in the glare of a hunter's
floodlight.

"This isn't good," Huang-ho whispered. Which must be the under-
statement of the year.

"Formulate antibody to cancel the rogue guard."

"Impossible," another voice objected. "They are traversing overspace."

"The rogue guard will have to leave the overspace soon."

"Target mapped. Now building antibody."

The voices fell silent and the feeling of enormous presences and
intense observation was gone.

A gas giant loomed, its methane clouds lit by Syrthene. In the depths
between Lucifer's cloud bands, Gunnar saw lightning flicker. The bolts
must be as long as the entire River.

The gas giant became a half moon, a sickle and then they flew above
the night side.

"There!" Semele pointed. The long shadow of the giant world was
filled with rotating mandalas and cones made of blinking navigation
lights: every dot a ship.

"I'm calling the fleet," Huang-ho said into something that looked like a half-melted cucumber and must be some kind of microphone. "This is Field Marshal Huang-ho. This is…"

A face bloomed on the wall in front of him.

"Our projectors are locked on you. There is a word you must say. A single word. A shape can be falsified rather easily. What kind of shoes was I wearing when we last spoke? When I gave you the assignment?"

Huang-ho threw up his hands. "How should I know? I'm a man! I don't notice such details unless they were stiletto heels and you were wearing fishnet stockings. Which you most certainly weren't."

"That will do as password. Follow the beam to my yacht."

Admiral Uzbar's yacht was gold-plated, bearing a Valkyrie with a flaming sword as figurehead. Gunnar thought it a good choice. This was pure Whelm: meant to impress, and a much more effective command center than a ponderous flagship. And the twin Thribolt projectors would make short shrift of any lesser ship than a dreadnought.

Their ship touched the airlock, melded with it and started to contract. The moment the outer door opened, the bubble was no bigger than the waiting room of a swift-bahn stop.

When Gunnar looked back over his shoulder he saw their living ship disintegrate behind the clear airlock door. Twinkling threads drifted away.

"Contact lost with the rogue guard," the voice said and Gunnar felt the muscles in his neck relax. *Huang-ho's double is gone. He sacrificed himself to throw them off the trail.*

"Correction. Locked on the rogue guard again. The information content is low, only nine percent of the original."

"Is it worth it to follow him, then?" the other voice asked.

Can one feel without ego? Obviously, because the first voice now sounded peremptory, almost exasperated.

"The perfect masters require a perfect universe. Leave no contamination."

"Antibody completed and ready for interception."

Chapter XXX

From *Wise Sayings for the New Century*, the *Alastor Herald* interviews Connatic Oman Ursht.

The Connatic: Well, ser, one couldn't call my life exactly adventurous. It is mostly sitting down and signing papers.

The Alastor Herald: You are rumored to have a dozen mistresses and each of those girls counting herself lucky. They say you walk the streets at night, disguised as a drunken cooper or a banjo-strumming beggar, parading his dancing kiwis.

The Connatic: Let's call them secrets of state. And my wife wouldn't like me visiting all those charming ladies.

The Alastor Herald: Your wife?

The Connatic: She, like those ladies, is a secret of state and I'm not saying I *have* a wife.

The Alastor Herald: The Idite Succession has always frowned on nepotism or family rule. They usually adopt an outsider as the new Connatic. It is said you weren't even born on Numenes?

The Connatic: Chevalier has claimed me as the bastard son of a cardsharp. Which is a great and fine compliment in their eyes, by the way. The Rhune concede that Lusz makes a fine castle for any Marune grandee. Yethro proclaims that I must be one of their aristocrats because the lady Samantha, who was seen on my arm at several festivities, has a face pale as ivory, framed in platinum blonde curls. (Shakes his head) How the scandal-sheets like to speculate! Lady Samantha is in fact a highly-regarded weapon-mistress, and one of my most trusted bodyguards.

The Alastor Herald: A final question, and perhaps an indiscreet one. The face you are wearing, it isn't your own? I've studied pictures where you congratulated the nine year old winners of spelling bees. Others, of you cutting ribbons red or blue. Each time your face was, well, call it severe, but never exactly the same. When I put them through face recognition there was no correlation at all. They may look like the faces of brothers but the program couldn't even see them as second cousins.

The Connatic: (smiles) Call me a secret wrapped in an enigma. That is how my citizens like to see me and I'm happy to oblige.

There were a hundred hologram faces hovering at the edges of the stateroom, voices soundlessly jabbering, hands gesticulating.

The Admiral and her science officer formed the only crew, which was exactly right. See the yacht as the fleet's bow, the Admiral standing at the railing with her spy glass, issuing orders which are flagged to the rest of the fleet.

The Admiral and Huang-ho knelt down in front of each other, touched hands. Gunnar saw them stiffen and enter an information trance. Huang-ho commenced to speak faster and faster until his words became a high-speed shriek, impossible to understand for anybody else.

He stopped three minutes later, rose. "So, now you know almost as much as I do."

"Tell me what to do," the Admiral said. "You are the Field Marshal and I assured the Connatic of your competence."

"The Cursar and his family let the jinn out of the bottle. I'll have to stuff it back in." Huang-ho touched his brow. "The guardian left instructions in my head. I can't access them right now but they will unreel in the right place and at the right time."

"Something dire is following you," the Admiral said. "It will make you less visible if you don't resemble the guardian too much. Where do you have to go?"

"Sanmartin. That's Alastor 2529. Why? Don't ask me. I get the feeling that the guardian will be making it up on the go. What little is left of him has no solid plan of action yet. Only hope." His arm rose, and his fingers jerked, grew rigid as if holding an invisible pencil. "Get me a piece of paper fast. Anything that writes!"

"The whole stateroom is interactive. Just extend your right index finger."

Glowing letters appeared in the air with every chop of Huang-ho's hand:

COPY THE NINE SIGILS OF THE JUSTLY BROKEN

PROTOCOL FROM THE SAMORAVO STELE

IN THE MUSEO ARCHEOLOGICO

Huang-ho's hand relaxed.

The Admiral frowned. "Some Elder inscription? And isn't a stele some kind of grave marker? Wait. Why go all the way to Sanmartin? There should be photographs of the stele in the Bibliotheque."

"Of a potent Elder artifact? I think not. And if someone tries to sketch it, he would quietly go mad before he's halfway." He clicked his tongue. "I hope my little bit of guardian makes me immune."

The science officer wasn't that easily diverted and touched the copy of the Bibliotheque that all warships carried.

"I see. No pictures. And it won't be easy to transport. If it is really coated with stabilized neutronium, it will be as heavy as a mountain." He nodded. "They found it orbiting one of the murdered worlds."

Semele frowned. "Murdered worlds?"

"When the Elders found any budding star-faring civilization, they didn't attack them. They just took their sun away and left them to freeze in the dark."

The Admiral's yacht was luxury incarnate: chandeliers cut from fossil ivory and lanterns filled with electronic fireflies, a rug so deep Gunnar almost had to wade through it.

Admiral Uzbar stopped in front of a door that must have been cut from an ironwood tree, with growth rings no more than half a millimeter apart. The famous Silenus quote was picked out in gleaming bronze, which made the function of the room crystal clear:

Kiss me,
My nymph.

Kiss me forever,
But please,
Let me come up for air
Once a century!

"This is our Peacock room," the Admiral said and added: "Have fun."

The door closed behind her and the four-poster bed seemed impossibly large.

Gunnar looked at Semele, suddenly horribly shy. There were a thousand kinds of female beauty: the balloon-breasted cowgirls from Chevalier, ladies carved from gleaming jet on Masai-na-Ona, the pale sylphs from Yethro.

His lover was eagerly adapting to the room, he noticed: the colors of the immense peacock plumes chasing each other across her bare arms, making her face an iridescent mask. They offset her gray eyes perfectly.

"You're beautiful," he said. "Perfection itself." *I'm babbling!* "Because you are Semele. Because there is no one else like you."

She touched her throat and her clothes peeled away, folded themselves on the chair.

"Truly? Show me then."

A snap of her fingers and the interactive room, which came perilously close to Turing grade, did Gunnar the same favor.

He saw Semele looking down at his crotch and realized that showing her wouldn't be any kind of problem.

The star-trotting vagabond would no doubt be able to describe the near-perfect night in all its lurid details.

Gunnar woke up very early in the artificial morning, and spent a full ten minutes just staring at the face of his beloved. She snored and it was a sound as elemental, as reassuring, as waves rolling in on a pebbly beach. He reached for his communicator, put it on 'scribe'.

"Your eyes are moonstones,
Luminous in the night.
Your breasts…"

He swept the words away when he saw that her eyes were open. They looked much better than moonstones, luminous or otherwise. They were as chameleon-like as her skin, altering with every bat of her eyelashes.

"Hi," he said and pulled her closer.

"So you are a poet," she said. "Show me next time. There is nothing wrong with writing nice sentences about your lover. But if you really want to please me, you should carve them into the tusk of a boar that you've personally speared."

Chapter XXXI

Advertisement on the light-board of the Teatro Grandissimo of Heligopolis, Sanmartin:

The Extravaganza Company of far Lusz
is delighted to present:
Rambo the Barbarian, a tragicomic opera,
with the original score
written by Silenus!
Semday night only.

"We jump in and out of the Überraum like a hare with its tail on fire," the science officer said when another sun loomed, only to snap away a heartbeat later. A nebula rose above a row of rotating starments. Next, the yacht grazed the clouds of a giant world as azure as fabled Neptune. "I hope it will muddy your trail and make it harder to find you."

"One can always hope," Huang-ho said.

Seven days later a triad of stars glowed in front of the bow. One was a seething blue giant, the others ordinary G0 suns.

The science officer waved his hand and the screen zoomed in to show a world like a mottled emerald.

"Sanmartin started out as an ocean world with only a score of islands. The colonists seeded the ocean with algae and waterlilies. It was a bit too successful as you can see. You can now walk from island to island on a thick mat of decaying algae. The handbook promises that you won't notice the smell after a fortnight. It is whispered that there are giant crocodiles lurking beneath the waterlilies."

"What kind of world is it?" Justine asked. "The people, I mean?"

"Let me see. The handbook awards them an M3. Devotedly mercantile. Merchants. So, you can leave your projac on the ship but seal your ozols in a panzer-glass money belt." He nodded. "I'll fab some on the printer."

"They are pickpockets, you mean?"

"There is an ancient Earth saying: A fool and his money are soon parted. They consider every visitor a fool."

The yacht set down on a space-field that was surrounded by scores of souvenir booths, and kiosks that sold tickets for a hundred sweepstakes and lotteries, some of which might even give out prizes. Gay banners with 'New!', 'Free!' and 'Only three left!' snapped in the breeze.

The smell hit Gunnar like a slap in the face, the moment the air-lock opened: weeks old mackerels, bubbling night-soil and fermenting seaweed.

"That booth," the science officer pointed, "they sell nose-plugs," and he set off on a stumbling run.

An official stepped closer, studied the golden figurehead and the leaded glass windows with evident satisfaction.

"This is a prime parking place," he told the Admiral who was clad in her usual black uniform and slightly scruffy combat boots. "You can tell the owner that the fee comes to a thousand ozols."

"That is pretty steep."

"A thousand ozols a day, lady."

"I'll be sure to inform the Connatic. I'll also recommend that the Whelm removes its protection from this world. We certainly can't afford such parking fees for our patrol boats. The starmenters will be most interested."

"Starmenters?" The official frowned and only now seemed to grasp the *gestalt* of the spaceship: not only the inset jewels, but also the ribbed mouths of the Thribolt projectors, the gold on black hornet symbol.

His grin became a sickly smile. "I was only joking. For the Whelm…"

"For a *Grand Admiral* of the Whelm on a *state* visit," Patriska Uzbar corrected him.

"Nothing." His hands fluttered. "No fee of course." He hastily pasted a certificate on the door and scuttled away.

"Being an admiral means a lot of boring paperwork but it has its perks," the Admiral said.

In the distance, towers rose like crystals of smoke quartz. Small ornithopters flapped around them: this was a low gravity world with a rather dense atmosphere.

"I phoned," the science officer told them. "The Museo Archeologico is closed on Semday." He spread his hands. "Even for an admiral. It is a private collection: the director is out, mat-running, and he left his communicator at home."

"Mat-running?" Semele asked.

"You sprint across the seaweed. That alerts the crocodiles and the sharks. The idea is that you run faster than they can batter a hole in the seaweed and eat you."

"You just run? You don't try to harpoon the lizard or something?"

"Well, the smaller ones are only seven meters long, but the wildlife team photographed one of twenty-six."

"Well, then you would just need a really big harpoon!" she protested but followed him onto the monorail after a final, yearning glance at the undulating weed-fields.

"Take your filthy paws off me!" Gunnar's money belt snarled.

A boy jumped back, glared at him. "I didn't do nothing! You can't prove anything."

"We don't have to," the science officer said. "It remembers. The next try leaves your fingers five smoking sticks."

The boy got off at the next stop.

After the yacht, even the Millionaire's Suite at the Grand Budapest Hotel seemed kind of cramped to Gunnar: a bed only three meters wide and nothing but seven year old Lord Guhlpfeffer champagne in the cooler.

Gunnar's communicator chimed.

"I got us tickets to the opera," Huang-ho announced. "Rambo the Barbarian. Very famous."

"What is an opera?" Semele asked. "Should I wear my bullet-proof vest?"

"I think not," Gunnar said. "We had operas on Numenes. People sing and dance. Ladies wail when their secret lovers get skewered by their brothers."

Semele perked up. "And then they take revenge? Horrible revenge?"

"I seem to remember that quite a lot of people get killed in this opera," Huang-ho said. "Starting with the first act when the airships sweep down on Rambo's palace. He was the King of Vietnam and the Shayriffs of the Many Starred Wizard killed his parents, took his sisters. At the end of the first act he sings: 'They will be avenged!' While standing on a heap of corpses and raising a bloody battle-axe."

"Good!"

"And carrying a bow up to the Box is frowned upon."

This was a truly ancient story, Gunnar realized. The Gaean Reach was a dream of the future still and men had only just set foot on the moon. Such a colorful barbaric time! And no Whelm or Connatic to curb evildoers.

King Rambo stalked across the stage, wearing the black bandana and dog tag of an Avenger. His sword-wielding lover Black Mamba was sung by a rather dowdy middle-aged soprano, not exactly the raving beauty the choir called her. Perhaps Rambo preferred older women?

He liked Rambo's projac, a massive weapon that launched impressive swirls of plasma and bolts of crackling electricity. The trapeze act was breathtaking: especially the part where Rambo almost lost his grip when the rope suddenly turned into a hissing snake.

After the final act, all returned to stand on the stage, even the dead. Shayriff Teasle the Grim with his leg and wrist broken, supported by the skewered Many Starred Wizard, Black Mamba on the arm of Rambo.

Semele jumped up, clapped.

"Bravo! And now burn down their own White Palace, ser Rambo!"

Sanmartin must be one of those rare twenty-four hour day worlds, Gunnar decided. The morning light woke them and there was nothing artificial about the light.

Semele stood in front of the window, marveling.

"Look, there is the sun again and we just saw her going down! How strange, a Great Day that is the same as a Small Day." She shook her head. "It feels hurried. I could never live that way."

Gunnar came to stand next to her. You could almost see the sun rise, an enormous red globe that was growing brighter by the second.

"Like actually seeing grass grow." She bent forward. "Those buildings, are they really swaying?"

"Looks kind of scary, yes? Well, there was no way to anchor them, with the ocean floor three miles down, which is why they're held up by repulsor plates. If the power ever fails, they will keel over and sink instantly." It was almost word for word what the science officer had told him yesterday when he asked the same question.

Breakfast could only be called lavish, a true bonterfest. Platters of steaming crabs and diced eels, a small roasted crocodile with a marzipan skull held between its front teeth, sea melons and savory mushrooms.

"Our director returned," Huang-ho announced. "Minus a hand. But as he told me, 'You don't run on your hands! And I'll use a prosthesis until they have grown me a new one.'"

He reached for his communicator. "I'll ask him if he has opened the museum yet."

A face appeared. The archaeologist wore the sideburns and data-crown of a true pedant. His glasses had numbers and symbols endlessly scrolling down. Gunnar felt instantly reassured: this man would be a walking encyclopedia, probably as erudite as the science officer. And he specialized in the Elder Culture.

"I tried your ancient trick, my clever friend, and it worked. Plastered latex mixed with antigrav on my stele and peeled it off. A perfect impression of all the symbols! And you were right that I could look at the mirror image without going mad. Not that I understood them any better." He pursed his lips. "You still want to see the original stele?"

"I..." Huang-ho began and then his hand reached for his fountain pen and wrote "YES" on the table cloth. "NUANCES MIGHT GET LOST AND I'M IMMUNE."

"That is your, uh, passenger speaking? Good, I'll be landing in ten minutes then." The face snapped out, but Huang-ho's hand kept moving. "THE ANTIDOTE HAS LOCATED US. HE WILL BE WAITING WHEREVER YOU GO."

Huang-ho stared at his own message. "Adolpho curse them!"

"Wherever you go," the Admiral repeated. "Well, fleeing isn't an option then. No reason to miss our appointment with the director."

"Anything that lives can be killed," Semele stated. "Look, he's the antidote, yes? The dark copy of Huang-ho. Flesh and blood, and therefore vulnerable to an honest crossbow quarrel."

"I admire your optimism."

The director met them at the platform on top of the hotel. His ornithopter seemed a rather flimsy affair to Gunnar: a dozen beating dragonfly wings, surrounding three benches. It hovered next to the edge of the platform, three meters distant, and the surface was a long, long way down.

"Get in! Get in!" the director urged. "Time and tide wait for no man!"

Gunnar breathed in, took a running leap and landed on a swaying bench.

"Ha!" the director exulted. "On we go! Isn't this a perfect, an *excellent*, day to die?"

The sky had turned a greenish blue and the sun had grown fierce, dazzling. Even a side-glance left Gunnar with dancing afterimages.

They swooped past roof gardens, balloons painted with the faces of leering demons and smiling Madonnas. He stared: the Madonnas weren't cradling babies, but baskets filled with gold pieces and crowns.

Snatches of lively tunes or of solemn marches reached Gunnar's ears. The streets were filled with strolling shoppers, dancing priests with sharks' masks, beating huge drums with human femurs.

This clearly was a world more frantic than Phaedra, ozol and fashion driven, where wearing the same gown or shoes as your neighbor was a major disaster.

The towers of the city receded and the endless algae fields of the outback opened up in front of them. Gleaming waterways crossed the green, like the cracks in a verdigrised mirror.

Gunnar pointed his macroscope: the silver waters seemed agitated. Another notch on the magnifier and he discovered the sleek forms of crocodiles gliding in the depths, sharks cruising.

A quarter of an hour later the director pointed. "Our destination."

A dome lifted itself above the horizon.

"Why such a distance from the city?" Huang-ho asked.

"The acreage is cheap here. What with the sharks and the crocodiles, no? And an ozol saved is an ozol earned."

High above the museum, the usual readable-from-any-direction sign proclaimed:

❋ THE ELDER CIVILIZATION! ❋

They tore whole suns from their orbits!
They created the Grand Rainbow!
Half of our worlds were once theirs.
Gaze at their awful secrets

~ HERE! ~

Below the HERE hung an urgently blinking arrow.

"That doesn't sound very scientific," the science officer complained.

"They don't want to be educated. All Sanmartins are louts, and you could use their heads for drums. There isn't any brain inside. I have to be sly and use sex and sensation."

"Sex?"

"Every Lesterday we hire a troupe of pole dancers. The only way you get to ogle them is after you have walked past all the exhibits." He sighed. "Still, sometimes a visitor lingers at the stone guns or at the nine-headed dragon carvings, and reads a part of the explanation."

The ornithopter unfolded its landing legs, touched down running and halted just before it smashed into the wall of the museum.

The director took off his goggles, peered at the entrance.

"A visitor! How nice."

The man waved back, walked in their direction.

An alarm bell went off in Gunnar's head. It was the way the stranger walked, the gait quite familiar. He grabbed his macroscope, zoomed in.

The visitor wore Huang-ho's face. Almost. The tattooed tear sat on the right cheek, not the left.

"It's him! The antibody!"

Semele's arrow was the first to hit the impostor, but the panzer-glass quarrel bounced right off, skidded across the landing ramp. The projacs of the others just refused to fire.

He's like the Galleons. Nothing high tech works in his vicinity, and he's a perfect copy of Huang-ho, wearing the same bulletproof cape.

It was as if Gunnar's realization was all the museum's repulsor plates needed. The museum wallowed, bounced up, and then sank straight down. A waterspout rose, but all waves were instantly damped down by the sluggish mat of algae.

"So much for seeing the original," Huang-ho sighed and stepped from the landing platform onto the algae mat. He took a dozen steps, halted with one foot on a giant waterlily.

"Come get me," he called to his mirror image.

"Perfection must be served," the creature said with a voice that was strangely remote.

There is no real sound. He's speaking right into our heads.

The antidote spread his arms. "Let me embrace you, my brother. We will both shine like a sun and then sift down in a plume of ashes. Thus perfection will be served."

"Oh yes, perfection must be served," Huang-ho replied. "Just come to me then."

The antibody had stepped from the ramp, and was taking the shortest route, straight across the mat.

"Yes, just keep standing here," the science officer said to Huang-ho, and nodded as if satisfied with a difficult equation nicely solved. Ten steps, twelve. Five meters behind the antibody a triangular fin rose up, and no one was even slightly inclined to cry: "Look out! Behind you!"

A maw opened, studded with teeth.

There wasn't even an outcry, only a rather definitive crunch. The gray snout sank once more below the green, the fin vanished.

"He's dead?" the Admiral called to Huang-ho.

"The pressure is gone. I no longer have that feeling of being stalked."

"You think that was it?" the Admiral asked. "They are done with you?"

"Only for now, I'm afraid." Huang-ho lifted his right hand, wriggled his fingers. "Nothing. No new messages."

The Director opened his pouch, unrolled a sheet of latex. "We have this at least, my friend. The print of the stele." His eyes shone. "How refreshing to encounter a living artifact of Elder tech! The fulfillment of my fondest dreams. Nothing desiccated, nothing fossil, but alive and alive, ho!"

"If he had touched me, the explosion would probably have killed you also."

"Yes, yes! Go out in a blaze of glory! Who wants to live forever anyway?"

Chapter XXXII

From *Restricted Worlds, the Observations of a Star-Trotting Vagabond* by Yuri Hopkins, writing for the *Alastor Herald*, monthly magazine, now with Mirricyllai-approved horoscope.

Like a falling leaf, the ship zigzagged down to the single spaceport of Jorsalim, Alastor 1639, her star drive moaning in a most distressing way.

"We'll have to replace the (incomprehensible technical term)," the captain declared. "Defibrillation of the meta-gears, for the layman. Won't take longer than three days. Four at most, and five if we have to grow new ones."

I was the only one to debark: Jorsalim wasn't exactly a Restricted World, but it carried a T9 label: fanatically religious and intolerant of any heretical talk. Sounded just right for an article.

In the distance, the white walls of the City of God rose, with the hundred meter high Pearly Gate.

Two customs agents were strolling in my direction, their projacs ornamented with angel wings and glowing eyes, but probably no less functional for all that.

"You fell from the sky," the tallest one stated. "Up there lies the dark domain of Shaitan and all his demons. Because Heaven is here, with the City of God for every good soul to enter."

"I'm not a demon, but a mortal like you."

He reached for his projac. "None of us is mortal here! We are all saved!"

I raised my hands. "You misunderstood me. I came here as a pilgrim, seeking enlightenment!"

"Enlightenment? Do you believe that the Mother of God

should be venerated as a goddess? Standing above her Son and the prophet Moshe Himself?"

"I'm deeply ignorant. Please tell me."

"Well, of course not! That would be like me washing my good wife's feet, wouldn't it? Now, those Kabbalahsians, they peer into the Nine Holy Books and count letters, reverse the words instead of merely intoning the prayers. No wonder they ended up with Maryam a Goddess."

"We booted them out and they fled to their own hellhole," the other explained. "They lie that Maryam has written her own name in the rock and that Kabbalah must thus be more holy than Jorsalim itself. Sheer balderdash! Never go there! They'll fill your head with nonsense and your soul will swim forever in the dark."

"Our next stop will be Chevalier, I think."

"Kabbalah hangs in their sky like a rotting pumpkin. Beware. Better to kiss the red, red lips of their cowgirls than to gaze upon that abomination!"

The Admiral put the yacht in an orbit that kept them just behind the single moon. Elder tech remained tricky, and it wouldn't do to lose a major planet.

"Here we go." Huang-ho unrolled the sheet in the control room and waved them back. "Don't look. Not if you value your sanity."

"Gibbering idiot time, you mean?" the Director said. "I glanced at the mirror image and even then my eyes wanted to roll back. I heard voices chanting from the marrow of my very bones. Voices never meant for human ears."

The sheet rested on a circular panzer-glass table, and it felt as if there were ripples pushing Gunnar away, waves that distorted space itself. He didn't try to sneak a look. Since the Galleons, he knew there really existed things a human wasn't meant to see.

"I've got it memorized," Huang-ho finally said. "I hope…" He shook his head. "Not a nice experience. Like munching razor blades. Red-hot razor blades."

He pointed his projac: the sheet flared, burned with blue and yellow flames. A second shot, and only ashes were left.

"What exactly did you learn?" the science officer asked.

"Call it the right protocol. A way for a lesser organism to address a higher guardian in an emergency. He will probably still be killed, but the higher guardian will at least listen until the messenger has finished speaking. While he's speaking, he'll be as one of the Elder Race himself."

"I see. Like addressing the god-emperor of Nueva-Gondwana with a mere 'Ser', because his palace is on fire." He frowned. "Say, you can talk to the Galleons then?"

"Oh no! Only a perfect master can talk to a perfect master."

Huang-ho sounded aghast, Gunnar noticed. *It must be the nine percent of the guardian imprinted on his brain.*

"You have his memories," the science officer insisted. "What exactly are the Galleons? Are they the remnants of the Elder Race? Or is it the crew of the Galleons?"

"Sorry. I haven't the slightest idea. I don't think the guardian's rank was high enough to know. To be *allowed* to know such arcane mysteries."

"Keep the peasants dumb. Don't let them learn anything."

"I don't think he was anything as advanced as a peasant. More like a watchdog. One who broke his chain while he only should have barked. Which is why we now have those exterminators stalking us."

Huang-ho raised his right hand and once more fiery words streamed from his extended index finger.

"THE SONG OF RETURNING TO THE FIRST AND MOST PERFECT SHAPE," he wrote.

"That's it?" the Director asked. "No other clues?"

" 'Carved in worldwide stone and plain to see,' a voice whispered. But it sounded kind of tentative. As if the guardian wasn't quite sure."

"I love those ancient detective tales!" the Director declared. "Mazes in mazes! Clues in an unknown language, yes, written in blood by a dying man on the wall of a locked room." He pursed his lips. "Carved in worldwide stone..."

"I'll ask the Bibliotheque," the science officer said, rising.

"No need," Gunnar said. "I saw her every morning from my window as I woke up on Chevalier. Kabbalah, Alastor 1643. The Carved World. It is Chevalier's sister planet: orbiting their sun together. Always glaring at each other."

"Alastor 1643," the science officer said. "Here it is."

A globe coalesced, grew sharp. Kabbalah still as gray as Gunnar remembered it, with the enormous polar caps of reddish ice taking up about eighty percent of the surface. A single continent straddled the equator: it was a curiously flat highland, some twenty-five miles above the eternal ice.

"Carved World?" the science officer asked.

"Zoom in and you'll see."

From ten miles up, the first hieroglyphs and words emerged from the gray pumice. At five miles up, you discovered that no ravine was natural: each had been cut deep into the crust, all the way down to the bedrock.

"It's very cold there," Gunnar explained. "And the top of the highlands sticks right into space. The colonists carved the ravines in the shape of their hieroglyphs, filled them with soil and air."

"Kabbalah is like an anthill," Justine said. "All the time these people are tunneling, like fire-ants in rotten wood. There are close to seventeen billion of them now. Living down in the twilight and the dark. Like pale grubs."

"The whole world is covered with poems?" the Director asked. "I would really like to see that."

"The Elder Culture is your expertise," the Admiral said. "Which might be useful." She licked her lips. "How about a commission as science officer?"

"With unlimited access to your Bibliotheque? And I get to carry a Whelm-grade projac?"

"Certainly, Colonel."

"Count me in then."

Chapter XXXIII

From *Restricted Worlds, the Observations of a Star-Trotting Vagabond* by Yuri Hopkins, writing for the *Alastor Herald*, monthly magazine, now with Mirricyllai-approved horoscope.

For once there were no monsters, nor ancient but still trigger-happy war-machines to avoid on Kabbalah. The 'Restricted World' status had been greatly desired by the inhabitants themselves. "To write down the awesome poems and admonitions of the One True Goddess, unhindered by Wrong-believers and Hecklers," as the petition to the First Connatic went.

A single Whelm cruiser orbits their world to keep uninvited visitors away. Not that there are that many.

I hadn't intended to visit Kabbalah at all, but I was forced to leave Chevalier post haste after a misunderstanding, and there were no star-liners departing for the next two weeks.

The Kabbalah Embassy proved little more than a shack, with the shuttle parked behind, in a field of yellowed sedge.

I paid my thousand ozols-per-diem a week in advance and had my head depilated. Next, the soles of my feet were coated with smart repulsor motes. That way I would always drift 34 centimeters in the air, never desecrating the holy ground. I could also declaim all seventy-three stanzas of *A Child's Greeting of Her Awesome Shadow*, so finally there was no reason to refuse me a visa.

"Not many want to visit our wondrous world to seek wisdom," the single employee said. He sounded doubtful.

"I'm a writer," I declared. "A whole world etched with poems sounds wonderful!"

"Some visitors grumble that they can't read the poems. That even our holy carvers don't know what they are writing." He spread his hands. "Those are words from the Goddess herself! *Of course* we can't read them!"

———※———

The face of the officer from the Whelm-cruiser orbiting Kabbalah filled the screen. He wore a uniform Gunnar only knew from historical war games: dead black, the cuffs arterial red and the golden hornet more like an eagle than an insect.

The ship itself was also utilitarian: as ugly as an ore carrier. The Thribolt projectors looked quite functional: they hadn't changed in a thousand years.

"No way can I just let you land that over-ornamented float. You go down to Chevalier like any other visitor, buy a visa and board the shuttle."

"I am Admiral Uzbar," the Admiral argued, "and he there, he's the Field Marshal himself!"

"There is no such rank in the Whelm, lady. And our ship, we are an independent command. By appointment of the Connatic himself. We have been guarding this world for *sixteen* generations and I won't be the *first* to…"

Sixteen generations. Gunnar could very well believe that: the other officers on the bridge had exactly the same kind of snub nose and eyes. The women wore their dishwater-blonde hair in a single braid, while the men, without exception, sported drooping mustaches, the left side a finger longer than the right side.

"Do the math," the commander said. "While I'm willing to concede that you're probably no starmenters, the point is that we have seven projectors locked on your ship and you only carry two."

The Admiral sighed. "We'll take the shuttle."

It felt deeply strange to be back on Chevalier, eerie. Gunnar had been eleven when he left, old enough to make girls the most puzzling creatures in the Cluster. And now he stood in the hot breeze, holding the hand of his girlfriend.

All the girls of his childhood would be married by now; mothers, or at least pregnant.

The Kabbalah Embassy lay in the middle of the drylands, a hundred miles from the nearest farm.

Ambassador Sesterman didn't look like a pale grub, no matter what Justine had said about his countrymen: he was as brown-skinned and freckled as any Chevalier cattle driver.

"It must be the peak season," the ambassador drawled. "Had another traveler just last week. The one before that...Ten, fifteen years ago. But perhaps the last one wasn't a true seeker of wisdom? The day after I returned, judge Pearson came along. It seems my passenger had danced with his daughter under the May tree, twice. And everybody knows that is as good as a proposal, so..." He grinned. "That judge, he came carrying a noose in his left hand and a marriage certificate in the other!"

"Was she beautiful?" Semele asked.

"A bit peaky. Thin and pale." Sesterman nodded. "She must have had some Yethro blood." He looked them up and down. "Now, that would be a hundred ozols a day. A hundred a person. And you must pay a week in advance. That is including the shuttle trip."

"That seems quite reasonable," the Admiral said.

"For that writer guy, it was a thousand a day. And I had him recite *A Child's Greeting of Her Awesome Shadow* until he did it letter-perfect. Took him eight hours and all the time he was looking over his shoulder!" He grinned. "Told him an unbeliever wasn't allowed to touch the holy ground and coated his soles with repulsors. Believed me, too!"

"Coyote could learn from you," Gunnar said, which was high praise indeed on Chevalier. "When does the shuttle depart?"

"Why not right now? It isn't that I have to wait for the rest of the passengers."

The shuttle was positively ancient and its drive most curious. Gunnar had heard about a pulsed fission drive but had never expected to ride one.

The basic idea was to explode a whole series of medium-sized atomic bombs in a reaction chamber to generate thrust. That went on until you reached escape velocity. It made for a bumpy ride.

Behind the diamond front window, Kabbalah grew from a pale half-moon to a grubby shield. The drive stuttered once again and they swung to the night side. Below them, the canyons were filled with eerie glows, no two monster hieroglyphs the same color. It reminded Gunnar of his first sight of Phaedra, with the difference that these colors seemed much colder, quite uninviting even.

"I wonder how he thinks to land," the science officer said. "Going up is easy, but slowing down without an atmosphere to brake…"

Right then, a dozen repulsor plates emerged from the underside of the shuttle. They fired up until the ferry descended in a swarm of swirling ball-lightnings.

They set down in a wide field of mushrooms.

Gunnar walked down the gangway, made his customary jump — gravity here was at least half again as much as Phaedra's — and then took a deep breath.

The air didn't smell cave-like or musty at all, more like the seashore just after a rain shower.

He looked up: the walls of the canyon rose for miles, studded with balconies and walkways, many-tiered temples with glass pillars. Ivy reached down in a hundred green waterfalls, its leaves the size of blankets, its flowers wafting down a mist of pollen. The whole canyon was lit by the glowing clouds at the three-kilometer mark.

"This is really something," Semele said. "Like a park, but with every toadstool polished. And there are seventeen billion of them, Justine said?"

"We never went here," Gunnar confessed. "The Chevalierans warned us it was like crawling through a cave. That their citizens scraped soggy mold from the walls. And we believed them."

"Ser?" the Director asked. "In what letter or word did we set down?"

"They are connected, a poem of about four dozen words," said Sesterman. "That comes to a length of a hundred miles. According to Hirag Mosdemar, a poet from the third dynasty, the poem goes like this:

Midnight spreads
Her black wings.
I wait
In my yellow pavilion.
For you
I have lighted
An isinglass lantern.
Dawn paints
A blue line
In the sky
And you haven't appeared.
So I fill the porcelain urn
With amanita wine
And drink it
Down to the last dregs."

"Amanita?" Semele said. "Isn't that a deadly mushroom?" She clacked her tongue. "How dramatic. Just because she didn't come? Perhaps she overslept? He must be crazy. And you dug up a hundred miles of rock to create this stupid verse!"

"Well, there is another interpretation." Sesterman spread his arms once more, lifted his chin:

"Morning has broken,
I take up my dagger.
The dagger
I have honed
On a whetstone
Made of your broken teeth.
They say
Revenge is a dish
Best served cold,
But I'm too thirsty
Right now!
I will fill
The porcelain urn

With his blood
And drink it
Down to the last dregs!"

"That sounds a lot better," Semele said. "But how could that be the same poem?"

"Only the Goddess knows the true sound or the meaning of her hieroglyphs. Thus, our world becomes a mighty tome of poems we can never exhaust." He frowned. "You are not convinced?"

"Call me a practical girl, ser. I like things to stay what they are. Not to wriggle away and change into something else the moment I turn my head."

Chapter XXXIV

From *A Starmenter's Life* by Sagmondo Bandolio, as told to Yuri Hopkins:

> "... and the dexax explosions opening up like shy flowers in the first warmth of spring," the rebel leader said. Seeing the expression on my face he added: "Don't worry. Your guns are here, and they're not metaphorical at all."

The whole landscape breathed an almost reverent hush, which quickly got on Gunnar's nerves. Pale butterflies the size of handkerchiefs fluttered past, but there wasn't a single bird singing, even though he saw them soaring in the upper reaches. The few visitors spoke with voices that seldom sounded louder than a whisper, and you couldn't hear their footsteps on the flagstones at all. They walked with their shoulders hunched, as if they would like to retract their heads like anxious turtles. *Afraid that the sky will fall?*

"What is this?" the science officer asked. "Some kind of Zen garden? A place to meditate?"

"Our prison," Sesterman replied. "You would probably call it a place of exile. Here, those miscreants end up who refuse to sing along with the morning prayer or who take the Goddess' name in vain."

"I understand. You live pretty close together, don't you? All this room must give them the screaming heebie-jeebies. Galloping agoraphobia."

"They aren't allowed to scream. The pastors would cut out their tongues."

Suddenly the endless fields of mushrooms seemed deeply sinister to Gunnar. No doubt most of them were poisonous or hallucinogenic, and they would be the only things to eat here.

A pity the Connatic won't allow the Whelm to interfere. Not that any outside intervention will help. Those wretches would probably be the first to take up arms against the infidel invaders.

"Enough about these sad territories," Sesterman said. "Follow me and I'll show you our true city. The glories of Maryam's sheltering warrens."

They walked down a path paved with flagstones, each of which was bearing a hieroglyph, doubtlessly unique. Sesterman clapped his hands and a door slid aside to show an elevator the size of a Hussade field.

Except for a lady cradling a naked mole-rat in her arms, the elevator seemed empty.

A beep, and they accelerated so fast that Gunnar's knees buckled and he had to sit down on the soft floor tiles. Of their group, only Semele remained standing, tight-lipped.

A dazzling point of light rose in the central column, with a recorded voice announcing the stops.

"Twenty-three: Red-fire fields and the Falleyn Water-gardens."

"Seventy-nine: Residence of the Lady's Voice in Exile."

"Hundred and four: Asmadill's Most Devout Emporium for all your prayer-ware."

They swept past all of them until, at the two hundred and ninth level, the doors opened. The floor rippled and sent them stumbling outside.

Instant pandemonium! Thousands of citizens milled around, prancing and declaiming poems or skipping like water-striders on their hover-disks. The tunnel must be at least twenty meters high, fifteen wide, and it dwindled to a point somewhere at infinity.

The din was indescribable: a hundred voices shouting and singing, sea-silk cloaks swirling, plumed hats bobbing. It made the streets of Sanmartin look like quiet country lanes.

The Admiral clutched Sesterman's arm and shouted: "How far to the inn?"

"Half an hour at most. Longer if we get caught in the rush hour."

"Can't we hail a taxi? A rickshaw?"

"The Goddess gave the more fortunate among us feet and sturdy legs. Why not use them?"

They passed a shop, its window filled with racks of projacs and hunting guns.

"The Right to Buy Weapons is the Right to be Free." The familiar slogan shone like a beacon and elicited a stab of homesickness.

"What?" Semele asked.

"They have a Weapon Shop here."

"Nice. Let's have a look."

They all halted in front of the window. It felt like a momentary shelter from the storm.

"Great projacs," the Admiral said. "Look how small those batteries are. Must be single shot."

"Not at all," the science officer said. "You can burn down an army, but they only fire in self-defense. That is the only reason the Whelm tolerates them."

In the back of the shop a huge portrait was hung, showing a woman of royal mien. Her nose was an eagle's beak, her lips determined. She fairly radiated charisma.

Not a dame to cross, Gunnar thought.

"Empress Innelda," the Admiral deciphered the rather ornate script. "Never heard of her."

A siren warbled, echoed down the entire street. Sesterman cursed, threw up his hands: "We should have taken a different route. That is the rush hour for this level."

Doors opened and disgorged an endless stream of workers in red uniforms and bureaucrats in elaborate wigs and pointed slippers.

Before, they had been able to skip and dodge and make some progress: now they were reduced to a shuffle, with barely enough room to put down their feet.

Three hours later they arrived at the Most Respectable Outworld Inn and stumbled past the panzer-glass doors. It felt like escaping from a raging flood-river, and gratefully climbing onto the banks.

TAIS TENG

Two men were sitting in the lobby, nipping goblets of fermented mushroom punch.

One of them rose, beaming. He held a fancy communicator with the *Alastor Herald* logo. "I know you people! You invited me to your wedding. Officer Huang-ho wasn't it? And your lovely Justine."

"The journalist. Well met, ser Hopkins. Was it you dancing under the May tree?"

"They should have warned me. I have three ex-wives already and I wasn't shopping for a fourth." He nodded to the other man: tall, black-bearded and bald, with eyes that seemed almost luminous. "I was interviewing my friend. I'm writing his biography. He has led a most interesting life."

"I should think so!" the Admiral cried. She had her projac out, the safety thumbed off. "That is Sagmondo Bandolio! The infamous star-menter. There is a price on his head on a hundred worlds."

Sesterman intervened. "Not on Kabbalah, Admiral. We granted him sanctuary, and the Whelm has no authority here."

"I paid three million ozols to the ambassador," Bandolio explained, "and he smuggled me in on his shuttle, together with my friend from the *Alastor Herald.*"

"Well," the Admiral said and holstered her projac. "One can't always be on duty." She waved to the bartender. "More punch please." But Gunnar could see she wasn't pleased.

Semele sat down in front of Bandolio, put her elbows on the table. "How many men did you kill?" There was no censure in her voice, only interest.

"In person, dear lady, no more than a dozen. That was when I was still a young man and knew no better. Look, families don't pay ransom for dead people. Slavers aren't interested in hacked-off heads." He pursed his lips. "Now, you would be prime merchandise. I could easily get two, three thousand ozols for you. And the next week you would strangle your master and escape. Then you would probably pull a Gersen on me, spending the coming ten years trying to locate and kill me." He shook his head. "No more raids and slave-taking for me. I'll buy me a nice cottage with seventeen rooms and a koi carp pond. Start cultivating roses."

"You're kidding, yes?"

It felt strange to sit at the table with such a famous man. Like meeting the Connatic in Justine's old Golden Catfish bar. Gunnar had played both sides in the official Whelm war games, had *been* Bandolio and Gazzardo. There had always existed a bond between a Whelm soldier and the human monsters he was hunting. Gunnar understood Bandolio better than he ever would a merchant counting his ozols or a basket weaver inspecting his willows.

Bandolio folded his arms, eyed them.

"And what brings you here, to this backwater world, two high officers of the Whelm? You can tell me. I'll never leave this world again. You'll probably put another dozen ships in orbit to prevent me from escaping."

"Sorry," the Admiral said. "I'm not writing my autobiography yet. There are some secrets I'd rather not share with a starmenter."

"I quite understand," Bandolio said. "I hope to see you at breakfast?"

"That text we are looking for?" Semele asked. "What would it do? The first text from Sanmartin would grant you an audience with someone very high up."

"I have been thinking and, well, call it mining my false memory," said Huang-ho. "THE SONG OF RETURNING TO THE FIRST AND MOST PERFECT SHAPE is some kind of lullaby. The Elders reverted themselves, became like the happy beasts of the fields." He waved his hands. "No, don't protest, Semele, or look incredulous. We had that on Earth. Wealthy city dwellers masquerading as shepherds and sleeping in the damp moss. People going back into the woods, clad in animal skins and eating berries they plucked themselves.

"Good, the Elders became animals again, still immortal of course, and if anything disturbed them, they would re-evolve in a heartbeat and become hyper-tech warriors again.

"But such a system could go wrong. It was bound to fail once in a while. One sleeper just waking up to sentience for no reason at all. No enemy to be seen.

"Then the Keeper of the Sleep would bow over him, hum this lullaby in his ear and he would sigh, sink back into his happy animal dream again without waking up any of the others. All of this is metaphorically speaking of course."

"There was text written down on my stele," the Director mused. "A kind of backup. And because the stele was made of neutronium, it was close to indestructible. We are looking for a text again, and this time carved in the crust itself. Which normally would keep it legible for millions of years.

"Let's see. There must be hundreds of thousands of spurious hieroglyphs on the surface by now. That shouldn't matter. We know most of the Elder hieroglyphs: we can easily pick them out from the fantasy ones."

"A map," Semele nodded. "We need a map. And a very detailed one."

"I made one, of course," the science officer said. "When we orbited Kabbalah. I then let the Bibliotheque scan it for Elder sigils. There weren't any to be found, and I went down to the one meter level."

"Right," the Director said. "Let me think. How would Lady Sheila Holmes have proceeded? When you have ruled out the impossible, take a pipe of opium and sleep on it, I'm afraid.

"A map. The best new map doesn't show anything. Because…That is as far as I can deduce."

Semele nodded. "So we need an older map. The oldest. The Kabbalahsians keep tunneling and burrowing. They would have erased the original hieroglyphs with their own fancy nonsense words. If we could get the original survey, the text should be intact."

"Ah, then we just ask Sesterman to take us to the National Museum," the Director said. "Every world likes to show off its humble beginnings. Tell you how far they have come since they put up the first Quonset huts and geothermal tap."

The science officer started typing on his portable Bibliotheque, looked up.

"That won't work, I'm sorry to say. This is a T9 civilization, you see, deeply theocratic. They didn't make their world: the Goddess did, then placed them here. In times immemorial, just after the universe was created.

"There's no place for history here, for plucky explorers discovering this world. Or an original survey. Saying otherwise will probably get you pushed off the highest balcony."

Gunnar could see how the gestalt was shaping up here: the Director with his tens of thousands of hours solving ancient detective cases, the science officer who could look up anything he didn't know, Semele who saw every secret as fleeing prey and would never give up. Like the first time, with Semele and Huang-ho, he felt close to useless.

"So they won't have any historical maps," Semele said. "That would show the world was once different, lesser..."

"Poems," Gunnar heard himself say. "Each poem is a map, yes? If we ask for the most holy poems they will probably turn out to be the most ancient. And every poem is part of a map. We can put them together. No, wait, the very first should be the Elder text. The one that set off all this burrowing."

"How elementary!" the Director exclaimed.

Chapter XXXV

From *Wise Sayings for the New Century*, the *Alastor Herald* interviews Connatic Oman Ursht.

> "Certainly, I could mobilize the whole Whelm, at enormous cost, and destroy the starmenters once and for all. But what is the use? All those sunless planets and planetoids would still be there, waiting, and there are a million evil men and women born every second."

———ᴍᴍ———

Gunnar lay tossing and turning on his mattress. He finally rose and descended to the lobby, opened his endless book.

Lamoraal seemed to have acquired a more or less permanent companion: princess Salya Thunderstar who bore a silver bow and only drank dew or the blood of a freshly killed hart.

Gunnar felt some chagrin. Was the book trying to please him or had it finally run out of plot lines?

> *"Love," the princess mused. "Do you love me, Lamoraal?"*
> *"Well," Lamoraal temporized, "that is to say... "*
> *"I hope not. Love only complicates things. I prefer simple lust."*

Ah, the book hadn't modeled her on Semele after all.

> *"As do I." Lamoraal felt a weight lifting from his shoulders.*
> *"I will still kill you if you look at another female, though."*

Gunnar could almost hear Semele say that. Not as a threat, but as a simple statement of fact. He turned the last page.

"Do you have many sons?" the princess asked.
"I guess so. But none of the mothers ever showed them to me."
"A bit hard, with you three countries away by the time they
discovered they were pregnant." She smiled. "I won't make that
mistake. This time you'll stick around."
"You mean you are… "

What had happened to his book? The princess pregnant and Lamoraal a goddamn *father*? What would be next? Lamoraal's son in kindergarten and chasing butterflies?

Gunnar closed the book, pushed the reset button, then looked at the last page again.

"Silence," the princess hissed. "I heard something."
An eerie cry echoed through the ravine. The white trolls had
found them again.

Ah, that was better. He sank down in the cushions of the sofa and read on.

At breakfast the starmenter and the journalist proved to be gone.

Sesterman shrugged: "I can't say I blame Bandolio. Writing a book should be private. Like carving a poem in a sheet of marble, surely? It distracts if you feel the gaze of the hangman in your neck, measuring you for a rope."

"You recited the poem we landed in," Semele said. "We would truly like to see the other poems. Surely there must be a place where you collect them?"

"You mean the Rhapsodion? Every poem ever carved is kept there. Our best copyists scratch them into clay tablets which are then glazed and fired." He pointed to three inscribed tiles on the wall. "Like these."

"We can see them? I mean, we are outsiders. Perhaps they are too holy for our eyes?"

It was the very first time Gunnar had seen Semele batting her eyelashes. But it seemed to work.

"Nonsense! Why would we deny you the truth? The marvelous words of the Goddess? You are more than welcome."

"I have been studying your hieroglyphs," the science officer said. "While no two are the same, there is one I see returning as the first part of every poem." He turned the screen of his communicator to Sesterman.

The hieroglyph was extremely elaborate, with a hundred curls and hooks. It reminded Gunnar of the QR marks master Ooka made them copy out at the Start of the Great Day ritual. He stared at it: there was something he just wasn't getting, which he should have recognized. *Palimpsest.* The word rose, then slipped away again.

"That is the first sign the carvers dig out in the pumice when they start a new poem. The name of the Goddess. It cannot be spoken of course." Sesterman reached for his own communicator. "I'll reserve tickets for you. The Rhapsodion is quite a popular destination."

This time they took the elevator almost to the top of the south wall. When they stepped out, the air was mountain-thin and it made Gunnar gasp for breath. Black flecks danced in front of his eyes.

The science officer plucked a handful of disposable one-hour-breathers from his pouch and slapped one on Gunnar's face. He eagerly sucked in the oxygen, and his sight cleared.

No snow, and the sky was black, studded with unwavering stars. Arctic pines bordered the entrance of the Rhapsodion, bent like old men, reindeer-moss their trailing beards.

The sigil of the Goddess rose nine meters tall above the entrance, and Gunnar instantly felt a pressure against his eyeballs, as if the sigil were emanating invisible black light. *Just like when Huang-ho unrolled that sheet of latex.*

He reached for his macroscope, peered through the lenses.

The sigil shivered: part of it grew misty and then the macroscope switched itself off with a petulant click. *Something Elderish. Like the Galleons, it interferes with human high tech.*

He ran after the group, clutched the arm of the Director.

"Look up at the sigil, ser! Parts of it are Elder hieroglyphs. All those curlicues and hooks. The whole sigil of Maryam must be a palimpsest, an overlay over a much older text."

The director studied the sigil, shook his head. "I should be ashamed. Blind as a mole, that is me. They just pasted the symbol over the original text." He kept looking. "If I disregard the Elder signs, I get something much simpler. 'Theyz,' the Hebrew word for 'goddess'."

"So we already have part of the text? We only have to subtract the Hebrew?"

"I'm afraid not. If it is anything like programming a computer, even a slight mistake or omission makes it worthless. No, we still have to get the original."

Picture endless corridors hung with palm-sized tiles inscribed with wise sayings and poems. That would be bad enough, but you can't read any of those poems either. Nobody can, but the ambassador is halting every twenty meters to recite an especially nice haiku or ballad. But it gets even worse: you have to pretend to enjoy your trip.

Semele must be a consummate actress, Gunnar thought: she clapped her hands, tugged at the arm of ser Sesterman and pointed to tile after tile. She even giggled as his translation bordered on the naughty. Semele hated dirty jokes. "Don't snigger and nudge about it," she would say, "just take off your clothes and do it."

"But now I want to go to the most famous poems of them all. The most holy." She spread her hands. "I don't want my attention flagging before I've heard the very best."

"You are quite right. One shouldn't gorge on *champignons Provençales* while the black truffles are still to come!" He opened a door. "This way. We are taking a short-cut."

They went down a spiral staircase for at least seven levels. Grit crunched beneath Gunnar's boots and dust rose with every step as if the stairs had been sprinkled with talcum powder. Clearly this part of the Rhapsodion was seldom visited. *Good. Nothing recent.*

Half an hour passed, an hour, and Gunnar's feet started to hurt. The higher gravity was taking its toll. *I must be growing a fine crop of blood blisters. Why are we taking these stupid stairs? The elevator stopped at all levels.*

Wait. Perhaps this isn't a regularly accessible level? A secret level?

• • •

"We are there." The ambassador produced a truly antique key, one with a glowing Laverdom circuit, put it in the keyhole.

"Tell me the password," a shrill voice ordered.

Gunnar saw Admiral Uzbar stiffen. *No machine may speak like a human.* And this was clearly a generated voice, not a recording. *Would they go as far as having an AI, a sentient computer, to protect this room? But why then did he bring us here?*

"Have a look," Sesterman said as the door opened and he stepped aside to let them pass.

A small battered space-boat sat on a pedestal. Gunnar recognized it as a Model 9B, the cheapest, almost disposable ship still used by less well-funded explorers. Model 9B scouts were climax-tech, impossible to improve, like a stone ax or a Kalashnikov.

"Have a good look," Sesterman said. "That is the ship that discovered our world. And in front you see the map, the false survey the locator used to hoodwink our Eminences."

Gunnar stepped closer: the Mercator map showed Kabbalah almost pristine, only the center marked with the sigil of the Goddess. He turned around. "There must be an earlier…"

Sesterman had stepped back and now stood behind a slab of doped panzer-glass: it would absorb the discharge of any projac short of a plasma-thrower.

"I knew that this so-called journalist was a spy from Jorsalim, the moment he entered the embassy. It may not look like much, but our security is up-to-date. I found dust from Jorsalim still clinging to the soles of his boots. His blood sample showed traces of fermented usgardill, and that fungus only grows on Jorsalim."

Don't say anything. Let him talk.

"When he greeted you, I knew that the six of you were also in the conspiracy." He chuckled, but there wasn't much merriment in it. "For eight hundred years, my family has kept the secret that could destroy our civilization. Hugo Maheen found writing on the new world, fifty square miles of deeply carved words. Cryptic symbols, but certainly not written by the Goddess."

"Hugo drew the sigil of the Goddess," the Director guessed. "Right across those symbols."

"Yes. It must have taken him a dozen flights to carry in all the dexax. Our Eminences were completely taken in. Foolish old men! And the remaining symbols, they took them for the words of the Goddess and started carving their like."

"Wait!" Semele called. "We aren't from Jorsalim. We wanted to see the original map. The one from before Maheen spoiled the original writings."

"There isn't any other map. This is the one he sold to our Eminences for seventeen million ozols. The map and the right to colonize one of the most worthless worlds in the whole Cluster!"

He raised his left hand and the sheet of panzer-glass became a mirror.

The science officer thumbed off his communicator. "There aren't any hidden exits. I probed the walls: three meters thick and solid melt-stone." He tugged the hatch of the Model 9B open, poked around inside.

"Forever batteries," he said three minutes later, shaking the dust from his cuffs. "And the air-maker looks functional. We won't suffocate."

"Even if we get outside," the Director said, "their shuttle is the only way off this world."

"If the ultra-phone still works we could signal the Whelm ship in orbit," Semele said. "No?"

"This ship is simply too old," Huang-ho answered. "Eight hundred years ago they still had to use messenger rockets with a tiny star drive. No faster-than-light radio at all."

"I see." Semele plucked the string of her bow, a sign she was deep in thought. The 'plink, ploink' almost drove Gunnar to distraction but you didn't interrupt a trancing temple girl. "What if we activated the drive right here? I mean, a star drive puts you in a quite different universe. Perhaps in one where this wall isn't there?"

"There have been experiments," the science officer conceded. "None with any survivors, if I recall right." He touched the screen of his communicator, moved his fingers in fast-speak. "Yes, an explosion. Quarter of a megaton sized." He looked up. "There are cheaper ways to achieve that effect than blowing up a drive."

"It was just an idea."

• • •

When Gunnar awoke on the third morning, the air smelled mustier. *Just my imagination. The air-maker is working fine. It is probably our own stink. An air-maker removes carbon dioxide and splits the oxygen off again, but it doesn't do anything about the smell.*

Semele stirred next to him.

"Gunnar? Is it hotter than before?" She sighed. "I'm complaining. We spent too much time in staterooms and seven-star hotels."

It is hotter and it stinks like a pig-pen. He looked around; the others were already up, but nobody was wearing a uniform, and before an admiral strips to her underwear…

The science officer was even walking around on his bare feet. The day before he had at least been wearing his socks. He had called the Admiral "Patriska" twice already, which showed that even he was losing his decorum, or even worse, his Whelm discipline.

"New antidote constructed," the cold Elder voice suddenly spoke in Gunnar's brain. He had a sudden vision of a Huang-ho double, growing in some hidden cellar corner of Kabbalah, like a man-shaped mushroom. It was clearly a complicated process: organic and slow. Bone for bone, the flesh budding from the skeleton, stringing muscles.

The picture wasn't only in Gunnar's brain. Huang-ho's head snapped up, his eyes widening. The Admiral shuddered, then reached for her projac, thumbed the safety off.

Huang-ho lifted a hand, shook his head. *Don't say anything. Just listen.*

"Locating the target," the second voice said. It was the lesser being, the flunky who had to do the real jobs, dirty his hands. "Searching. Searching. I have located the target."

All the little hairs on Gunnar's arms stood up. It was as if he sat hunched in the middle of a dark forest clearing, with a hundred green eyes staring from the underbrush. That they weren't staring at *him* didn't help.

"Place the antidote."

All projacs were out, Gunnar noticed, everybody scanning the room for a movement, for the sudden materialization of the false Huang-ho. He could be killed. The shark devouring him had shown that the antidote wasn't invulnerable.

"There is no need. The target is already isolated, with the water recycler ready to break down in one tenth of a rotation of this planet. Taking the rising temperature into account, he's scheduled to die of dehydration in three more rotations. Transporting the antidote there would be a waste of precious energy."

The voices halted and the sense of awesome, godlike presence faded.

Huang-ho holstered his projac.

"Well, it's nice to know we aren't worth the effort. That soon we will be safely dying of dehydration. That'll surely make me sleep easier at night."

"They don't know everything," the science officer said. "It is just an extrapolation. One that is probably based on us not knowing that the filter is ready to fail. Well, it was nice of them to warn us. I'll have a look at the recycler right now."

He climbed from the Model 9B six minutes later, scowling.

"Nothing to be done?" the Admiral asked.

"The ion exchange filter is crumbling, Patriska, and that skin-flint of an explorer packed no spares."

Gunnar licked his suddenly dry lips. *No more washing up. We'll have to hoard the water, enjoy every single sip.*

The air smelled worse than ever and it felt bone dry, pulling the moisture from his nostrils with every exhalation.

"Does anybody know how to compose a sestina?" Semele asked.

"Let me see," the science officer replied. "Yes. According to my abbreviated Bibliotheque, a sestina is a fixed verse form consisting of six stanzas of six lines each, normally followed by a three-line envoi. The words that end each line of the first stanza are used as line endings in each of the following stanzas, rotated in a set pattern. May I ask why this sudden interest in a rather obscure kind of verse?"

"When a sister-in-Diana is mortally wounded but still conscious, we are supposed to compose a death song. To greet Diana properly when we walk into her hunting lodge."

"Here, take my communicator. I called up the rhyming scheme for you. Also some famous samples. Like 'Ye Goatherd Gods'."

• • •

Time started to drag. One hour passed, two, three.

"To return," Semele mumbled. "No, I used that word already. Mirri, why can't we just die and that's it?"

"Could you please stop?" Gunnar snarled. "Or compose in silence?"

"All men are oafs," Semele told him. "They don't understand the power of a poem. A drinking song is about their forte." But she took up the science officer's communicator and went to sit in the open hatch of the Model 9B.

A chime sounded, a sound shockingly loud in the lethargic hush of the hot room. Gunnar grabbed his own communicator, but it was the Admiral's that kept ringing.

"Yes?" she answered, her voice hoarse with unbelief.

Yuri Hopkins, the star-trotting vagabond, appeared in mid-air, sitting on a bar stool, a goblet of something green and bubbling on the counter. A cherry with a small parasol drifting in the middle signaled that it probably wasn't lethal.

Holy Mirri, that drink looked cool. Gunnar even saw droplets condensing on the glass and wriggling down.

"Good morning. Glad I hacked your phone, Admiral. Well, they arrested us. Called us infamous dogs from Jorsalim and Goddess-deniers." He smiled. "I was in the company of Bandolio: we didn't stay arrested for long." He tut-tutted. "Putting us in an ordinary police cell. It took only three thousand ozols to bribe the jailer."

A second face shifted in.

"The ambassador boasted he had you safely put away and would be back in a year or two to collect your bones." Bandolio snapped his fingers and a virtual map rose from his hand-held communicator. "Your signal tells me where you are. Now this is how I see the situation: you want out and I want off. Off this planet. Without getting arrested the moment I'm free."

"You mean immunity?" the Admiral asked. "A pardon for your crimes?"

"That would probably be problematic. Not even the Connatic could grant me immunity without causing an outcry to be heard from one end of the Cluster to the other. No, give me a head-start of one week and a lifeboat."

"Sounds doable," the Admiral muttered. Then, in a firmer voice. "Right. I promise."

"Good. Getting you out is easy. The north wall of your cell sits on the canyon side and is only three and a half meters thick."

"A cord of demolition dexax?" Huang-ho said. He sounded doubtful. "Perhaps if we did it in stages? In about eight steps? That would probably leave us with only a few broken bones."

The starmenter grinned. "The Kabbalahsians have been carving rock for eight hundred years, scooping out entire canyons. They have found easier ways of cutting stone than dexax." He folded his arms. "Good, the rest of the plan. We get you out, but then the only way off the planet is their shuttle. Which will be heavily guarded."

"Get us out and we'll provide you something much fancier than a shuttle. A Model 9B scout."

The signal came two hours later.

"Stand well back," Bandolio's voice ordered. "This thing should only cut rock at this setting, but I'm no mason."

A black spot appeared on the north side of the room. It grew and then swiftly described a circle, five meters across. A vibration, and cracks raced across the whole circle.

Pebbles rained down and suddenly a breeze blew in, ice-cold. In the distance, the other side of the canyon rose, lit by the rising sun.

Bandolio and Hopkins let themselves down on monofilaments so thin they were almost invisible, landed on the floor.

"That was easy." Bandolio put something the size of an incense lighter back in his pouch. "I hope your ship starts at the first try because our jailbreak wasn't exactly unobserved."

The Model 9B eased itself through the hole, riding on its repulsor plates. The police sirens were loud enough now that Gunnar could hear them even through the hull of the ship.

The smell of burning insulation filled Gunnar's nostrils, made his eyes water. Blue and green sparks danced across the instrument panel.

"It doesn't matter!" the science officer cried, trying to wave the greasy smoke away. "The drive is intact."

The ship came free and instantly started to fall. The science officer lunged, threw a switch.

The canyon swiftly fell away below them while the whine of a badly adjusted agrav-spool set Gunnar's teeth on edge.

The canyon became a wriggle, a tiny crack, and then the horizon changed from a straight line into a curve.

"I ordered my yacht to meet us at the second gas giant," the Admiral said. "The one with the rings."

"Ordered?" Bandolio said. "I thought you and the science officer were the only crew…" He stroked his beard. "I see. You ordered your ship to come and it did. Launched itself, flew to the right spot. All but saluted."

"It isn't real AI," the science officer protested. "Barely sentient. And we only use it in an emergency."

"*Quis custodiet ipsos custodes?*" Bandolio muttered. "I'm shocked. You are no better than I! Worse. I never broke the First Law."

"We are the Whelm and we make the rules," Huang-ho declared. "Of course we need better weapons than pirates and reivers."

It sounded completely logical, Gunnar thought. When you want to stop evil men brandishing swords, you need a projac. Still, it rankled. Like seeing the abbot of a vegetarian sect dining in private on spare ribs and partridges smothered in truffle butter.

On Chevalier Gunnar had spent whole winter nights gazing at the rings of Zanegrey through his telescope. Even the cheapest macroscope would show him a thousand details more but he had ground and silvered the mirrors of his Cassegrain telescope himself. It had been delightfully low-tech, like starting your own fire with dried toadstools and flint, or constructing a birch bark canoe.

Zanegrey drifted closer until they soared across the rings like a skipping stone. A shepherd moon appeared in a gap between two rings. It was a jagged shard of ice, cratered and smeared with hydrocarbons.

"Stop here," Bandolio ordered. He held the stone cutter and a blue nimbus was pulsing around the muzzle. "I adjusted it some. It will only cut living flesh now."

"You are bluffing," the Admiral said.

"Why take the risk? Put your projacs on the floor and step back."

"And then?" Huang-ho said. "You push us out of the airlock?"

"Only after we have landed on the shepherd moon. And I have printed six throw-away spacesuits for you. Good for five hours. Your yacht should pick you up in half an hour."

"But why?" the Admiral threw up her hands. "I promised you a brand-new life-boat! I gave you my word of honor!"

"There is that ancient saying about one bird in the hand. This boat has a working drive and even the Whelm can't intercept a ship in flight. Also, you might reconsider, and even if you didn't … See it this way: I'm saving you from many a sleepless night, sera. 'How could I have let him escape?' your mind will wail. Honor lifts her chin, flaps her wings: 'You promised him. You gave him your word.' Duty retorts: 'You should have arrested him!' " He turned to the journalist. "What about you, Hopkins?"

"We were writing a book. One that might well sell a billion copies. Of course I'll come along."

The Model 9B drifted away from the ice peaks of the shepherd moon, vanished like a popped soap bubble.

Ten minutes later the golden spark of the yacht appeared.

How delightful to breathe air that smelled like nothing in particular and was just air!

"We got off that dismal planet," Patriska said. After their ordeal, they were all on first name terms with the Admiral. "We are still alive and that should count for something. Retreat to fight another day, eh? A pity Gunnar's old poems didn't work out. It was such a clever idea."

Gunnar bit back a reply. Such faint praise almost felt like an accusation. "The maps didn't go back far enough. The explorer must have destroyed the first map." And then the solution slowly coalesced, like a jeweled leviathan rising from the deep. "The maps are still there, Patriska, speeding away from Kabbalah at a light-second per second. If we move out 850 light-years, we should see the planet as it was before Hugo Maheen arrived."

• • •

Eight hundred and fifty light-years would almost bring them to the outskirts of the Gaean Reach, the Alastor Cluster no more than a luminous smudge in the distance. Time enough to play a score of games of Go, to read a thousand pages in your endless book.

Inside the Cluster, any star ship had to crawl along: thirty thousand stars packed into a volume no wider than the distance from Earth to Vega made for a bumpy ride. Think of an Olympic runner forced to move through a crowd of dancing Hussade fans. Bumping into even one of them would be fatal.

Weeks later, the voice of the science officer rumbled from the speakers.

"We just passed the final named sun. I'm switching the drive to maximum."

A sensation like a stumble in a dream and suddenly Gunnar could see the stars actually move: colorful sparks, slowly sidling in, then zipping past, faster and faster, like a hailstorm seen in the headlights of a skimmer.

He slumped back in an easy chair which was massaging his back to keep his muscles from going flabby.

"I'm still bored," Semele announced. "According to the scoreboard of the gym, I'm now an Artemis grade bow-woman. I can out-shoot Arjuna and skewer seven wolverines before the eighth tears out my throat. I could aim for the highest score, Hou Yi grade. That Chinese warrior who shot all those suns from the sky. But what is the use?"

"We could…" Gunnar started.

She shook her head. "No. For that you should sound a bit more enthusiastic. Sex isn't a stopgap for when you can't think of anything else."

A gong sounded and Gunnar jumped up.

"Starmenters?" he asked hopefully.

"Almost as good," the science officer replied. "We are at the four hundred light-year point now. Time to test your idea."

Chevalier's sun showed as a butter-yellow spark, a color that was unmistakable.

"Zoom in, ship," the science officer ordered. "Locate Kabbalah."

There was no pretense anymore that the yacht didn't have AI. The ship's brain was AI of the feeblest sort, however, no more than thrice as intelligent as a human genius and not even weakly godlike.

"Got it."

Kabbalah hung in the cross-hairs, a misty brown dot, no bigger than Gunnar's fingernail.

"That is the best you can do?"

"You should have seen what I had to work with," the AI protested. "Listen, a picture degrades while it moves over such a distance. It has to tunnel through dust clouds. Miniature black holes smear its light out in all directions." The AI drew a red circle around the hazy orb. "This here is a true work of art. Of truly amazing extrapolation and interpolation. Like you handing me a picture of a random rain cloud, and me interpolating it until I show you the face of the First Connatic, pores and all."

The science officer frowned. "But there are no pictures of the First Connatic. Nobody knows what he looks like!"

"I rest my case."

"What if we had a better telescope than the yacht's?" Semele asked.

"I used the telescope of an admiral's yacht. There are no better or more expensive macroscopes to be found in the whole Whelm."

"I used the wrong term." Her voice became slurred as she entered her trance. "What if we had a *bigger* telescope?"

"That might help. A telescope as big as a solar system."

It was like a ping-pong game: one player thrice as intelligent as a human, but ponderous, making a billion calculations per second. The other had only a standard brain working in overdrive, but she was much more agile, able to think of seven impossible things before breakfast, even one more than the Red Queen. A pity that most of those things were truly impossible.

"God's Eye," Semele said. "Alastor 72." There were red fever spots on her cheeks and her eyes rolled in their sockets. Gunnar felt a stab of alarm. *She's overheating! Close to a stroke.*

"Stop it, Semele!" he cried and ran to her, slapped her cheeks. "Come out of it!"

"Their hyper-telescope uses seventy million bowls," Semele slurred.

"Useless, my girl. Those are radio-telescopes. They'll see Kabbalah's magnetic field and nothing else. No pictures of the surface at all."

"How stupid can you be? Reverse it! Use all those bowls for a radar pulse. Radar will show the writings crystal clear. Even better than any optical picture."

"You are not thinking it through. Even if the pulse returned instantaneously it would still show Kabbalah as it is now. Not as it was 850 years ago."

Semele's eyes rolled up and she sagged in Gunnar's arms.

"Burst a brain vessel and her heart stopped." The science officer looked up from the medical tank. Semele hung in the thick gel, her chameleon skin a horrible mottled gray, her eyes staring.

"She's dead," Gunnar said. "She's gone."

It felt like missing the last step of a stair. A sickening disorientation that went on and on and never stopped, never would diminish.

"Don't look crestfallen," Huang-ho said. "Two, three hours and she's as good as new." He laid his hands on Gunnar's shoulders, squeezed. "Remember the healer's half an hour rule? It wasn't even half a *minute* before we got her into the tank. We're no longer on Chevalier where death is irreversible."

There should be a word for the sudden wrench from utter despair to incredulous hope, mutating into certainty that this wasn't even an emergency, that all was under control.

Gunnar burst into tears and then couldn't stop. Sobs shook his whole body.

"You'll go to sleep," the science officer said, "and when you open your eyes she'll be there." He raised his hypodermic gun.

Gunnar woke from a deep and dreamless sleep, completely rested. Semele sat at the foot end of his bed and studied him, her face strangely solemn.

"They told me you cried," she said. "Nobody ever cried for me." She walked to his side, kissed his brow. It was a deeply strange, almost sisterly thing to do. As if he were fragile.

"You are back," Gunnar said and started to cry again.

Chapter XXXVI

From *Restricted Worlds, the Observations of a Star-Trotting Vagabond* by Yuri Hopkins, writing for the *Alastor Herald*, monthly magazine, now with Mirricyllai-approved horoscope.

I didn't even get halfway to Looking-into-God's-Eye. They boarded my boat at the outermost world, a dwarf planet that was little more than a dirty snowball.

My visitors were scarily high tech, stepping right into my cabin without using the airlock: three stick-men, their skin dead-black and nine fingers on each hand. They looked quite fragile: as if I could break them across my knee with my bare hands. I would probably die before I could even touch them.

"You want what?" their leader asked. They had this clipped way of speaking, as if they had to dig deep into their memories to remember how to use such an obsolete system as speech.

"Well, I would like to look around," I said. "Visit your worlds. See your fantastic project with my own eyes. I'm a journalist, you know, I work for the *Alastor Herald.*"

"No worlds," they said, now speaking in unison. "Broke them up. Made them into ears and eyes. To see God."

"God?"

"Who made the universe. In the first picosecond of the Big Bang, one should be able to see his face, before he melded with his own creation. His face or claw. Tentacle. Whatever." They nodded, as in confirmation. "Which is why we need a truly huge telescope. One as big as a solar system. Our solar system."

I knew they had been building an array of radio-telescopes for at least ten centuries, converting their planets into bowls of ice and rock. The telescopes all worked together, forming a radio-lens seventeen light-minutes wide.

"And you have seen God?"

"Not yet. We need another thousand years. Perhaps even to break up all other worlds of the Cluster?" Their leader stepped closer. "Turn back. This is not for you. You are only human."

"And you are something else? Something more?"

"Such is the case."

Which they proved a heartbeat later. They vanished, and my birth planet Yethro, two hundred light-years from Looking-into-God's-Eye, hung in front of my ship. The message was clear: "Go home. Don't bother us."

—⟁—

A lastor 72: the low number made it one of the oldest colonized worlds of the Connatic's realm. It hung high above the Cluster, an eagle's eyrie looking down on the swirl of stars.

There wasn't a single planet left: a ring of sparkling haze orbited the sun. Even the little ice dwarf, where they had intercepted Hopkins' ship, was gone.

The science officer opened the Star Catalog, frowned. "Population: three? That can't be right."

"They must have killed off all their rivals," the AI said. "Academe, red in tooth and claw. Scientists will do anything for tenure."

The yacht's macroscope zoomed in: each light point proved to be a bowl, spider-webbed with superconducting panzer-glass.

The magnification jumped a power of ten and now Gunnar saw that the bowl was terraformed: mirror-bright lakes and green patches that might be forests. A measuring rod appeared next to the bowl and he realized his error: no lakes, but oceans. You could park the whole of Phaedra in such a bowl and still have room to spare.

"This is…" The science officer shook his head. "Impressive," he concluded. He had grown out his beard, and his hair curled over his ears. While they all called the Admiral Patriska now, he still remained just 'the science officer'.

"You wanted to go here, Semele," Gunnar said. "Insisted on it. I haven't asked why, because I was far too happy to have you back. Like it would break the spell. But I'm asking now."

"The radar idea was stupid. It wasn't me who made us travel on, but the AI. 'I'll tell you the reason when we get there,' it kept repeating." Semele shrugged. "We didn't have much choice. It wasn't like we knew any better place to go."

"It was just a hypothesis," the AI said. "I have now proved it." He zoomed in closer on a lake. It remained almost featureless; no trace of islands or waves.

"It's a mirror!" Semele shouted. "The bowls are mirrors after all! Optical telescopes."

"Were," the AI corrected her. "The conversion to radio-telescopes came later. Looking-into-God's-Eye started as an observation post for astronomers. They set out to locate and classify every sun and star of the cluster. As long as nine hundred years ago, their telescope was the most powerful ever built."

"They must have photographed Kabbalah! Made maps!" Gunnar looked at the glittering disc, surely the biggest artifact ever made by man.

"They'll never let us into their archive. They told Hopkins that they didn't want any mere humans here."

"Who says that we are mere humans?" Huang-ho said. "I believe they would gladly welcome an ambassador from the Elder Civilization. Being a billion years old we surely are a lot closer to the Creator than those newcomers." He spread his arms, looked at the ceiling. "I have felt them for some time. Our enemies. They must almost be ready. Yes."

The sudden pressure of unseen eyes, of passionless scrutiny felt almost familiar.

"This is the third time we grew an antidote," the major voice stated. "A third failure is unacceptable."

"The rogue guard's ship is still moving and therefore inaccessible," the other voice said. "I have strengthened the antidote, but where should I place it?"

"I looked across the rogue guard's time-line. Put the antidote *here* to intercept him."

At the "Put the antidote here" a picture flashed past. Gunnar grabbed it from his temporary memory, played it back in slow motion.

The Elders' antidote stood in the middle of a hall carved out of purple ice IV. Three night-black God's men surrounded him, their palms turned in his direction. A pulsing web of electric fire enveloped the antidote: he was clearly resisting an attack.

This is bad. They have upgraded him like they said. We need more than a super-shark to get rid of him now.

"We are back in normal space," the science officer announced. "Somebody switched off the drive."

Four dazzling vertical lines sprouted from the floor. They grew into doorways and three God's men appeared, their hands outstretched. The antidote stood in the middle, still surrounded by his defensive force field.

One of the God's men stepped back and threw a small hologram on the captain's lectern.

"This is what you came to get. A seventeen petabyte picture of the original Kabbalah, showing every rock and crack. Now take him away."

"He bribed you to bring him here," Semele said. "With what in Diana's name? You must be almost as powerful as the Elders!"

"He told us that his Elder makers had seen the face of God. That he would show it to us if we didn't stop your ship and bring him in here."

"But wasn't that what you wanted? What you have been striving for?"

Anguish flashed across the spokesman's face, the first human emotion Gunnar had seen.

"Not like this! Knowledge must be *earned*. It is the journey that counts. Not the destination."

Gunnar perfectly understood the God's man's fear, his loathing. Point to the highest mountaintop of the universe and tell the climber that you can put him on the very top in a heartbeat, in the twinkling of an eye. He would probably push you into a ravine if he believed you.

The God's men turned about, became lines of light again, and winked out.

Huang-ho closed his eyes, spoke a sentence that was mostly hisses and should never have issued out of a human mouth. Gunnar felt the power: such deeply wrong words, ice-words, snake-warrior words, horribly wise.

"Don't talk to me like that!" the antidote cried. He stumbled back, put his hands to his ears, but that didn't help. The words were too potent: Gunnar could hear them resonate in his own brain, thoughts rather than sounds.

"Stop it! Stop it. You can't address me like that! I'm not worthy! Not a Perfect Master."

Huang-ho is intoning the words from the stele, Gunnar realized. *The formula even a peasant can use to address a Perfect Master in an emergency.*

"Stop it! I can't stand it anymore. It makes me filthy, unclean."

The antidote's fingers grew claws and he hooked them into his chest, tore the rib cage open and plucked out his heart.

It looked like some savage Viking diorama, Gunnar thought, the open rib cage, the torn-out heart that was still gushing blood across the priceless angel-wing rug. He tried to hold back the vomit that was burning in his throat.

"Diana be praised," Semele said in the silence. "You shamed him to death."

"I don't think his master will bother us again," Huang-ho said. "They also heard those forbidden words. They will have lost all honor. Their rightful place."

"They will have to commit suicide," Patriska said. "Perform *seppuku*. Like an ancient samurai."

"From the frying pan into the fire," Huang-ho muttered.

"What do you mean, love?" Justine said. "I didn't memorize all those fancy sayings of the Connatic, like you had to do in school."

"I used the Protocol. Speaking those words made this an emergency of the highest order. I'm afraid somebody else heard them. Something much more powerful than the antidote-makers." He closed his eyes again to concentrate, listening to voices only he could hear. "The Keeper of the Sleep, she's slow, just waking up. Think of an archangel as big as a world, no, a sun. Sluggish but monstrously powerful. We'd better find her before she finds us."

"A kind of captain of those guards?" Patriska said. "I would place such a captain somewhere central. A view from a high place. A castle tower, a mountaintop."

• • •

TAIS TENG

A flicker in a corner, and one of the God's men stepped back into the control room. He inspected the fallen antidote, touched the cooling heart and tasted the blood.

"So he's truly dead. You stopped him. Good. But you promised to be gone." He fluttered his many-fingered hands. "Depart. Pollute our clear skies with your presence no more!"

Semele put her hands on her hips. She had to crane her head to look into his face.

"Tell us where to find the Keeper of the Sleep, their captain of the guards. Some place central, Patriska thinks."

"How blind are those who never drown in the night sky in wonder! What is more central than their biggest trophy hall? Go to the Grand Rainbow. Where else could she dwell?"

"Went as fast as he came," the Director said. He rubbed his hands and his face shone. He looked almost beatific, Gunnar thought, like a young boy who has just seen an angel. "Such a delightful puzzle! And even better, there is a time limit. Solve it or die. How Sheila Holmes would envy me!"

The ceiling of their bedroom showed the sky, where stars were zipping past like luminous hailstones. The God's man had wanted them *gone* and had thrown them clear across the Cluster.

Ahead, the Grand Rainbow emerged from a dark cloud of carbon and hydrogen. The yacht was moving much faster than light and the suns were circling the central black hole like panicked fireflies.

Semele turned her face to his. In the starlight she was very beautiful and wild: her chromophores made mother-of-pearl gleams flicker across her cheeks, her hair was as dark and lustrous as the voids between the stars.

My goddess, Gunnar thought, *and she loves me.*

For just a moment, no more than a heartbeat, he saw an alternate now. One where Lavoine had chosen to dance with him on Saint Dismas. Would she have made him her Suleiman? Would he now be lying under black satin sheets with Lavoine and her sister?

"I have been thinking," Semele said and the vision suddenly seemed something foul, the worst of all possible worlds.

"Yes?"

"Perhaps we should make a baby?"

Gunnar felt a stab of profound alarm, of sheer panic. Becoming a father, like on that aborted page about Lamoraal and his paramour?

Semele chuckled. "You became all tense. Don't fear. It was just an idea."

"I don't mean that I don't want to marry you. Or that I don't want a child. But it seems hasty. Perhaps we should wait to see how all this pans out?"

"You're right. Me with a big belly, while the Elders are snuffing out suns and hunting humans. Waddling like a walrus. Yes, better wait a bit."

The next morning, while Semele was singing in the shower, Gunnar gingerly opened his endless book.

> "I heard about an enchanted sword," princess Thunderstar said. "It cuts right through bronze and steel. No armor can withstand it."
>
> "I was rather thinking about the ironwood door of a treasure room," Lamoraal said. "Go on."

Gunnar read another three pages. There wasn't a word about the princess longing for a child. But wait...

> "And who are you?" Lamoraal asked. The boy could be no more than ten years old. He was clad in chain-mail and his dagger looked like Valerian steel, forged in the breath of a dragon.
>
> "You can call me Lamoraal. Lamoraal junior. I'm your son, ser."
>
> "Such a sweetie!" the princess squealed. "And you look just like your father."
>
> "And you are... ?" the boy asked, adding: "Fair lady," and clearly meaning it.

Gunnar closed the book. *Neat. Very neat. A new warrior to help them get that sword and the princess clearly likes him. She'll mother him, teach him a thousand lethal tricks, how to draw poison even from a stone. You won't be hearing her again about having a messy baby.*

Chapter XXXVII

From *Restricted Worlds, the Observations of a Star-Trotting Vagabond* by Yuri Hopkins, writing for the *Alastor Herald*, monthly magazine, now with Mirricyllai-approved horoscope.

Wender Humne covered a class two planetoid with an air-skin and filled his new home with soil and air. Then he added the ornamental plants and fruit-trees of a dozen worlds.

A boosted and quite illegal star drive tore the small world from its orbit. Three days later it emerged a quarter of a light-month out from the Grand Rainbow.

The Whelm would have shot the planetoid from the sky if they had seen it approaching, but now had to accept the *fait accompli*. Using potent energy weapons this close to an Elder artifact was insanely risky.

—

"All my sisters are happily married," one of Humne's daughters told me. "I'm the youngest and probably the most beautiful. Why don't you stay here?"

I laughed. "The view is certainly excellent. Twenty-six suns in the sky and then there is the Cerenkov-blue ring pulsing around the black hole. But, my dear girl, a stein of beer costs a hundred ozols here, a room sets me back a thousand. I'm on an expense account from the *Alastor Herald*, but..."

"You can marry me. Then the beer is free and my father won't begrudge us a bed."

"The morose waiters and the frowning gardeners, they are the husbands of your sisters?"

"Such is the case."

"Sorry, I'm a journalist, a writer, and even worse, a poet. Like Silenus, I won't be caged. But why don't you come with me?"

She shook her head. "My father would burn your little prospector's boat before you went a hundred meters up. He used an industrial laser to level the ground for the terrace, you know."

"But you would be inside!" I exclaimed.

"My father is a brute and he hates to lose." She leaned her elbows on my table and looked at me with eyes that almost made it worthwhile to become a gardener. "If you really are a poet, then write me a poem. One with my name in it. Tonight I'll knock on your door and you'll read me that poem. If I like it…" Some sentences don't need to be finished.

"I'll do that. But what exactly is your name?"

(You can find *Gertrude with Rainbows in her Eyes* in my small tome of poetry titled *Tavern Girls and Other Princesses*.)

—⚯—

"There is only one true crime anywhere, in any civilization," Huang-ho stated. "Getting noticed by the authorities. Well, we have been noticed."

"By the Keeper of the Sleep," Semele nodded.

Gunnar knew that overly alert look in her eyes. She was bootstrapping herself into the genius-trance, finding solutions for problems they didn't even know they had.

"Your using the Protocol is slowly waking her up. If there isn't any follow-up, she'll slap at you, still half asleep. Like a sleeper hearing a mosquito buzz." She pursed her lips. "Distance is no hindrance. Like those others, she'll know exactly where you are."

"When she wakes up," Huang-ho said, "I must be sitting right at her feet, repeating the Protocol again. Convince her to use the Song to calm the Galleons. I know the Protocol, I have the Song etched in my brain. But I don't have the slightest idea where to find her, except that she should be somewhere in the Grand Rainbow, as the God's man said. With twenty-six suns to choose from…"

"Why, she lives in the Command Center of course. In the middle of the quantum web."

"Please be a bit more specific?"

"How stupid can you be? In the One True Sun, of course!"

"No, I haven't the slightest idea what I meant with 'in the One True Sun'," Semele said when she came out of the trance. She shrugged. "I'm only human now. How can I understand what I oracled? And I can't trance for the next three days. I don't know if you can sprain your nervous system, but my nerves feel like unraveling bowstrings right now, ready to snap. Wake me up when we arrive at the tavern."

" 'In the One True Sun,' Semele said." Patriska frowned. "That is quite specific. Nothing about the Command Center orbiting said sun. *In*."

"I can skim the corona," the AI said. "We have half an hour before the field collapses and we fry."

"Well, we have to find the right star first."

"We are slowing down," the science officer said. "The God's man must have aimed us at Humne's tavern."

The wheel of stars now filled half the sky, with the suns no longer colored streaks but tiny disks.

"Your Semele, she's a real prize," Huang-ho said. "So much more than that little voodoo-girl."

"I know," Gunnar said. "Semele will probably throttle me if I look at another girl."

"Firm-minded women are the best. A man knows where he stands, then."

"I wonder...I wonder what Lavoine and her father are doing right now? If they provoke the Galleons one jot more, Phaedra's shores will probably be swept clean of Earth-life."

"I got an update from the fleet two hours ago. Nothing has changed. The river-valley is still wreathed in an opaque mist. Not a single radio-signal is coming from the surface."

"And the fleet?"

"Still hiding behind the gas-giant. Standing by, ready to evacuate Phaedra, but only if the mist clears."

"The Keeper?"

"Semele must be right about her residing in the Rainbow. The feeling of presence is getting stronger. My nine percent of a guardian is guessing that we have about three days left before she really awakens."

A transparent tunnel led down to the surface of Humne's Splendid Rainbow Resort. A girl was waiting for them at the entrance, her hands on her hips. She inspected them with a curled upper-lip. "Some more vagabonds and space gypsies arrive. I hope none of you is a journalist?"

Huang-ho shook his head. "I have never put a pen to paper or written a single poem beyond the title."

"I have had my fill of journalists," the girl declared, "and he seemed such a nice gentleman."

"What exactly did he do?"

"He left without me!"

"If it is the same journalist I'm thinking of," Huang-ho said, "he tends to leave abruptly when girls start talking about the color of their wedding dress."

There were swallows skimming just below the near invisible air-skin, a partridge clucking in the pear tree. Gunnar lifted his glass of punch. This could have been a perfect place, a perfect moment, with Semele leaning against his shoulder, and the breeze warm and perfumed with hibiscus. Being under a death sentence with but a single day left was rather spoiling it, however.

"The One True Sun," Semele said. She clenched her fists. "This is completely stupid! It isn't some riddle a nasty sphinx made up. It was so obvious I didn't even bother to remember it!"

"The One True Sun could be their home sun," Gunnar said. "I don't think it is really circling the black hole. The others are all trophy stars. You don't hack off your own head to hang it on the wall."

"A pity no-one has the slightest idea what their home sun was," the science officer said. "One of those suns must be false. Hollow, with only the outer layer burning. I probed them all: they look quite genuine." He hissed in annoyance. "We'll have to depart soon. I guess we can try three suns before the force-field or the armor gives up for good."

"The color of the One True Sun," Gunnar said. He almost had it. He lifted his right hand, frowned. "Don't say anything. Our first sun, it was yellow. Which was why we humans prized gold above all. Used it as the symbol for Sol herself."

"You are brilliant!" Semele pointed to the sun that was just clearing the hills. "That must be the one! The same color they always paint their basic symbol. It was on the sails: a deep brooding red with flaming green veins!"

The swift rotation of the worldlet lifted the sun higher in the sky and the terrace was flooded by an eerie crimson glow. The new sun was indeed a brooding red with green flames. For a heartbeat, they seemed to sketch the Elder copulating snakes symbol before the veins fell into another configuration. It was probably an illusion: so many dancing flames that you could Rorschach them into any shape at all.

"Set the controls for the heart of the sun." It had a strange resonance, words spoken long before the first human ship passed Neptune. Gunnar must have heard it on Chevalier, where they kept the ancient songs alive.

They dropped down from a great height. The compressed light made the suns circle like fireflies around an ultraviolet killing lamp.

"May Diana make our hearts staunch," Semele intoned. "Grant us our death with a grin on our lips." She lifted a fist. "Make us spit in the face of fate!" Her eyes were shining.

Gunnar rather envied her: he didn't see anything romantic in being fried like a suckling pig on a spit. His bowels felt watery, his legs shook so much he couldn't have risen from his seat.

A sun like a flaming emerald flashed past, a cornflower blue one took its place. They skimmed just above the plane of the ecliptic, the disc where twenty-six suns circled the black hole.

"Almost there," the science officer said and he sounded like Semele. Eager, no matter what would happen.

Gunnar felt a surge of chagrin. *This is an adventure. We are saving a whole world, perhaps all of mankind. Like in a game. Why can't I enjoy it?*

But it didn't feel like a game, not heroic at all. More like something deeply stupid you did on a dare when you were at most ten years old.

The One True Sun ballooned from a disk into a globe, filled the entire view-screen. Red light flooded the cabin. Dazzling green flames leaped.

Filters cut the light down before it seared their retinas, cut it down again by a factor of ten thousand.

The red light became solid, plastered against the screen.

It suddenly cleared and they emerged inside a hollow sphere made of burning snowflakes. Each snowflake was the size of a world, and was constructed out of other snowflakes, endlessly repeating until they must become as small as molecules.

Gunnar recognized the architecture: they were speeding through the fractal heart of a quantum computer, an artificial intelligence so potent that it shouldn't have lasted any longer than a microsecond before turning violently insane.

Perhaps it is insane. The Elders were berserkers, foaming at the mouth, destroying world after world.

"So those are the midges that awoke me." It wasn't a voice exactly, but something much worse than sound. The voice plucked Gunnar's nerves to form the words, burned them in the quivering jelly of his brain.

Think of blunt scalpels cutting your eyeballs, think of each word as tearing the living skin from your arms. Gunnar screamed, but his tongue refused to move. Distantly, light-years away, he heard Huang-ho intoning the Protocol. These words also hurt, but they pushed the greater pain of the Keeper's voice away, like pinching your earlobe for a momentary relief from a terrible toothache.

"I heard you the first time," the Keeper said. And suddenly they were just words, mere information. "Phaedra, I see. The perfect masters waking up, becoming less than perfect. Becoming like me." There was an immense sadness in that voice, a deep disgust for what she was forced to remain. Gunnar got the impression of someone having to stay outside while a mighty festival was going on: the Elder equivalent of surging music, fireworks and bristly boars turning above the coals.

"Valhalla," he heard Semele say. "All the warriors and gods are feasting, but she's like Heimdall. She has to stay outside to guard the Rainbow Bridge, to peer into the gloom for any approaching enemies."

"You're right, girl. They became beautifully simple and happy savages once again. Look at them! See how we started our life in joy most savage!"

And pictures filled Gunnar's head, emotions he could almost understand. There was the crunch of armor beneath steel-hard teeth, the metallic taste of cobalt-laced blood, a thousand times more exquisite than century-old port.

The Galleons of the ocean world Yusdalith had been like enormous Portuguese Men-o'-war, jellyfish-like colonies of polyps. Some of those polyps had grown into a living sail, others became the mouths, the stomachs, the hearts pumping nutrients to all the other members of the colony.

The Elders had started out as the hunters: they formed the tips of the questing tentacles. They were armed with stings to paralyze their prey and defend their Galleon. Their senses were the most acute, and soon they were leading the Galleons to the best feeding grounds. More as captains then, than as hunters and scouts.

Their tiny nerve-clusters ballooned, grew into true brains. The hunting tentacles became detachable, free-swimming, and the Elders learned to farm the fish, to train them to swim along with the Galleons.

With such a living larder, it became unnecessary to hunt, but the Elders loved the thrill of the chase, the fierce joy of fighting adversaries as dangerous as themselves.

And then one of those Elders must have looked up to the sky and realized that the stars were suns. Suns with worlds like Yusdalith, planets with oceans filled with prey, and even better, worthy adversaries, monsters with glowing eyes and jaws filled with poison fangs.

"You humans set out to conquer," the Keeper said. "To find treasure and territory. We were different. We just wanted to fight, to feel the joy of battle again." Gunnar felt the Keeper rummaging in his head. "The Vikings would have understood us. Or Tamerlane."

Gunnar saw water-filled ships jump like silver salmon from the ocean, swimming up into the dark. Yusdalith receded, became a bloody teardrop in the light of her red sun.

"We found enemies galore, some even worthy," the Keeper said. "But when we hung the last sun in the Rainbow, we felt a crushing emptiness, an indescribable ennui. We had been wrong to leave the

Galleons behind. As hunting tentacles, we had been effortlessly happy, joyous in knowing that we were part of something greater."

"So you decided to turn evolution back," Gunnar heard Semele say. "To become happy little tentacles again. The Galleons on Phaedra? Are they all that's left of the Elder race?"

"Twenty-six or twenty-six trillion: what do numbers matter? As long as the Galleons sail on in bliss, my race lives."

A projection of Phaedra appeared in front of them, the River a glowing ribbon. They swooped like a hawk and a Galleon expanded. For the first time, Gunnar saw every detail: the sails were anchored with ropelike muscles and there were hearts pumping below the armor-glass deck.

A tentacle surfaced, the tip a nightmare collection of hooks and stings, barbed arms. The frontal arms were lifting something metallic and lensed: a weapon, no doubt, and something made, constructed, not grown.

"They are awake now, ready to detach. Their technology is still quite low, mostly instinctive. A thousand years in advance of yours, at most. They can't pluck suns from the sky and hurl them through the dark. But they'll soon realize that the shores of their holy river are infested with parasites. That the whole home cluster is crawling with vermin."

"Make them slumber again," Huang-ho argued. "They must be desperately unhappy. Like..." he waved his arms. "Like waking up in the middle of the night, frozen and wet, on a soaked mattress. Without the slightest idea of where they are."

"I'm not allowed to intone the Litany. Only one of the Elder race is. I'm just a recording, a program, you understand. I can broadcast the Litany, put every reassuring word into their brains and make them slumber again. But as for speaking those sacred words..."

"I..."

"The Protocol gives you that status. To address me as one of my race. But what is the use? They'll sleep again but those pesky humans woke them once. They will wake them again."

"Not all humans," Huang-ho said. "Just a small group. Crazy folks. Unhappy people."

"A curious idea. Have they lost their roots like my people? The shapes and lives that once made them happy?" A pause. For a quantum computer that must be long enough to label all the stars in the Galaxy, write a billion-page sonnet. "The shape that once made them happy... Let's reach back."

A Neanderthal appeared, hefting a fire-hardened spear, wearing trousers made of ox-hide. "Still meddlers."

A Homo Habilis loped across the savanna, holding the thigh-bone of a wildebeest.

"Further back."

A small monkey with a banded tail sat below a shrub, plucking purple berries. His mate sat crunching a large beetle, spitting out fragments of the wing-case.

"Your first and most contented ancestor. You called them Proconsul. No fire and no artifacts. Good. Say the words and I'll give you humans a safer shape."

"Not all of them!" Huang-ho cried. "For most of us the Galleons are holy, the River taboo." He reached into the pouch the rogue guard had left him, and showed the Keeper the Suleiman insignia. "All the wrong ones are wearing this: your symbol and the blue scimitar."

"We'll see. Speak the words. You know the price? The Litany will brain-burn you. Wipe all your memories. You will be like a toddler at best."

"I didn't realize... It doesn't matter."

"Huang..." Justine said in a strangled voice. She rose, then sat back. She was a soldier, the wife of the Field Marshall, and sometimes a leader must stand in the frontline.

Huang-ho didn't say "I love you", or something useless and sentimental like a Chevalieran minstrel would. He just took a deep breath and spoke the first word of the Litany.

Chapter XXXVIII

From *Restricted Worlds, the Observations of a Star-Trotting Vagabond* by Yuri Hopkins, writing for the *Alastor Herald*, monthly magazine, now with Mirricyllai-approved horoscope.

Others might call it 'finding closure' or even 'a pilgrimage', but it mostly felt *strange* to visit Phaedra again. To see the lumens along the Esplanade shutting down, the air conditioning falling silent when the Galleon sailed past.

Cursar Justine ambushed me the moment I walked down the gangway of the shuttle.

"Welcome," she said. "I have reserved a room for you in the Residence." She eyed my rather threadbare traveler's overall. "I'll also get you some clean clothes." She nodded. "A rickshaw is waiting." The two burly guards she had brought along made it not exactly an invitation I could refuse.

———

Semele shook my hand, called her daughter.

"Yiske, this is the rascal I told you about. The one who was the partner of the starmenter who stole our spaceship."

Her eyes grew big. "Really, truly? Mother isn't lying?" Nothing is as gratifying as the wholehearted admiration of a five-year-old. "I want to become a starmenter, just like him. Later." She eyed the frayed hems of my trousers, my scuffed sandals. "My grand-mother said you were a millionaire? Because of that book?"

"Should I wear a crown and carry a gold-plated projac?"

She nodded.

"I have those of course. But I travel incognito."

"Ah." She nodded. "Like the Connatic." She pointed. "You

see them running there? That is my father and my grandpaw. Grandpaw hasn't many words, but he's learning new ones every day and he's almost as good a runner as my mother." She took my hand. "Let's go feed the monkeys."

—

Yiske's monkeys lived in a jacaranda tree behind the villa. They must be genetically manipulated because the fur on their chests showed a blue scimitar set into the infamous Elder sign.

"You can feed them. Here, I have a bag of walnuts. But not that one. Lavoine is kind of vicious. She'd rather bite off a finger than take a nut."

—⁂—

Numenes, the palace of the Connatic:

It wasn't exactly a vacation," the Connatic protested.

"No, more like a crazily risky caper." Esclavade snorted. "A ruler of five trillion shouldn't be that hands-on. Posing as a lecherous journalist and going gallivanting around the Cluster, visiting all the most dangerous places!" He threw up his hands. "And that starmenter is still at large!"

"Those restricted worlds were just to give me an alibi. And my *Observations of a Star-Trotting Vagabond* was the best-read series in the *Alastor Herald* this century. More readers even than *Sayings of the First Connatic*." He raised a hand. "But you didn't call me to ream me out. Or at least not only."

"Well, a rather curious message just arrived. From Pharism: Alastor 458. It had the 'most urgent' code from our Cursar."

"No, no! Don't tell me. No one should have to save the universe twice." He rubbed his chin. "My recent companion is quite competent and he has a brand-new face now and likes adventure. He was talking about, well, not atoning, but being on the side of the angels for once…"

Esclavade stared at him, aghast. "You don't mean…?"

THE END

Channeling Jack Vance

When I started writing, Jack Vance was big, huge, in the Netherlands. Me and my writer-friends, we wanted to be Jack Vance when we grew up.

Forget Isaac Asimov or Robert Heinlein or even clever Larry Niven!

Vance had that perfect mixture of wonder and suspense. No matter in what direction you looked in his worlds, you saw something deeply strange. The furtive Pnume, merging with the tan shadows, the fierce Dirdir, priceless coins ripening in seedpods...

The Grandmaster wasn't all that hard to imitate. Nicely ornamented sentences, a perhaps rather cynical but never bored way of looking at the world. Quite a few of my friends produced Vance look-a-like stories or even started whole novels. Strangely, after half a page, all those stories fell flat.

We could masquerade as him, put on his gaudy feathers but we weren't him. His stories were always incredibly information-dense, full of invention. He had clearly visited many countries, seen a dozen exotic cultures: that made his aliens and future cultures believable.

Wanting to become Vance seemed a worthy goal, something to aim at. Of course we all went off in different directions later, some of us straight into high fantasy (but Vance went there too, with *Lyonesse* and the *Dying Earth*), thrillers and detectives (well, like the master) or hard sf (*The World Between* with its careful terraforming is one of the best hard sf stories I know).

I wrote two *Dying Earth* stories for the Dutch homage collection WERELDBEDENKERS and wanted more. So I asked John Vance at Spatterlight if they were interested in a novel set in one of Jack's universes.

They were.

I had always liked the *Alastor* books, so nicely self-contained with the enigmatic Connatic in the background. I also loved the idea of the Whelm: overawe your enemy with your splendor and might, so most of the time you wouldn't have to fight at all. The gold-plated yacht of an admiral is a more effective weapon than any number of guns.

This novel would be a hybrid, a mixture of Vance and Teng, but I could try to use one of his patterns as a template for that Vance feeling.

Quite a lot of Vance's stories start on one planet, with the protagonist quite young, and then move over to another world. *Emphyrio* comes to mind, or *Night Lamp* and *Durdane*. He, or she, also often has a problem fitting in, especially if the culture is hidebound or obsessed with status. And there is some secret in the background, a mystery he has to solve.

Before I started my story, I reread the *Alastor* novels.

The open star cluster is possibly set in the same timeline as the *Demon Princes*. The Gaean Reach is mentioned, but the Beyond or the Oikumene are not. So the Alastor Cluster might be part of the now civilized Beyond.

I set the story a thousand years after the *Demon Princes*: the star drive is no longer referred to as the Jarnell drive, so there's probably more than one type of drive by now.

There are no computers or robots in the Gaean Reach. I decided that AI was just too dangerous and had been forbidden.

I have written quite a lot of space opera and hard sf before, but in this novel the universe was willing to conform to my story.

I wanted a black hole in the center of the Alastor Cluster, for instance, and was thinking about a good explanation. I googled one more time and discovered that most star clusters probably have one.

Phaedra orbited a brown dwarf and I found several good artist impressions of what they would look like. Good that I did: I hadn't realized they would be banded like Jupiter.

The length of the Great Day and the size of the brown dwarf in the sky turned out to be quite right after a helpful amateur astronomer, Rob Friefeld, did the math. I had done it by feel: using a lamp, a grapefruit and a tangerine as stand-ins.

I love world-building: for an interview, we once counted more than a dozen quite distinct universes that I have constructed. For my *Granterre* trilogy, there is a secret, more-dimensional Earth that stretches all the way to the orbit of Neptune.

In my *Loki* cycle the World-tree is real. When Charlemagne cuts it down with king Arthur's sword, the top ends up in the Middle East, close to the city of the jinns. A bit of a problem for Loki, because he needs a leaf to buy his lover free from the underworld.

I have also written in the universes of other writers, like Lovecraft's Cthulhu-mythos, *The Night Land* by William Hope Hodgson and Clark Ashton Smith's *Zothique*.

When I came up for air after finishing this novel it felt like I had visited a beloved mother country. I think this is how a musician, who is also a composer, must feel after playing a work from his mentor. It is of course my own interpretation, but still I hope there is an echo of the master.

Thank you, Jack.

Tais Teng

About Tais Teng

Tais Teng (1952) is the pseudonym of the Dutch fantasy and science fiction writer, illustrator and sculptor Thijs van Ebbenhorst Tengbergen. He shortened his name to Tais Teng to leave room for a spaceship or a grinning skull on the cover of his novels.

Tais has written more than a hundred and twenty novels for both adults and children. He has won the Paul Harland Award, the Dutch Hugo, four times.

His books have been translated into German, Finnish, French and English. One of his novels, *The Emerald Boy*, has also been published in the USA. He has sold thirty-five English short stories and novellas to magazines and anthologies. He also created quite a few American book and magazine covers.

Together with Jaap Boekestein, he is the originator of Ziltpunk, optimistic climate fiction set in the Netherlands.

As a sculptor, his dearest wish is to own a Star Wars laser cannon to carve some of Jupiter's lesser ice moons. Reading Jack Vance's *The Face* really made his fingers tingle with eagerness.

His English short story collections *Lovecraft, my Love* and *Embrace the Night and Other Stories* are available at Smashwords and Amazon.

English website:
    http://taisteng.atspace.com
Illustrations, book covers and commissions:
    http://taisteng.deviantart.com/gallery
YouTube channel: http://www.youtube.com/user/taisteng
Facebook: https://www.facebook.com/taisteng
Twitter: @taisteng

Colophon

This book was printed using 11,5 pt Adobe Arno Pro as the primary text font, with NeutraFace used for titles.

Special thanks to Rob Friefeld and Steve Sherman.

Book composition & Typesetting: Joel Anderson

Typographic design: Howard Kistler

Jacket blurb: Tais Teng

Management: John Vance, Koen Vyverman

www.ingramcontent.com/pod-product-compliance
Lightning Source LLC
Chambersburg PA
CBHW031954240626
47153CB00003B/978